ALSO BY TUPELO HASSMAN

Girlchild

Breast Milk

gods

WITH A LITTLE g

gods
WITH A LITTLE g

TUPELO HASSMAN

FARRAR, STRAUS AND GIROUX   NEW YORK

Farrar, Straus and Giroux
120 Broadway, New York 10271

Grateful acknowledgment is made for permission to reprint an excerpt from *Footloose*,
copyright © Paramount Pictures Corp. All rights reserved.

Library of Congress Cataloging-in-Publication Data
Names: Hassman, Tupelo, 1973– author.
Title: Gods with a little g / Tupelo Hassman.
Description: First edition. | New York : Farrar, Straus and Giroux, 2019.
Identifiers: LCCN 2018060815 | ISBN 9780374164461 (hardcover)
Classification: LCC PS3608.A8613 G63 2019 | DDC 813/.6—dc23
LC record available at https://lccn.loc.gov/2018060815

Designed by Abby Kagan

Our books may be purchased in bulk for promotional, educational, or business use.
Please contact your local bookseller or the Macmillan Corporate and
Premium Sales Department at 1-800-221-7945, extension 5442,
or by e-mail at MacmillanSpecialMarkets@macmillan.com.

www.fsgbooks.com
www.twitter.com/fsgbooks • www.facebook.com/fsgbooks

1   3   5   7   9   10   8   6   4   2

for Bradford

The high aspirations and ambitions of adolescence shrivel as life advances, and because many of its promises are unfulfilled, philosophers have urged that unless there be immortality our nature is a lie.

—G. STANLEY HALL, *Adolescence: Its Psychology*, 1904

I'll sing to you of silver swans,
of kingdoms and carillons.
I'll sing of bodies intertwined
underneath an innocent sky.

—ARIEL'S POEM, *Footloose*, 1984

gods

WITH A LITTLE g

THE MEASURE OF GOODNESS

If you were flying in a plane over Rosary, California, the first thing you'd see is me, a skinny white girl with messy hair and a big backpack, waving you on. "Keep going," I'd say. The second thing you'd see, on an afternoon when school was just out and the wind was starting to shift, would be teenagers closing in on a tire yard like bits of metal pulling to a magnet. Until we were all gathered there, negative and positive, and jumping from the force of being near each other.

If I told you a Genesis story fit for our teenage congregation, it would be just the opposite of the church-and-the-steeple rhyme my mom used to tell, her fingers the multitude gathered for worship. *Here's the church, here's the steeple, open the door, and see all the people.* In this version, the tire yard is the church and the best rhyme for "steeple" is "deep hole." In this version, you go in when the doors open, and you let them close behind you. As your eyes adjust to the gloom, you see all the Dickheads. And that doesn't rhyme at all.

Mo's brother, Tucker, started working at Fast Eddie's Tire Salvage two summers ago. Then he started working late. Then he started hanging out later and drinking Fast Eddie's beer. And the rest of us followed. Tucker begat Mo, Mo begat Bird, Bird begat Cy and Sissy and everyone else stupid enough to have a crush on him. Which would be me. My name is Helen. The Dickheads call me Hell.

So, which came first, the Dickheads or their girls? Which came first? Beer. The beer begat us all. Bespat us. It called our names. And we came running, flying, climbing fences, breaking curfews, spilling rhymes. Here are the Dickheads going nowhere, here are the Dickheads making dares.

We dared each other at first just to drink the beer, then to drink more beer, then to get the beer. More beer. Then we dared each other to do more of all the things we want to do but don't dare on our own. We got drunk together over and over again until getting drunk together became something. Until we became something. And on one of those early evenings as the light in Rosary was fading, back in the early days when the glow from those first beers still warmed us all the way home, we were christened. Sissy said, without thinking, maybe, "See you dickheads tomorrow." And it stuck, hard. Like we're stuck, here with each other. The best and worst of everyone we know, doing what we must but shouldn't, becoming who we are and always will be. Without thinking, maybe.

Dickheads forever.

COUNTRY TORE

Rosary's skyline is a graveyard. A line of crosses and bell towers march on forever, each taller than the last. It turns out that size does matter, and so Rosary's founders created an ordinance allowing no structure within city limits to have a higher reach than God's, as represented by the tallest of the many church steeples erected in His honor. And none does. Except the refinery. Rosario Bay Oil Refinery is exempt from the ordinance because it was here first and because without it, none of Rosary exists. The refinery has a pole rising from its center, higher than any of its smokestacks, which burn all day and all night over the crosses below. A red light flashes at the very top, warning planes away. It blinks there, far above it all, like a message left by God Himself that no one has bothered to check.

The city of Sky is Rosary's closest neighbor, just across a miles-long bridge built over the soggy delta and the bay, and it has a real skyline, jagged with buildings competing for the light. Sky also has real movie theaters and real schools. It has the real internet. And real scientific facts. In Rosary, the internet is policed, so we read our porn from books like the ancient peoples did. And in Rosary, dinosaurs and man lived together at the same time and fossil fuels aren't any of our concern. If the ice caps are melting, that is God's plan.

Get thee behind me, Science.

My dad is a member of the Council for the Peaceful Reconciliation of Rosary and Sky and it is worth noting that everyone on the council is from Rosary. In an effort to bring new business into Rosary, to bring any business into Rosary, the council sends letters to hopeful prospects from Sky and cities like it, explaining why the businessperson in question is being invited. I've seen these on our computer at home. They read stiff, the way no one talks. It's kind of like porn, really, because you can't believe anyone is going to take a come-on like this seriously. Except in porn, the come-on works. All the lonely, unlikely sex god has to say is hello, and the next thing you know there is a bra on the lampshade. But no legitimate business is jumping into bed with the City of Rosary, especially with an invite like this:

Mr. Boreal,

I would like to officially inform you that we hereby invite you, the following individual, Mr. Boreal, to visit Rosary to attend the biannual seminar, entitled, "Dr. Baker's Scientific Efforts on Faith and the Big Bang," to be held in Rosary, CA, by the Council for the Peaceful Reconciliation of Rosary and Sky. We would be honored by your participation at our conference, given your work with the Sky Observatory and its resulting tourism.

The conference will also invite other scholars from various fields to participate in this event. We have appreciated the work you have done and sincerely feel that your participation will contribute to the success of this conference.

The Council will pay in full for room, board, transportation, and your other sundry expenses in service of the Peaceful Reconciliation of Rosary and Sky.

Yours respectfully,
Elijah Dedleder
Council Member

The Reconciliation Council's learning curve, if I'm being generous, is as flat as my chest. There is not a soul in Sky, saved or damned, who doesn't choke with laughter at these letters, who doesn't immediately toss them in the trash or the shredder. Sky is done with turning the other cheek. Has had it up to here. The bridge is burned. The ship has sailed. There are no metaphors left for all the ways that Sky is done with Rosary's bullshit.

I was just a kid during the election that created the first rip in the seams of this country, this county, even in some families. And with every election that came after, we the people unraveled. The leaders of Rosary stepped right up like they'd been waiting for just such an opportunity and set about joining church and state while separating the rest of us based on race and sexual preference and other things that make them wet their pants with fear. After years of lawsuits from the City of Rosary on the supposed behalf of "minors taken advantage of by the irresponsible availability of unnecessary elective medical procedures in Sky," the city no longer welcomes any of us. Sky finally found a way to give Rosary a taste of its own medicine, by telling us who they think belongs. And who doesn't. Rosary citizens can't go to Sky for any of life's basics—birth control or an R-rated movie, even if you are seventeen, not for anything at all. Not unless we have a fake ID with a Sky address on it. Or are in documented medical distress.

Believe me, we all try to document our distress around here as carefully as we can. Only, maybe not in the ways you would think.

INCANDESCENT

The bulb is bare and hot to the touch. It's old-school, the shape of a cartoon idea, and throws a brighter kind of light than the new ones that last forever and won't burn the house down. There is no hiding before it. And that's good. Mistakes are made in the shadows.

"Your only job," Tucker says when I sit down, "is to hold still and not block the light."

Then he unwraps a needle. He makes a big show of pulling the wrapper open, the way he's done with each of the wrappers already empty under his table. Sterility is a sign of his professionalism. I'm the third to sit here tonight, to take off my shirt or pull up my sleeve or turn the chair around and lean over it with my pants down. Now it is my turn to look at the wall and pretend to study the old map hanging there because I am so bored and I feel no pain.

Tucker dips the needle into black ink, our only option, and as the needle touches the soft skin of my forearm, the motor of his homemade tattoo machine whirs out a word into my skin that is copied from my mother's own handwriting.

It starts with a looping *l*, bent on leaving.

I feel pain.

The motor sounds like those in the sewing machines lining the tables in home economics at Rosary High. It's a gray noise underneath plastic, faint and determined.

Next, an *o*.

I am not bored.

Then, a comma. Not unlike those that God supposedly favors in place of a period. Not unlike their reminder to take a breath and carry on.

But this noise is not the one we are used to hearing. The sewing machines with Rosary High girls bent over them—the way our sisters and mothers bent over them before, making the same aprons, napkins, place mats, tablecloths—that sound is the sound of the past.

The sound of Tucker's motor is the sound of the future, with a capital *F* and a capital *U*.

LO,

Tucker saved money from two Rosary summers slinging tires at Fast Eddie's to buy the parts for this tattoo machine and for secret trips to Sky's tattoo shops to watch and learn. And then he took off. Whenever he sneaks home to visit, he posts up at Fast Eddie's, and so long as we pay for the ink and let him take pictures when he's done, our tattoos are free. Dickhead discount.

He dips the needle. Starts the second word.

A small *p*.

This is all completely illegal, of course. Because Tucker can't get a license here.

A little *e*.

And because we're teenagers.

A little *t* and *a*.

The very last thing we have control over is our own bodies.

A little *l* rising up, like a sail caught in a wind.

THE LAST WORD

In Rosary, the kiss of God wetting a babe's forehead in baptism is the only approved bodily modification. Because God doesn't make mistakes.

A small *r*.

If He'd wanted those words or flowers or birds, if He'd wanted that arrow on you, He'd have slung it there Himself.

A small *i*.

As the little dot above the *i* takes the shape of the tiniest flower, I beg to differ.

An *s*, an *e*, an *r*.

If God is allowed the postscript of baptism, if He forgot something so important as salvation's own bar code, who's to say He didn't drop a stitch elsewhere? If Pastor Ted is doing His work at the baptismal font, it seems to me like Tucker might be doing

His work here too, with his stolen batteries and clean needles, in the dazzling white light that chases out the shadows. This pot of ink might be just another font we dip into to add what God forgot.

PS

Tattoos will be outlawed in Rosary soon. Not just creating them but having them. The Rosary Bible Thumpers will get a doctor to say they cause anemia, or are contagious, and he will be believed. They will have to be camouflaged, hidden, the way piercings are. If by some anti-miracle a Rosary High student scores a piercing, it has to be removed before school lest a flash of metal cause a distraction from our studies. We don't have uniforms, but there are many rules like this at Rosary to make us uniform.

For now, tattoos are discouraged in the usual boring ways, with laws and licenses and red tape. Tattoo licenses aren't issued in Rosary. Period. A rig like Tucker's can't even be built here unless instructions are brought in from the outside. The batteries used to run it are the same as those used for fire alarms and children's toys, but they are still kept locked up in every store across this city, just like condoms and cans of spray paint.

This is my first tattoo. Right over the thin blue vein running up the inside of my left forearm, the one you would have to break open if you were ready for the mother of all spoiler alerts. That's not my style, but like anyone kept in a cage long enough, I know the escape routes by heart. This one is the perfect place for a reminder to myself, a modification I think God would approve of.

My mother existed once. And here she lives again, in these letters on my skin.

The cursive is traced from her tiny handwriting in the front pages of our Bible. Not that she ever wrote this exact phrase. The *lo,* comma included, is hers, from her favorite verse, Matthew 28:20, her favorite line, copied in the front of the Bible under my birth date, "And, lo, I am with you always, even unto the end of the world." This is the *lo* she would use when she looked out the window and saw the sun rise, or heard a bird sing, the small prayer she uttered for any of a day's moments, her reminder to wonder at them.

The rest of the cursive I gathered from the letters in the names and birth dates she had written down over the years. Gathering them into two words that I could imagine her saying, words I wish she had said, to finish that prayer she was always in the midst of. Her reminder to pay attention to the wonder of my own creation.

LO, PETAL RISER

I make flowers out of paper. There, I said it. The first step is admitting you have an arts-and-crafts problem. Pages from old books, sheet music, recipes, you name it, I can fold them in complicated and precious ways, until they look like all the best flowers do. Temporary. The best flowers don't last. They open early, call the world to their scent, and fade.

Just like some people.

My bouquets last forever, though, just like Mom taught me to make them. She and I, on every rainy afternoon, bent over squares of wrapping paper, my fingers clumsy with the folds at first, skipping important steps. When I was ready, we moved from wrapping paper to construction paper to art paper, then to anything, coupons, letters, medical bills. And after she died, for a while, to no paper at all.

But I missed her. And this. Growing new life from old paper.

And now I make flowers on afternoons at the Rosary Psychic Encounter Shoppe when I'm supposed to be working, but I'm really eavesdropping on a session. I make them during class when I'm supposed to be studying, in my bedroom at night when sleep has forgotten me. I wrap different weights of paper together for depth, use different sources for meaning, a textbook or the phone book, a flyer from a telephone pole, for proof that meaning is what we make of it.

And then I throw them away because the person I am making them for is gone.

FALLEN

There is a body in the dirt and weeds of Rosary's empty lot. The lot is near the end of the main drag, where something important should be, something to save Rosary's failing economy. But it has sat there empty for at least my entire life. Except for that body. And I might be the only one who knows, who sees it there. As the afternoons wear on into the future, I imagine myself lifting up and away from here, taking a god's-eye view of a place God has refused to keep His eye on.

There's the cluster of churches at the other end of San Pablo Boulevard, Rosary's main road, and in the midst of them, Rosary High, a movie theater, and the Country Store, whose *S* was lost to gravity or apathy years ago. Putting all of that in your rearview to come down this way, it feels almost like escape, especially since San Pablo runs more and more parallel to the freeway as it goes, until chain link and stubborn bushes are all that is left between them.

Our city is in love with that freeway, the houses push up against the businesses, the businesses push up against San Pablo, San Pablo pushes up against the chain link, and the chain link pushes up against freedom. On the other side of the freeway is Rosario Bay, with its small beach no one goes to, its single bridge no one drives on, and up above it all, Rosario Bay Oil Refinery. The bridge to Sky and the freeway intersect right beneath the refinery's eternal red light. And that's it. Nothing to see here, especially right here, on the other side of town from God. But then, in the empty lot.

Furrows and ridges of dirt and some forgotten plant life conspire into the shape of a human form. Barely human. Making it out is like finding pictures in the clouds on a windy day, like reading fortunes from tea leaves at the bottom of a cup. It requires a good imagination and a loose focus as the shape drifts, shifts, and settles. As it becomes less human and more monster, a monster with wings.

One wing reaches toward the squat stucco building painted the color of shadow, the one with me inside of it. The other wing brushes into the narrow parking lot of a bright white building across the way, the color of sugar. It is like the wings will knock our buildings down. Or, it is like they want to gather them up, hold them tight.

It is like this monster, destroying and terrible as it is, is more of an angel. Or was, once. When you fall, you have to land somewhere.

The angel's eyes are two concrete blocks half buried in the ground. Above them rests a halo of discarded metal bent jagged as flame. As I'm trying to decide if the tire tracks below the wings are a heavenly robe or a hospital gown, the shadow of a plane cuts like a knife through its side. And it's gone.

PREVISION

From my perch on a wooden stool behind the counter, I watch the angel disappear along with the daylight. I see a lot of Rosary's comings and goings from this spot where I keep the shoppe's books after school. There are the regularly scheduled donut pick-ups across the lot at the Donut Hole. There are the unscheduled walk-ins here at the shoppe. And there is the angel, drifting in and out with the shadows, wanting to hold us all together or lay us all to waste.

I don't know that anyone wakes up in the morning with plans to have her fortune told. It's a thing a body decides as the day slips away and takes with it all its expectations, all the power and hope it rolled in with. People pull into the Psychic Encounter Shoppe starting in the late afternoon, surprised to find themselves there but hungry for something a donut cannot provide and faith does not ensure. What they want is that sweet little illusion of control, and my aunt Beverly, resident psychic, serves it right up.

When a car pulls into the shoppe's lot, I close the curtains around my counter to give the illusion of privacy. The curtains are made from Aunt Bev's old sheets, tie-dyed, and when they are fully closed, there's a comforting feeling of being cocooned in rainbow vomit. I pull my feet up onto the rung of the stool so the sight of my frayed and graffitied Converse peeking out from under the tie-dye won't ruin the mood. I listen to the shy voice of a new customer admitting to a weakness for the future. I fold their shame into a rose.

DRINKING GAMES FOR TEENS

Thanks to the refinery's constant smoke and flame, the sun doesn't set in Rosary so much as it crashes for the night. As the sun gives up in Rosary today, Peggy, she said her name was, finally stops thanking Aunt Bev for all the truth she's been given, for Aunt Bev's odd reassurance, "You will always have money, but then you will always lose it." This is the psychic's refrain, and Peggy, having eaten it up, is better now. When she leaves, Aunt Bev pulls my curtains open, drops money in the safe. She washes her hands like a doctor wrapping up after an exam. Then she dims the light to rest her eyes, and in the fresh darkness, a new mystery unfolds in the empty lot.

There is something between the angel's wings, a bulky shadow, and it doesn't move.

Aunt Bev settles on the couch with a small green pillow over her eyes. I bring her a glass of water, then grab the broom as quietly as I can to gather all the psychic dust left by Peggy and her desperate need. I sweep it outside and then slip out the door after it.

It's quiet out and I can hear my feet crunching on the dry, packed dirt, so I slip off my shoes and carry them. I will risk a little tetanus to be a better sneak. The shadow in the lot is lit from inside with a floating warm light and in ten more barefoot steps I am close enough to see that this shadow has a rain flap and is staked to the ground.

I knock on its zippered door. With my voice. Because it would be stupid to knock on a tent.

"Knock knock."

The light inside stops moving and there's rustling, shuffling. The sounds of something being hidden. Then throat-clearing, and in a tone that is trying to reassure me that there's nothing to see here, that I've interrupted nothing, a greeting. "Just a second."

I recognize Cy's voice, from wasted afternoons at Fast Eddie's Tire Salvage, of course, but before that, from wasted weeks at Bible camp last year. That was when he was first trying to be a Dickhead but couldn't really cut it. When he still liked to be called Cyrus.

Cy's mouth is all braces. And braces just don't fit the reputation of a badass that most Dickheads want to pretend they deserve. Braces tell a story of many, many trips to the orthodontist, with a parent, and Dickheads deny hanging out with or obeying parents. Braces tell a story of hygiene and care. Dickheads don't wash because that would destroy the stink that grows underneath their balls, stink they like to reach down and gather onto their fingers and then rub on other Dickheads' faces in the genuine hope of making them puke. Braces tell a story of giving a fuck. And Dickheads don't do that.

They also don't have tents.

Once Cy figures out which zipper goes which way to actually open the door, he looks relieved to see it's me. He peeks his head out to make sure I'm alone and whispers, "Come in."

I climb into the tent and offer a standard Dickhead greeting. "What the fuck, Cy?"

Cy is sitting on a fancy sleeping bag and moves over for me to join him. It's silky under my hand, plush, a burgundy color. I didn't know sleeping bags came in burgundy. His super-cool flashlight sits steady in the middle of the tent now like a lantern, pointing up at the plastic sky. It's nice in here.

There's a pillow.

None of these are accessories that will improve Cy's Dickhead reputation.

"I got kicked out," he says. The story of getting kicked out doesn't match any of the stories told by the braces that shine across his teeth. I don't know what to say.

He reaches behind the pillow. The pillowcase has orange flowers planted across it, and looking at it makes me wish for my own bed, has me feeling tired of all the Cys and Peggys of the world, of all their confusion and need.

There's more of that rustling as he opens the paper bag he's stashed and pulls out beers. We crack them open and say, "Fuck Fast Eddie."

We have barely made it through that first beer when there's a banging from outside, metal against metal. It is coming from the direction of the shoppe and I realize that I forgot to lock the door when I left. I scramble my way out of the tent, whispering a scream at myself, "No, no, no."

I run across the lot toward the shoppe, its front door, and the man standing there with a hammer in his hand. It shines like hot iron under the shoppe's red porchlight as he swings it against the door one more time. He doesn't hear me coming and I'm already in the parking lot when Cy climbs out of the tent after me, his flashlight on full blast. With Cy's light behind me, my shadow falls giant over the shoppe's front window, the palm painted there on the glass. The man and his hammer freeze. And then he runs for a truck I can just make out a little way up the road.

Two nails have been driven into the gold and silver mandala Aunt Bev painted on the shoppe's front door, and hanging from them is a piece of cardboard. Written across it in bright red marker: LEVITICUS 20.

Aunt Bev is on the couch, right where I left her, but she's sitting up now. When she sees the look on my face, the cardboard in my hand, she holds her fingers to her temples and says, "Let me guess." For a real psychic she does a pretty good impersonation of a fake one. She moans and rolls her eyes back in her head. "I'm getting something . . . a white man. With a hammer. And something about my being an abomination of all that is holy? Does this mean anything to you?"

She's trying to make me laugh with that question. The psychic's stock-in-trade. *Does this mean anything to you?*

But this does mean something to me. It means that anonymous letters aren't enough anymore for the Thumpers who want Aunt Bev gone, scared off like the last Rosary psychic, like the last Catholic family and their church, like anyone who doesn't speak English like it is the first language they ever tasted and ain't it great. They all ran off, were run off, exhausted by Rosary's hate. Or worse. If the threats are being walked right up to the front door now, what's to stop them from turning the handle, from going right inside?

Locking the door would be a good start.

Because when Leviticus is delivered after dark with red ink and hardware, it is a threat. Leviticus 20, the Bible's instructions about how to handle those doing evil in the sight of the Lord, "stone them with stones," it says. Not very poetic, but it gets the point across.

None of this is news to Aunt Bev. She already knows. She probably knew before I left the shoppe, maybe that's why she looked so tired. And she didn't tell me. Because I'm supposed to know this stuff myself, but I was distracted by Cy's stupid tent and I was drinking a beer and I forgot to lock the door. Selfish. So selfish to forget that in this town, every threat comes with a promise.

Before I can say any of this, Cy comes into the shoppe, his flashlight still set to blinding. "I think he thought I was the cops, he was running so fast."

As Cy clicks off his light, Aunt Bev takes LEVITICUS 20 from me, uncurling my fingers from around the cardboard. She rips it in half, drops it in the trash, and says, "Stones, maybe, but this"— she nods toward the garbage can—"this will never hurt me. Now go on with your friends. I'm going to bed."

As she heads for her room, she adds, "Lock the door this time."

A GULP OF SWALLOWS

Sissy. She's blond and curly, always, I don't even know if it's natural or not. It's pretty glorious, though. She's usually quiet, but when she's not, she's saying something so weird, it's funny. Or so funny, it's weird. She's too pretty to be as funny as she is, a fact we have all learned from the movies.

Sissy's at the end of the greasy corduroy couch that sits in the center of the tire yard's cement bay floor. Next to her is Bird, and everyone always knows right where Bird is. You can't take your eyes off him. Especially if you want to. Believe me, I have tried. Then Mo, and she's half under Bird or half over him, somehow half of her is always missing along with half of her clothes, which are always too few, too short, too cold. Half of her face is behind her hair, which is blond too, like Sis's, but flat and stringy, like she's always just come in from the rain. I get cold looking at Mo. Aunt Bev says pay attention to that, the feeling in your body when you're with someone, the temperatures that repeat around them. I just think that Mo should put on a sweatshirt.

Next to Mo there's Cy. Or there might be me. Sweatshirt on, hood up, bundled against the chill no one else seems to feel.

On the table in front of us, which is not a table but a stack of pallets, there are beers. On the floor around us, there are beers. Under our backpacks with our supposed futures inside, there are beers.

Cy. Bird. Mo. Sissy is lying across the couch, her head partly covering Mo's legs, which are bare below the tattoos on the inside of her left thigh, little *v*'s floating up and up toward her vagina, vortex, vying for some kind of warmth up there. Sissy is humming "Amazing Grace." It's not unpleasant.

Cy and I have the map that slides behind the cracked plastic case on the wall by Fast Eddie's office. It's one of those old-time maps from when the tire yard was just a gas station without a city on a road to somewhere else. We're choosing different destinations based on how far we think we could go on a single tank of gas in my dad's retired post office jeep. This will never happen, involving, as it does, us, driving, and somewhere else. The game is to guess the mileage. Whoever's guess is the farthest off from what we measure using our pinkie fingers as guides against the map's legend, that person has to drink.

Sissy. Mo is focused across the warehouse, watching for Bird to come out of the bathroom. Cy is on his feet, taking this chance to move into Bird's spot, which is empty now and still warm, so he can grab the last beer from the bag at Mo's feet. Sissy's response to this is made clear by the impressive belch she makes after she beats Cy to the beer he was wanting and drains it in almost one gulp. She crumples the can in her hand and throws it at Cy, who sits back down where he was.

Cy is Bird's disciple, made in his image or whatever, except less handsome and less tough, or maybe it's just that he actually has something to lose and Bird does not. Mainly, he is kept busy taking orders from Bird or waiting to take orders from Bird. In their spare time, Bird and Cy beat up on each other for fun. When Bird isn't going to school, he calls Cy and Cy stays home too. Like a good little shadow. Otherwise, they are the same, white—like we all are, like it seems all of Rosary is now—young, and dumb as the used tires wasting around us.

Sissy. Mo. Cy is bent down tying his shoes like his life depends on it. The longer he takes, the less climbing he has to do. Cy is afraid of heights and Bird is climbing the tires, a series of steel racks that are bolted into the walls of the warehouse, which means Cy has to climb too.

The used tires are sorted onto these racks according to a plan that's only clear to Fast Eddie and maybe God. Brand or style? Or wear? It might be about whether you can see the top of that president's head when you stick a dime in the tread. I'm not old enough to vote yet, but so far this seems about the only practical use for a president's head that I've heard.

Bird is going to hang upside down from the highest rack of tires until the top of his head is filled with blood and he'll look so peaceful doing it that pretty soon we'll all join him. Me, Sissy, Mo, and Cy. Upside-down Dickheads. If we let our shirts fall, let gravity cover our faces, if we don't tuck the hems into the top of our pants to hide our tits, Eddie will come out of his office and toss us beers. The game then is to catch them and drink them upside down. It's harder than you think.

TEENS GONE WILD

The tire yard's customers call him Ed. We don't call him anything. We flash our tits, we get our beer. We say, "Fuck Fast Eddie," as we cheers, and then we swallow them down.

No one worries about being caught when the bay of Fast Eddie's Tire Salvage turns into Fast Eddie's Teenage Wild Kingdom. When school lets out, the last bell rings into the wind changing direction over Rosario Bay and the smell from the refinery begins its afternoon tour of streets and houses. The smell is so bad that no one wonders that Eddie's door comes rolling down by 3:30 p.m., and no one wants to go outside and see where the kids have gone anyway. We run to the tire yard from our different directions, over the back fence, through the side door, jump into the bay from the front lot, but once inside we all do the same things. We climb the walls of tires, swing from the rafters, and wait for the beer to pour once Bird or another Dickhead jumps onto the door, holds on there as his weight rolls the big metal door down, shutting us in with the wasted tire smells, asphalt, and spent rubber. It gets in our hair and soaks into our skin, but no one can smell it over the smells from the refinery in the afternoon air.

Climbing on the spent tires that are waiting to be burned or retreaded or for one more chance at the road, soaking up the petroleum through our skin, getting drunk on cheap beer, we don't worry about being caught because we already are. We'll know how these tires feel our whole lives, whether we succeed at rolling out of here or not. We see it at home, when we go there, we see it on the faces of parents too tired to hope.

My dad wasn't always one of those tired kind. When my mom was alive he was different, whole. When she died, though, he fell right apart, and I've been collecting the pieces of him since.

NIGHT OF THE LIVING DAD

Parents come in all kinds of monster. My mom, for example, is a ghost.

My dad is basically a zombie, like the kind in those old movies from back when zombies were a piece of cake. Dad is just another sad old white person in his Sunday best. Too single-minded and slow to be dangerous, he ends up being more annoying than anything else. He just keeps on trudging.

If I were going to put Dad out of my misery, I'd start by cutting him up into tiny, thoughtful pieces. I'd cube him, like the top chefs do on television. Hold his flesh down tight under my fingertips, my knuckles a guide for the blade. Then I'd place these pieces of him far from each other, a distance too hard to travel without a brain to scoot them along. I'd keep his hands away from his wrists, put one shoulder under the kitchen sink, an elbow under the back porch. And even if I did this, he wouldn't change. One hand would still crawl toward his wallet, still pull out his bank card to help preserve Rosary's heritage and then again for every infomercial about starving children, still pull out a wad of cash for the collection plate on Sundays. Giving out money is as natural to Dad as holding his dick while pissing, the cash arcs out in a stream.

I could bury his feet on either end of the block. And even if I did this, worked through his tendons and gristle, tore him apart, his feet would still stuff themselves into his orthopedic shoes in the morning, walk themselves to the retired postal jeep that we pretend is a car a normal family might have, and push the gas pedal down until he arrived at the post office to work another shift on the march toward infinity. Or retirement. Same difference.

Would anyone at the PO even notice if Dad's feet came to work without his face because I'd hidden it in our mailbox? And when some other gray-skinned zombie shuddered up in his little postal jeep, picked up Dad's face, rode around with it all day, and then dropped it in the bin back at the station, would that finally be enough to put the postmark to Dad's dead-letter life?

Probably not. Probably no one would notice the difference. And I probably won't dismember my dad today even if I would be doing him a favor. Today I'll keep him together.

Again.

WAYS TO CLOSE A PRAYER

When Mom was first in and out of the hospital, I was too young to really get who was in charge. It was supposed to be them, Mom and Dad together, the big bosses. Mom and Dad and sometimes God. But the way Mom and Dad talked about her getting better was confusing. They didn't seem to agree on who to trust, argued quietly, politely as ever, about where to put our faith. Like faith was some kind of cash we'd been keeping under the mattress and now we needed a safer spot for it in case the house burned down. They talked about God, like before, like always, but also about doctors, lots of them, and their words all kind of ran together, so I did my best to sort it out.

I would go through the official bedside-with-parents prayers, the ones Dad started leading me through because Mom was too tired to tuck me in. Mom's church, the one that used to fly through the air at bedtime, brought alive by her two hands, sat closed and quiet in the embroidered pockets of her robe, all its people wrapped around a tissue she never seemed to let go of anymore. At bedtimes now, it was the Church of Dad, a serious place where nothing rhymed. I would go through those prayers with him and then, once the light in the hall was off, I'd slip out of bed, knees back to the carpet, and pray for real.

I would start by crossing Rudolph's white feet on top of each other and petting him until he started purring. A cat's prayer, I figured. Then I'd whisper into my folded hands what I couldn't say with Dad listening.

Doctor God, it's me again.

Thank You for taking care of Mommy like Daddy says You are.

I know You are busy and have all the sparrows of the field to keep an eye on, but I was hoping that You could please not be late anymore to Mommy's appointments and keeping her waiting with the sick people and that same old copy of Family Circle *with the meat loaf recipe, especially when she is getting better and is always early.*

It makes her tired. And I hate meat loaf.

Amen. And in Your light.

And if You could point some of that light to the insurance stuff she has to work on instead of playing with me, just enough so all the papers would catch on fire and burn up like your bushes in the Bible, that would make us all feel better too.

In Jesus's name. And when He takes over Your practice, maybe He could get some new magazines.

SHADOW OF THE VALLEY

All my prayers didn't work. Neither did Dad's.

Before Mom was sick, when she would tuck me in, she'd stay by my bed until I was asleep, or she thought I was. She would kiss my forehead, pulling the blankets up one more time before she turned away. I'd open my eyes then and watch her go, watching until she turned off the hall light. Just as she flipped the switch, I'd close my eyes tight, so the light would burn her shape into the darkness, a blazing pure white against the black of my eyelids and the night, more real than any electricity. That's how prayers with Mom felt too. Like the God we were talking to was bigger, brighter, more powerful than all the darkness around us.

Nothing else ever felt as real.

RELIGIOUS ORGANIZATIONS

The city of Rosary's Yellow Pages contains twenty-seven churches. The main thing these churches have in common is an inability to have the letter *t* appear in their names, or anywhere in their listings, without turning it into a cross at least once. The idea of Jesus Himself hanging right in there for our sins must appear smack-dab in the middle of an address or the center of a pastor's name. God help those who can't help themselves.

Under *C*, for *Crosses and Their Misuses*, and under *F*, for *Fraternal Organizations and General Fuckery*, you'll find *The Council for the Peaceful Reconciliation of Rosary and Sky*. The council takes up most of Dad's time on Thursday evenings and the first Saturday afternoon of every month. Its focus is on ideas like reform, family values, increased revenues, and extending the benefits of its own membership. Dad's job as a council member seems mostly to be about writing extremely awkward correspondence.

The letters are mainly to people who were made to feel unwelcome when Rosary was first incorporated, when McClure County broke out into angry red cities just like this one, the way a teenager breaks out in zits. The people who would have none of Rosary's anger and isolation, these are the people Rosary wishes would return, so we can prove how nice we can play if you just give us a chance. Rosary is like that bully in the schoolyard who looks around when the dust settles and says, "Where did everybody go?"

BEAT CUTE

Violence does help pass the time. In this way, Bird is like Rosary High's own time machine. A day might be dragging on, the clock clearly broken, and the next thing you know, Bird is smashing someone's head into a locker and it's time to go home. He usually reserves his best efforts for the Thumpers, but sooner or later we all take a turn.

Today, it's mine. And I'm not alone. There's a new guy at school. He is hard to miss in his XXL button-down and a precisely knotted tie that screams hard-core Thumper. At least, that is what I'm thinking as we pass each other in the quad and he smiles down at me like he cannot wait to share the Good News. His look is so sincere, so open, that even I am kind of caught up for a second, and this is the exact moment when Bird decides to welcome him to Rosary High by knocking his head and my head straight into each other. Hard. Hard enough that the new kid throws up, chocolate milk and red licorice, all over the three of us. A pretty weird diet for high school.

Not that I know he's thrown up, because I'm passed out on the hot cement of the quad and dreaming of sugar melting in an Easy-Bake Oven, the black scar ruining the pink metal and my mouth watering. When I open my eyes, it's to Bird kicking this kid in his big, soft stomach, Bird saying, "You messed up my shoes, you pig," and the new guy not saying anything, even when Bird kicks him again, his chocolate and sticky red Converse leaving streaks on the fancy shirt, streaks that look like smears of shit and blood, and even when Bird kicks him again and shouts, "Is that all? What else is in you?"

The new kid says nothing.

And he still doesn't say anything when a girl I've never seen before either, with long brown hair and tight jeans, comes up behind Bird, flips her Technicolor bangs back, and says, "Spencer Doncaster." Like she is taking roll. Like she is dying to get her ass kicked too. And then she says it again.

"Spencer Doncaster, that's my brother you're fucking with."

Only teachers call Bird by his real name. And even they look a little scared when they do.

When Bird turns around to explain this to the new girl, she hits him across the face with the long side of her forearm before he can. I am thinking that this is a really good way to break an arm and I am hypnotized by the mess of silver bangle bracelets flashing and jingling in the sun as she swings back and hits him again. Her bangles come away as red as licorice with Bird's blood and he can barely push "Fucker" out of his swollen lips, lips still too kissable, more kissable than is right.

She leans down to her brother and strokes his head. "Win, you okay?"

He doesn't answer her. He speaks to me.

"Hi."

That smile again.

"Hi," I say. And, "You got a little something on your shirt." All I can manage before teachers are there with Jay, Rosary High's security guard, and we are all escorted to the principal's office.

REPENTANCE

"Helen." Dad is out of breath, which is typical, his shoes squeaking across the tile as he lurches over to me, leans down, and looks in my eyes to see if I am okay. "Helen?"

He seems to be himself and I am relieved. Sometimes, by the end of the day, Dad is falling apart, and I spend some time bringing him tea, making up things about school that seem like they might have happened to a person who wanted to be there, that seem like he would feel good hearing. But this is only lunchtime and he looks good. I nod at him and scoot to the end of the bench so he can sit down. He can be a total embarrassment—he is a dad—but sometimes even when he isn't being embarrassing, when he is wearing his postal uniform, I have a hard time talking to him. Since the day he picked me up from fifth grade, took me out of a math test so we could go to the hospital and say goodbye to Mom. He knows this and sits in silence.

Now we are only waiting for the parents of the new kids to arrive so they will have someone to represent them in the principal's office, in this reconciling we are always expected to have whenever there is an incident of "campus violence." I heard Mrs. Curran, the secretary, giving directions to Rosary High when she called the number in their file. The Epsworthy family has just moved to town.

And coming down the hallway is their leader.

"Don't even think about repenting, sinners, you don't have time for that shit. Excuse me. You don't have time for that crap. This place is going to blow sky-high! Get a load of that!"

Once we become friends, I learn that Winthrop and Rainbolene Epsworthy never expect their mom. Even though she is alive, mostly, she never leaves the house. Their dad, though, is almost never in it. He drives around Rosary in this van painted with sheaves of wheat and LOST CITY BREAD written on the side, bought from some bakery where they used to live in Alaska, near another refinery there. And though there is a speaker mounted to the top of the van that connects to a microphone he uses freely to broadcast the troubles of his current lost city, Rosary, all of which he relates to the existence of Rosary's oil refinery—and to boost the sales of the life insurance policies it is his business to sell—this isn't enough for him. Mr. Epsworthy needs to be heard.

When Mr. Epsworthy sees my dad, he narrows his eyes and sniffs. As if he knows all about it, what it is to fall apart every day and have your kid put you back together and how that can kind of stink. The vomit on Winthrop doesn't faze Mr. Epsworthy at all, though. He hugs Winthrop and Rainbolene before he even says a word to them, holds Winthrop's cheek to the light to better see his bruises, and then touches his shirt where the cloth has dried red.

"It's not blood, Pop," Winthrop says.

Mr. Epsworthy sniffs up and down Winthrop's shirtfront. "A little blood," he says, "but mostly . . . licorice?" He has a very good nose.

Winthrop nods.

"Your mom packed licorice in your bag today." Mr. Epsworthy doesn't sound like a crazy person anymore, or an insurance salesman. He sounds like a dad. And like all the dads I know, especially my own, he sounds like he has just lost a fight.

Winthrop nods again, and for the first time since I opened my eyes in the quad and saw his face, I think he might cry. "And I ate all of it."

Mr. Epsworthy puts his arm around his son, and then Winthrop looks less like a giant man-baby, roly-poly in his stomach and face, stretching his ruined shirt and bursting the top of his dress pants. He just looks like someone's kid, being held like he needs to be held, until we hear Principal Harrison opening her door and Mr. Epsworthy lets him go.

A FAKE CHINESE RUBBER PLANT

"Before I call in Spencer and Mrs. Doncaster, I want to have a quick chat with your two families in private," Principal Harrison says, so we follow her into her office as if we have a choice. First Winthrop and Rainbolene and their dad, then me and mine, who is dragging his feet, as usual. There is barely room for all of us between the file cabinets and a too-tall, sad plant leaning in toward the lamp on the desk like it could possibly get the nurturing it needs from that light, enough so it can uproot and walk out of here.

Harrison's chair wheels screech like someone just put the *Haunted House Sounds* album on in the library next door and she clasps her hands over a stack of papers that might have been there since before computers were invented. Her joined hands in this pose of patience let us know that she is going to be very reasonable about this.

She aims her reasonable self first toward Winthrop. "Winthrop. Are you all right?"

He looks pretty bad and, based on what I saw between him and his dad in the waiting room, I expect he'll lose it when he talks about Bird beating on him. But he doesn't talk about Bird at all.

"Nothing happened, Mrs. Harrison," Winthrop says.

My dad groans when he hears this, but no one pays attention when postmen groan. Winthrop and Rainbolene's dad is lost in reading the earthquake safety poster on the back of Harrison's door, sometimes laughing out loud and saying softly, "Get a load of that." And Rainbolene, who is twisting her bracelets around her wrist, scratching blood off the silver, doesn't even look up.

"Excuse me?"

"Nothing happened, Mrs. Harrison. I fell."

"But . . . there's blood." She looks at his shirt, linen, I think, and a pale pink. Too nice for Rosary High, and so Rosary High, in the form of Bird's fists and feet, made sure it would never be coming back.

"It's licorice." Rainbolene offers this without looking up. "That's licorice on Win's shirt and some chocolate drink. Slim Kwik? It's not blood." She looks at the clock above the door. "Can we go now, Mrs. Harrison? I don't want to miss final period because my brother is clumsy."

"Mr. Epsworthy!" Harrison says then. Her effort at patience collects like spit in the corners of her mouth but her eyes do not rest even for a moment on Rainbolene. There is no earthquake safety poster to prepare Rosary High's principal for the fact of a student like Rainbolene in her midst. One who knows herself and what she's capable of so well, one who makes the very fact of Principal Harrison, and the gates she is there to keep, perfectly irrelevant.

"Find an interior wall!" Mr. Epsworthy giggles. "Cover your

head!" But he pulls himself away from the poster he's been reading and says, "Principal"—he reads the nameplate at the edge of
her desk—"Harrison." And he makes a short bow as he says her
last name. "It all boils down to this . . ."

As soon as Winthrop and Rainbolene hear these words
they sit down together on the small bench under Harrison's
sad fern. Then Winthrop gives Rainbolene a little push and he
pats the seat that has opened up between them. He gives me
that smile, one that says either he's here to save my soul or
we're going to hell anyway, so let's make the most of it. And
I sit down.

Mr. Epsworthy says, "Roanoke."

Rain looks carefully at her nails then, they are short and
perfect and painted a light green that reminds me of lime snow
cones. I realize that she is studying her nails because she is trying not to laugh.

"Everybody loves Atlantis, there's a hotel named after it, for
crying out loud, but Vegas hasn't cornered the market on Sodom
and Gomorrah, all the lost cities are celebrated, in fact, all the
lost things."

Principal Harrison looks like she's the one whose head is
hurting.

"Do you watch any crime dramas, Mrs. Harrison? Any police
procedurals?" When he says these words, "crime dramas" and
"police procedurals," Epsworthy's voice slows down, falls into a
whisper. It is riveting for one second and then it is boring, and
that seems to be part of the plan. "Everyone is in search of the
perfect crime, the perfect criminal, maybe her own perfect
escape. We lovers of the lost continents are in search of the perfect decadence."

As he returns to the ancient cities, his voice rises again. On
either side of me, Winthrop and Rainbolene move their mouths
in chorus with him as he says, "Transcendent decadence."

Harrison tries to interrupt him, but her protests turn to silent blushing at his next words.

"Orgies! Indulgence! In these stories of what we've lost, there are no children. We want to know that they deserved it, those populations that disappeared, so there can't be any children. If there were children among them, then they must have all been innocents, which means we are going to have to try harder, to be like them, to be worthy." His hands lift. His fingers wiggle.

Epsworthy's version of the chosen ones reminds me of my mother's clasped hands, the pretend people there, wiggling. I see her lifting her index fingers together, touching their tips. *Here is the church, here is the steeple.* Her wedding ring flashing in the light from my bedside. *Open the door*—she'd flip her hands over—*and see all the people*, and as she wiggled her fingers I'd snuggle into the blankets, heaven right at hand, all around me in the form of my mom and Rudolph, my partner in prayer. Rudolph loved this show as much as I did, we'd watch Mom's fingers together, hypnotized. *Again*, I said to her, always, *again*, and she'd do it again and again until I was ready for sleep, safe in the idea that eternity was in my mother's grasp.

"Again," I say. Out loud. That bump on my head must have done more damage than I thought. And I am so embarrassed. But not as much as when Mr. Epsworthy turns to me and repeats what I can't believe I've said.

"Yes, by God, again, there's a smart one there. It's all going to happen again." And he lifts his hands to the pressboard sky of Harrison's office once more. His fingers are the people of a lost colony that has nothing to do whatsoever with schoolyard bullying, a colony ascended to the stars.

We all fall silent, transfixed by the tiny rapture before us. Harrison's eyes follow those fingers to the perforated ceiling, and Dad, well, there's nothing he likes better than the end of days.

Even though he's all but worn out from rising again, he's excited for everyone else to join him.

Mr. Epsworthy takes a deep breath. Gathers himself. "Does that answer your question?"

Of course it doesn't answer her question about what happened in the quad, but it certainly has made it so she isn't going to ask Mr. Epsworthy another one, probably ever. I feel like I should applaud, and I push my hands between my knees so I won't. I look at my dad, standing as still as stone, as dead as Epsworthy is alive, and we all wait for Harrison. She has started tidying the withered pile of papers on her desk, positioning her stapler just so.

"Well." She clears her throat. "I think we are close to wrapping this up."

Has she forgotten about me? I hold my breath. But no such luck. The haze that Epsworthy created in the room to protect his own children doesn't cover me.

"Helen, let's hear your side of the story." She takes in my safe position between Winthrop and Rainbolene and then points to the chair right before her. "Join me."

As I stand, Winthrop whispers in a tiny cartoon voice, "I'll miss you!" and Dad tries to catch my eye, to stare me into doing what I know he thinks is the right thing here. For Dad, *right* always means the biblical right, black-and-white right. When I don't look at him, he keeps angling my way, until he almost falls over.

Dad and his scripture. He was raised a believer and always walked the talk, that's why he came to Rosary in the first place. But since Mom died it's like he's had a Bible transplant for a heart just to save him from any new story being written there. He's curled up in the Good Book like a tired old dog on a sofa cushion, grateful that someone somewhere has the answers, nose to tail, just waiting for the end.

Harrison's nameplate is plastic, not metal like it is pretending to be. I focus on that so I won't have to see my dad's God-fearing eyes. His daughter-fearing eyes. And I tell my side of the story, just like she asked.

"That's it, Principal Harrison. Winthrop fell."

Dad forgets himself then. Says, "Hell!"

He never calls me that. For obvious reasons.

"I practically fell on top of him. It's lucky I wore black today." I pluck at my black stretch pants, smooth my hands over my black hoodie, feel where the licorice-and-chocolate vomit has soaked into the fabric, hardly noticeable except to my fingers. I wear black every day, of course, but I dig my feet into their black Converse and dare her to call me a liar.

Instead, she puts her head in her hands while Dad sputters in the background, caught in his own trap. "Hell!"

Dad tries to leave others to their sins, even me. He leaves salvation to the sinner and her God. That's why I don't have to go to church if I don't want to. And I don't want to. And it's why he just stands there in Principal Harrison's office while I weave a tangled web, shaking his head and saying over and over again just one word: "Hell."

Poor Dad. For someone so devout to have me for a daughter and with the Devil's playground for a nickname. That is a curse. Helen was my great-grandma's name on my mom's side. According to Aunt Bev, Great-Grandma had the gift, but so far as I can tell, the only gift that comes with my name is being able to trick my dad into cursing in the principal's office.

THE 9IFT

Aunt Bev's shoppe is around the corner from us. Her bedroom and bathroom are in the back, both crowded with books and icons and a surprising number of cowboy boots. Up front there's a stove and a small fridge next to the cash register, and the usual suspects: a round table with a velvet cloth, a crystal ball, and a box of tarot cards wrapped in purple silk. But don't let the shoppe's extra *p* and silent *e* fool you, Aunt Bev isn't here to annoy you to death. She bought the storefront already named from the last Rosary psychic, who left, sick or scared of Rosary's resistance to her work.

And don't let the "psychic" part fool you that much either. The back of Aunt Bev's shoppe is open for business as much as, if not more than, the front.

Aunt Bev doesn't try to hide anything from me, she says, because I'll see it all soon enough. I don't know if she means I'll see it soon enough because I'm growing up or because she insists I inherited Great-Grandma Helen's gift and then a "backhanded blessing" on top of that when Mom died too young and became my eyes in the sky, a guide I am supposed to be able to rely on someday, some other day that is never today.

I see it all either way. Aunt Bev can read fortunes. She can do other things too, with paper and rose water and tears, cast spells maybe. But her gift isn't enough to make ends meet, what with the Thumpers trying to take away her business license and littering her front step with scripture and hate mail.

Or maybe Aunt Bev isn't broke, just bored. Of Rosary. Isn't everyone? What I am sure about is that the ink in the shoppe's ledger turned more black than red when she turned her hours upside down, started giving readings later at night, in private, and started conducting more business in the back bedroom than at the front table. She says, "They really listen to you, if you let them get close. If they think they know you, they let you know them." She says it is all the same. Intimacy is intimacy. And that she chooses which customers to make fall all the way under her spell. She hardly has repeats for this kind of work. "Catch and release," she says. If there's any regret for one she wished she hadn't let go, I can't hear it.

I've been hanging out at the shoppe since Mom got sick, when Aunt Bev started helping Dad take care of me full-time. I do her accounting while she works or rests between clients. "You gotta keep good books," she says, and shows me how to account for "research," also known as taking her niece to the old movies they run in Rosary, because "you have to know what stories people are feeding themselves, what stories will be getting in the way." She teaches me which of the IRS's categories are best for writing off sage and incense, "home office" or "business expense." And she has me put some perfectly useful receipts aside. At the end of each quarter she burns these in the smudge pot. As an offering, she says. To keep the real balance.

In her own way, Aunt Bev is just as devout as Dad except that where Dad holds the Bible, Aunt Bev has a pack of tarot cards bent at the corners, greasy with the oil of fingerprints and hope. And she's never had to bother being born again because she never let anyone stop her from living in the first place.

Dad's fear is that I'll succumb to this temptation of prophecy, like Aunt Bev did. As if it were that easy. He's afraid that I'll become her apprentice and take over for her when she retires.

She says he'll get over it.

They can go ahead and arm-wrestle for my soul all they want, I've got other mysteries on my mind.

I peek between the curtains drawn around the office-kitchen nook, see how Aunt Bev lets her hand linger over the bloodred velvet that covers the circular table when she is reading a palm, holds it a bit longer depending on the customer. I see when she brushes against a hand as the customer chooses cards. Some of these sessions finish faster when she invites the client back for an extended reading after hours, which is my signal to close up the register and go on home. The next day I come in to see a charge slip that is double the usual reading fee, triple, even four times the usual payment. Aunt Bev says that you can't put a monetary price on a spiritual exchange, but clearly she is working with some kind of algorithm, one far advanced of the math I'm learning at Rosary High.

At first I thought the customers must be feeling Aunt Bev up, that they were French-kissing and messing around. I was too young to imagine what the different charges could be for, and Rosary internet, when Dad finally allowed us to have it, is zero help, quarantined as it is against sites that aren't authorized by the City of Rosary's Information Neutrality Office. In middle school, things became clearer. I learned from what I heard in the halls. Then, thanks to the staticky Sky Radio program geared to teens in distress that I can just barely tune in here at the shoppe, everything fell into place.

It goes something like this: Aunt Bev charges double for a hand job, triple for a blow job, and quadruple for the trump card, as shooting stars spew over the lovers' heads. Meanwhile, I'm sitting alone behind tie-dyed curtains with a crush on the world's wrongest boy and I've never even been kissed.

ACE OF WANDS

Bird and his mom are finally invited into Principal Harrison's office from the conference room, where they have been secluded like this is some kind of grand jury appearance. As they walk in, the office shrinks. We are all pressed against each other. I scoot the chair in closer to the desk and I'm glad I'm sitting down, because Bird is right behind me. I can feel the heat from his body. I can smell him, a stinging cleanness like bleach seeping out of his skin. I pull my sweatshirt around me. I'm freezing but then I'm too warm. Bird sends my body in all directions at once, cold and hot, empty and full. I can keep my distance at the tire yard and usually at school too, but here I am lost in the bright smell of his sweat, the violence like cologne. Mouth dry, underwear not.

And what is there to say? It isn't the first time, won't be the last, even though Mrs. Doncaster, Bird's mom, acts like it is. And

Principal Harrison doesn't have any ammunition, since we all lied. She can't even force us to make the insincere apologies we've learned by heart or gag our way through the corresponding required statements of supposed forgiveness.

All of those words aren't for us anyway, but for them, for Mrs. Harrison and the parents in attendance. So they can sigh with relief and carry on with pretending that they've totally aced this role model thing. But not today.

Pretty much everyone at Rosary expects to get beat on by Bird at some point. It's what he does. There are a few of us, though, who hang out with him despite the risk, or because of it. Because skin on skin is honest and in Rosary the only way we're legally allowed to experience some of that is through violence. Even Security Guard Jay will tell kids to "leave room for the Holy Spirit" when they stand too close in the halls. The way he says it, like he's being recorded, makes it clear that protecting us from touching each other in any way is a part of his job description.

Jay is more like a guy who collects shopping carts at a grocery store than a security guard but he's here anyway. Securing us. Or guarding us. Whatever it is he's supposed to be doing, what he does is be nice to us, hold the doors open when we go in or out, and stop us from full-on fucking in the halls. Whenever someone starts a fight he's on it, but if anyone starts making out behind a locker, he waits as long as he can and then runs really, really slowly in that direction, making sure his keys jingle and the walkie-talkie on his belt, which connects to Principal Harrison's office when he pushes the button, is squawking away. But he doesn't ever push that button until a teacher shows up or there's blood. It's almost like Jay trusts us to figure out our shit on our own. And that is precisely not what they are paying him to do.

Next on the list of useless ideas had by the Rosary High

School Board is the zero-tolerance rule for fighting. Everyone who is in a fight, or near a fight, or saw a fight out of the corner of their eye, no matter who started it or why, is put on an automatic three-day suspension. From school. At home. It's almost as if, unlike Jay, the school board doesn't want us to figure anything out. It's almost like they want us to fail at learning to fight, at learning to protect ourselves, because the next thing you know, we'd be protecting ourselves from them.

PUNISHED

My three-day Rosary High vacation begins with Dad leaving for work, the door finally closing on the last of his many reminders about the studying he thinks I will do today. And then silence.

And more silence.

Aunt Bev will still be asleep. The tire yard isn't open to Dickheads until school is out.

Silence.

I might actually study.

And then the phone rings.

Even after the meeting with Principal Harrison, even while I was giving Winthrop and Rainbolene my phone number, while Bird's mom and my dad were talking, I didn't notice Winthrop's voice. I do notice it on the phone, though. There is no way to hide from its depth and strength, nowhere else for it to go but straight into my head, and when he says, "Helen Dedleder, this is Winthrop Epsworthy speaking. Do you want to come over to my house and not study?" I can even hear the smile on his face.

CITY BLOCKS

I grab my backpack in case Dad makes it home before I do and needs to believe I'm off somewhere studying. As I walk the five blocks to Winthrop and Rain's house, I take in the new flyers plastered on the telephone poles lining San Pablo Boulevard.

Rosary's main street is one of a handful still named after some saint or other. The Rosary Bible Thumpers are pissed that the Catholics landed here before them and got to do all the murdering-slash-saving of the souls who were truly here first. What's worse, this means the Catholics had the privilege of officially renaming everything. Part of what Dad does on the Reconciliation Council is the tedious paperwork required to officially rename bits of Rosary in ways that are more evangelically inclined. He's very proud of Jesus Saves Parkway and Good News Avenue, but he refuses to consider my idea for the renaming of San Pablo Boulevard as What Would Jesus Drive.

The Thumpers can't stand that Rosary is named after a favored Catholic accessory. But what is a rosary except a bookmark for prayers? When this tiny suburb of Sky sprang up around the refinery, the oilmen were in such a rush to make their dollars, they grabbed for the name of the nearest landmark, Rosario Bay, whitewashed it, and were ready to go. Next, they threw up all of our houses at once. I mean, like, vomited them up. Spit them out. Each one the same. No one ever has to ask where a bathroom is in someone else's house here. We know the way because the layout in one house is just like the next, from the grain of the paneling in the hallway to the bushes in the front yard and how high they grow. We could unpack each other's groceries, fuck each other's husbands or wives, and never realize that we didn't actually make it home. Each of our houses is like one of those beads strung up on either side of the plastic Jesus weighing down all of Rosary, eternal in their sameness. Any shine they once had was rubbed away from years of worry until they became as identical to one another as our parents wish we would be to them.

MASTURBATE THEATRE

Winthrop and Rainbolene give me the tour of their house, all except the Epsworthys' bedroom, where Mrs. Epsworthy is "taking her midday rest," Rain says, with only the slightest eye roll. And their house is just like mine, except they are living the two-bedroom version of Rosary life and we have three, one for the little brother or sister I never got to have. And except that where our porch has the same polite nothing on it as most Rosary porches, the Epsworthys have placed a stone pagoda and their yard is dotted with dandelions.

My dad goes out at night with a tiny spray bottle of weed killer and murders the dandelions when he thinks no one will notice. As far as I know, this is the only time he succumbs to pride. And here is an entire plot of them, the sins of a Rosary lawn, for all to see. And here is a pagoda, with no explanation at all. And in the Epsworthys' kitchen, right in the middle of the day, we eat ice cream. I can't decide if I've wandered into Sodom or Gomorrah, but I finish every bite.

And then.

We still have two and a half days left without school.

The Epsworthys have an old stereo with a dial tuner and we sit around for a while on the living room floor, trying to get Sky Radio to come in. Every Rosary teenager, Thumpers too, tries for Sky Radio on any device they can access. It's worth listening through the static because the doctor and his sidekick talk about sex and answer questions about sex and make jokes about sex and have live porn stars on to talk about performing sex acts for a living. Like all of these sex-related actions are choices a body can make with no shame. And most important, the hosts give shout-outs to Rosary kids like they know we're listening. Like they know what we're listening for.

It won't come in and I'm suddenly saying, "I can get it at my aunt's shoppe if you want to come over there sometime." I don't want to explain Aunt Bev, don't want to lose these new friends if the fact of her will drive them away, but I think this thought after I've already opened my big mouth.

"Your aunt's the psychic, right?" Winthrop says, and when I nod, barely, like maybe I can still hide this information by being noncommittal, he says, "Cool." And then Rain says, as if she already knows about Aunt Bev too, "But what are we going to do now?" She kind of meows the "now," like a bored little kid. It's like everyone they know is related to some witch or other, so my situation is no big deal, and the acceptance of these two people settles around me like dandelion fluff from a wish I didn't know I'd made.

"We could put on a play," Winthrop says.

Rain jumps up. "Meet me in the bedroom."

In their bedroom, Win and I sit on the floor between their beds and Rain comes in with a big metal box and shuts the door quietly so as not to wake their mom. A minute later, and we are surrounded by Mr. Epsworthy's collection of dirty books, reading lines out to each other, and I am laughing so hard it feels like the first time.

SPEAKEASY

After we have read through most of Mr. Epsworthy's stash on the first day of Rosary High Porn Camp, I invite Winthrop and Rain to the tire yard. Which is kind of an awkward invitation to present.

"Hey, do you guys want to go to Fast Eddie's Tire Salvage and break the law with that guy who beat up Winthrop, a couple of weird girls, and an old perv? Is that something that sounds good to you?"

I don't put it quite like that.

When it gets to be 3:30 and I know the Dickheads will be on their way to Fast Eddie's, I make this slightly more enticing offer: "Hey, after school some of us get together at the tire yard and drink beer. Do you want to go?"

———

Since Winthrop and Rain didn't rat Bird out in Principal Harrison's office, I know they will be welcome. Or what passes for welcome in Dickhead language.

Allow me to translate.

When we arrive at the tire yard, Bird nods at Rain and gives Winthrop a "What's up?" This is a standard greeting in many dialects but when spoken at the tire yard to a newcomer it translates roughly as "Fellow Traveler, you are welcome here."

Bird doesn't expect an answer, and when he does not receive one it is revealed that the Epsworthys must have encountered other Dickheads in their travels and are familiar with our customs.

We sit down, and Bird pushes the bag of beers at his feet toward us. In Dickhead this translates basically into "I have done you a wrong, which I now acknowledge. I would like you to forgive my past behavior. I share with you now the tools of forgetting."

Accepting the tools of forgetting without comment, as is appropriate, Winthrop and Rain open them and drink.

Dickhead initiation successful.

DETAILS

Rainbolene is not Rain's given name, in the usual sense. Rainbolene is the name she gave herself when she gave Winthrop all her butch clothes and started growing her bangs low over one eye. She dyes a bright strip through them, the color of a tropical fruit, and she smiles like she's turning letters on *Wheel of Fortune* when she's kicking someone's ass.

Rain knows all kinds of facts about how to be found "beautiful according to our current societal norms," like how part of the reason Vanna White is so famous is that she has a weirdly giant head and people subconsciously find this attractive. And Rain knows how to use these facts. She can put on eyeliner better than anyone I've ever seen in real life, but she can't legally grow tits until she's old enough to get a prescription for them, for the hormone boost she needs. In Rosary, that age is never. But at eighteen, she can leave this city for Sky. Until then, there's this. There's us. Still life with Dickheads.

MY SO-CAULED LIFE

Having a witch for an aunt doesn't exactly put you on the fast track for popularity at Rosary High. Whether or not she is actually doing anything illegal by the standards of the law or the Lord, Aunt Bev is seen as an outlaw here, at best. She's the Devil herself at worst. Somewhere in the middle, she's a weirdo, and guess what that makes me.

Mom's family was first-wave Rosary and Aunt Bev left as soon as Great-Grandma Helen was safely in the ground. There is some debate about who was disowned first, Grandpa and Grandma Hill or Aunt Bev, but I know for sure that she was never invited back, and as far as the elder Hills knew, no one ever spoke to her again.

Aunt Bev made it to Sky, bought a used Toyota truck, and started driving it up and down the coast, picking fruit and telling fortunes on the beach, on the side of the road, at bars. Even though she left Mom behind, to go to high school, to fall in love, they never lost touch. Aunt Bev called her little sister from phone booths on the road and Mom answered when she could. They talked whenever Mom was alone, figuring out when this would be thanks to Aunt Bev's psychic connection and via a sequence of intricate signals—hang-ups after so many rings to let Mom know when Aunt Bev would be calling. Coded responses from Mom, who would be sitting by the phone when it rang, to let Aunt Bev know their parents were now in the room. The sisters' commitment to each other, always strong, was strengthened by these many repetitions of "I'm sorry, you have the wrong number," and "No, thank you, we are not interested," and like all bonds of forbidden love, it was built to last.

When Mom was first sick, Aunt Bev returned to Rosary for good, much to every faithful Thumper's dismay. She planted her crystal ball permanently then, taking over the shoppe and signing her name, Beverly Hill, on the business license right above the words *FOR ENTERTAINMENT PURPOSES ONLY*. The Bible is clear on its position on soothsaying, but party tricks, apparently, are allowed.

"Truthsaying," Aunt Bev insisted. I was seven years old. I felt forty. My mother was sick and my weird aunt who wanted me to look into the bottom of a teacup would never stop talking in riddles. "We did not come into this life to be soothed."

She put the cup in front of me. She managed to drink almost all of the tea that was in it without swallowing the few leaves at its bottom. "You just have to find the way that gets you through."

I didn't understand her. Who could understand her?

I took a deep breath. The tea smelled like jasmine. "Through to where? To God?" I was pretty sick of talking to Him, to God. Capitalized. Like a brand, a product. Another in the never-ending series of Rosary television commercials advertising salvation. And until my mom got better, I wasn't buying it.

Aunt Bev shook her head but gave no other answer. Just turned the cup counterclockwise, slowly, three times. The porcelain rubbed against the velvet of the tablecloth like Rudolph purring, and as it spun, the tea leaves swirled at the bottom. It was hard not to look at them, to watch them settle. When they did, when the last one finally slipped into place, my eyes danced for a second and jumped. They lost their usual focus, the sight that works in the world, gets you from point A to B without falling over, stops you from stabbing yourself in the face with your fork when you're eating dinner. Then my eyes became as still as the leaves in the bottom of the cup, and those leaves were all I could see. But I didn't actually see them at all.

Aunt Bev said, "Tell me."

That first time: a butterfly. It was almost perfectly made but for the tiniest tear out of one wing. I can see it even now, down to every scrap of jasmine making up its body, the straggling leaves pointing like antennae.

Later, I saw other creatures too. A limping bird. A tailless lizard. And when all of them were injured somehow, wounded, I told her if all I am going to see is pain, I'd rather do my math homework.

That afternoon, she pulled out the bank ledger. And I learned two crucial lessons: one, profit and loss are equally important. The other, never run your mouth around Aunt Bev.

"It's a language," she'd say, as she threw the *I Ching* and asked me what I saw. As she spread her tarot pack out like a fan and then pulled out cards for me to look at more closely. She talked to me about all of its currencies. Sticks. Coins. Swords. Cups. "But your own language." And I didn't see any wounded animals in them, but I didn't see anything at all. The lines on Aunt Bev's palm were only wrinkles. Her crystal ball, only glass.

Finally, before Mom's cancer got deadly serious about taking her away one piece at a time, I read tea leaves for Aunt Bev, for real. And then I never wanted to read them again.

"Why would you wear only half a bra?" I asked her, looking up from the teacup slowly. Returning to the room was like looking up from a book when someone is talking. Part of me was still holding my place in that cup.

She'd been waiting for me, her own cup of tea read through, its message kept to herself, as usual. And I didn't need a gift to see the color of her face change to a sick kind of yellow when I asked this question.

She recovered, too late, said, "Tell, then ask."

Statements first, then the question. That's the number one rule of fortune-telling. Even if I'm not sure what I'm seeing myself, the customer will be able to place it, or create a place for it, if I lead them well. This is the part where trust comes in. Trusting whatever you saw. It's the hardest part to learn. The Rosary Bible Thumpers would be surprised how much faith is required to keep the shoppe's supposedly godless heart beating.

I used my best grown-up psychic voice then, thinking that maybe I'd finally done it. After all of these afternoons, I was on to something. I made the statements describing what I saw and asked the only question that is allowed. "There's a clothesline, and hanging on it, a bra. Half of a bra. Does this mean something to you?"

This was before I thought about bras enough to even reject wearing them, before I knew that cancer could return and spread and how it, like just about everyone and everything else, loves breasts. And so I walked right into this ugly mortal truth with my otherworldly vision. Aunt Bev's poker face slipped, the only time I ever saw it fail her, but I wouldn't understand what I'd done, or seen, until a year later. After the first surgery.

That day, Aunt Bev squeezed my hand across the table, and though her eyes were full, she focused on the work, as usual, and gave me a different kind of bad news.

"Helen, the tea leaves are your guide. No mistake."

Not tarot cards with their pretty fairy tale of lovers and squires and horses, not a crystal ball sparkling with magic. Nope. Soggy old tea, wet with the spit and worry and wishes of some dumbass not brave enough to go out and make a future for themselves.

Gross.

HAND CANCEL

Dad's fortune has run out, but he wasn't always like this. Like most dads, he was something else before, more like a man. And I can't put my finger on it. Not anymore. When we remember something, that's a memory. But there's no word for the thing we can't recall. So there is no word for what Dad is now. Or there is.

Dad is a forgot.

Have you ever gotten in the car, backed out of the driveway, made it all the way to the stoplight, and only then realized you were still wearing your slippers? And went on to where you were going anyway? If you have, then you know what it is like to be my dad. At first, you can't remember to change before you leave the house. Later, you realize no one cares if you do anyway.

He's pale and shuffling and quiet. I almost don't know how he carries on. But then I do. God, of course, but also, the union.

Unions aren't favored here in Rosary, but until Rosary secedes, like some Thumpers wish it would, we're stuck with at least one, because when Rosary got its own PO, the postal workers union came with it. Dad can never get fired from the post office, no matter what a terrible job he might do. Neither rain, nor sleet, nor death warming over will deter him from his appointed blah blah blah. Even right after Mom died, when he was too depressed to shower or shave, when he stank like sadness on a turd, they didn't send him home. And I'd wash him up, help him strip down to his boxer shorts, striped blue like his uniform, swimming around his skinny legs. I'd put him in the shower, slide the door shut, and talk him through it.

"Time to get cleaned up, Dad," I'd say, perched on the toilet, rubbing the fuzzy seat cover's yarn between my fingers, its yellows and oranges settling under me like an interior-decorating sunset. "Take off your boxers and toss them over."

And Dad's response, "Unghhhh."

"Move around so you get wet everywhere, okay?"

"Unghhgghg."

"Is your hair wet, Dad?"

"Unnhnnh."

"Pour some shampoo into your hand now, the purple bottle, and rub it around in your hair until there are bubbles."

"Mmmmmph."

THE GOOD NEWS

The treasure chest of porn that Winthrop's dad hides so poorly in his bedroom closet contains actual books, not dirty magazines. The covers have all been torn off, so if there were some saucy images under the titles, those are gone too. Words only. Mr. Epsworthy is old-school. Besides, even if we could somehow get porn here, Mr. Epsworthy says the internet gives you cancer. I don't know what kind of messed-up disease you can get from whacking it to dirty books, hand rot with a side of silverfish maybe, but he seems fine.

Winthrop and I read through the entire collection before the end of our three-day suspension, taking turns reading to each other or teaming up and performing a scene together for Rainbolene's benefit. I mean "performing" as in reading aloud like an old-time radio play. Winthrop and I are not actually performing the various ridiculous sex acts we read about. That would be weird.

And somehow reading pornographic stories aloud together is not weird. That's right.

That is, if you can even call them stories. It's mostly that there are these women who are falling all over themselves to bonk as many strangers as they can while they talk about it the whole time, the bonking. They're always remarking on the bonking and the remarks fall into five main categories.

Directional: "Right there in my pussy."

Observational: "My nipples are on fire."

Hyperbolic: "I love your monster cock."

Encouraging, in the manner of a stereotypical cheerleader: "Yeah, oh yeah."

The fifth category is only sounds, moans that the pornographic book's author has tried hard to faithfully render: "Unhnnh."

Reading this dialogue out loud is a crucial friendship-building activity. We work hard at keeping a straight face while we do it and mix things up by employing British accents or singing the words out, or reading them like one of the poems assigned in Ms. Millen's English classes with all the weird line breaks and no punctuation:

> *right*
> *there in*
> *my pussy my nipples*
> *on fire I love*
> *your monster*
> *cock yeah oh*
> *yeah u*
> *nhnnh*

When there isn't the riveting dialogue, all the characters sound like my dad did right after my mom died. Like he still does during the holidays or the weeks before Mom's birthday. It turns out that depressed dads and people who are fucking so hard they've lost their minds sound exactly the same, like a keyboard attacked itself.

POSTAGE DUE

I know it's weird to be in charge of your dad's showers, of getting him from one task to the next, to be the sun that rises in his mornings and the crease in his uniform, the fine-edged blade of his razor scraping against his neck. I know there are programs for daughters like me. Even in Rosary. But to get to those programs, to even walk in the door, much less raise your hand and say your name, first you have to survive your childhood, and in most cases that means your parent has to survive it too.

So you run the shower.

You test that the water's not too hot. You clip his gross toenails and no matter how many times you do this, needing the strength of both hands to close the clippers over their mess, or how often you tend to them, his toenails still make him look like he actually did crawl out of a grave. Maybe your mom's. You wash his underwear and that means you see and you touch the stains there. One of adulthood's little secrets. You grow up about five years in that first moment over the washing machine, your dad's dirty shorts in your hand. Shit stains are how adults are made.

You know the mole on his right shoulder intimately, monitor it for changes, can match it up with yours, in nearly the same spot, and you think about whether you should have yours removed, to get away from him and this sadness you might have inherited, or if you should get a tattoo around it, a temple to your connection on your skin. The waving inky lines of the USPS canceling the stamp of it so it can't be reused. So it can't be sent anywhere else ever again. Just like a body, stamps are designed for one trip only. The postmark city and the date in the circle beside it always the same, the day Mom left us and time stood still: *April 11, 2013, Rosary CA.*

EPISTLE

My mom. Breast cancer. At least that's how it started. It isn't a new story. It wasn't a new story then either. I was nine. I wasn't too young to know that she was going, but I was too young to see that Dad might slide away, was sliding away to join her and his precious Holy Father in Heaven, so that finally even the USPS suggested a medical leave of absence because he'd missed too many days just sitting in the dark at home while I was at school, then throwing frozen tater tots into the cold oven when he realized that I was home and that he had at least one mouth to feed.

It was Aunt Bev who was paying attention and it was Aunt Bev who finally took over soon after the issue of Dad's medical leave came up. One night, after Dad had gone to bed and I was brushing my teeth at the kitchen sink, so the light from the bathroom in the hall didn't wake him—as if anything could wake him—Aunt Bev let herself in with her key, one that saw very little use. Despite sharing the same favorite person in the world, Aunt Bev and Dad are only a teenage girl's arm-length away from all-out religious war. Which is to say, unless it is because of me, they don't hang out a lot. So it was a surprise to see her walk in the door.

She shushed me, the finger with the silver serpent ring against her lips. Then she pulled off her cowboy boots—she always wears cowboy boots—and padded around me in the kitchen until I finally moved out of her way and just watched. She filled a big metal pot, the biggest one we have. It used to hold a whole chicken in the time when Mom made soup every week, then the chicken stock that she would drink slowly, then slower, then not at all. Aunt Bev rinsed the dust out of it, filled it, put it on the stove to boil, and added a few drops of rose-scented water from her bag.

She went down the hall.

Dad wasn't snoring but making that moaning sound like he does sometimes. I thought Aunt Bev was going to wake him or quiet him, maybe soothe him, put her hand over his mouth, smother him. Instead, her hand went straight under the pillow and she pulled out a stack of letters I didn't know was there. A handful of letters held together by extra-wide, extra-strength, USPS-grade rubber bands. Dad even reached for them, his nails scraped across the sheet as Aunt Bev moved away, but he didn't wake up. He slept like the dead.

Back in the kitchen, Aunt Bev turned off the light and the house went completely dark except for the blue flame of the stove curling up around the bottom of the big pot like it had been missed. She sat down on the linoleum and unwound a shawl from her neck, her lucky one. She would say her "blessed" one, and then tell you a story about climbing a mountain, starving herself for the length of a waning moon to get it—be given it—from a shepherd who lived there. It is dark green with red goats pasturing across it and she laid it on the floor that night and then unbundled Dad's letters and unfolded each of them. Even in the gaslight I recognized my mom's handwriting on the pages, the way she dotted the *i* in her name with a tiny flower, one single bloom sprouting up in the middle of Evie.

And then Aunt Bev tore those letters into strips. The flowers too.

She loves me. She loves me not.

Letter by letter, a pile of word parts grew high on the fabric, on the linoleum, on the floor of this house that my mom and dad bought together the year before I was born, when the last of my grandparents died and they had only each other and a tiny inheritance to make it possible. I can still hear the sound they made, the strips of paper ripping. Like leaves fallen from trees. Like feet falling on snow. Like the past coming apart. Like letting go.

And that's when I really cried for my mom. She'd been gone for a year and I had cried, of course, but this was the first time I couldn't stop myself collapsing. I was sitting on the floor and I pulled my knees in tight, trying to stop from falling. I rocked into myself and Aunt Bev did a thing then, she reached for me, like you'd think she would, but she reached for me with strips of the torn letters in her hands. And she wiped my face with that paper and when the first strips were soaked she threw them in the pile and reached for more. The pages were so old by then, softened from folding and refolding, that Mom's letters might've been a tissue from the pocket of her own robe.

All those strips of paper and all those tears went into the pot on the stove and the pot boiled all night. The heat from the flame and the metal warmed the room and eventually I stopped falling, tumbling forever. When I landed, I was on my own kitchen floor, so I curled up where I was and slept. I'd wake now and then, the shawl tucked around me, the goats climbing up and through my dreams. Aunt Bev would be sitting there on the floor, cross-legged, watching me. Or she'd be standing, stirring. Sometimes she'd be talking to herself as she did this, whispering, and then she'd adjust the flame, higher, always higher, past where the dial should go, beyond the heat anything man-made could be capable of producing.

In the morning, she strained the pot into the coffeemaker. She rolled the mush of paper into a ball, squeezed it until it was dry and small enough to fit in a pocket, then she knotted it into the scarf that was back around her neck. She put a filter and coffee grounds into the coffeemaker, setting it to brew. She filled Dad's favorite cup, the one with First Corinthians 13 in blue letters, and brought him into the kitchen, where he sat and drank the cup through without noticing a thing, without even asking why Aunt Bev was there. Dad's fingers wrapped around First Corinthians as he lifted it up to ask for another cup and another, and each time he did, Aunt Bev was there with the pot.

Dad used to break First Corinthians down for me, quick and sure of his mind and his faith, of me. He'd talk about forgiveness like an old gambler sharing tells. Like he'd never lost this game of doing the right thing, never been caught holding a grudge. He'd quote from the Bible, "Love keeps no record of wrongs." And then, as if from some old Wild West movie, he'd add, "Only the Devil keeps score, my darling girl. Keep it all at zero and you are the one who wins."

I pushed around the *o*'s in a bowl of cereal and watched while Aunt Bev filled Dad's cup. He had a pretty terrible thirst. And when all the coffee was gone, Dad was, I guess you could say, awake. More than awake. My dad was back that morning. Or, a dad. A version of one. He wasn't exactly the same. It was the end of something and the beginning of something else. Like most things are.

DELIVER US

I started making Mom's paper flowers again to avoid the life-threatening boredom of Vacation Bible Camp. I've been lucky so far. Last year was the first summer I was forced to attend. "It means a great deal to me," Dad said, in an awkward formal tone not unlike the one used in his council letters. Dad and Aunt Bev had obviously had a conference to determine the path of my life, or my summer, anyway, and they had reached a compromise. If I was going to spend the rest of the year in the arms of temptation, as represented by the Rosary Psychic Encounter Shoppe, then I could spend two precious summer weeks held safely to His bosom at Bible camp.

To top it off, Aunt Bev, a person who has never taken a vacation before in her entire life, went on vacation. She had a long meeting with my dad, a meeting held privately so I couldn't burst in, and then suddenly decided to go away. For the same two weeks, it so happens, that the Life Fellowship of Rosary holds Vacation Bible Camp. God might laugh when we make plans but I'm pretty sure even He doesn't laugh at Aunt Bev.

Vacation Bible Camp isn't really a camp. It's basically Life Fellowship, where Dad worships, and Mom used to, opening up for two weeks straight of an otherwise beautiful summer to cram down the throats of Rosary kids any religion that might not have been adequately crammed in during the school year.

Because if there's any space left at all, the Devil will fill it.

Along with a great deal of sermonizing, for some reason the camp also involves contests presumably meant to help us feel like the God of our fathers is hip and cool and fresh. The contests range from seeing who can eat the most jalapeños fished from a bottomless jar filled with tiny hot peppers and a nuclear green fluid that looks awesome coming back up, to who can walk across a room blindfolded without breaking any of the actual raw eggs that are rolled onto the floor amid a mess of Styrofoam peanuts after the blindfolds are in place.

Because these are totally the things we teens do together when left to our own devices. Good, clean fun. And food wastage. The competitions are interspersed with "lessons." Lectures on the evils of ingesting too much of the popular culture that has been created to cause our souls to burn. Lectures on the joys of walking in the light of the Lord no matter what we step in.

It was during one of these lectures last summer that Cy became an official Dickhead.

I was pretending to listen to Pastor Ted go on. And on. But was quietly ripping the Song of Solomon out of the Bible I was holding so I could fold its pages into a bouquet. Bible pages tear quietly and easily and fold perfectly. I've made about twenty roses of this chapter now, the only sexy one, and I was just about to slip these pages into my pocket when something flew across the pews, landing right near Pastor Ted. That something was a rubber band from Cy's braces.

And it was fantastic. A moment to include in future camp brochures advertising the *Treasured Memories to Be Made on the Path to Salvation*.

Pastor Ted stopped speaking. He'd been talking about a show none of us watch at all or would admit to watching anyway because it is for children, and how this show is full of messages from the Devil. There's a cat on it who is always getting into hijinks and, it turns out, the cat is a servant of the Devil himself, a vehicle to "boost hell's own ratings." The whole idea is hysterical, especially the bit about a cat doing anything for anyone other than itself. We all laughed, and the laughing must have loosened a rubber band in the mess of wire in Cy's mouth.

I didn't mean to do it, but I turned with everyone else to look at Cy. At how red his face was. At how he closed his mouth tightly then, his lips disappearing, and how he looked like he wanted to disappear with them. At how Bird laughed so hard he fell between the pews and how Cy finally thought to start laughing too, at himself, and earned his Dickhead status.

In between the lessons and the lame competitions, there was free time after lunch when the Pastor left us alone in the cafeteria. Twenty minutes while he went to the rectory to eat his lunch. And sob.

Twenty unsupervised minutes.

When the Devil got busy.

Thanks to Pastor Ted and one of his more remarkably boring lectures on how God is found in "inner space" and the temptations of the world are found in "outer space," the act of making out in a closet was renamed. What was known as "Seven Minutes in Heaven" to our parents' generation is now "Going to Outer Space." Heaven may have been the ultimate destination for the previous generation, but we grew up on space travel.

Houston, we need a condom.

CONDOM NATION

The first time Bird and Dad met it didn't count as meeting, that day in Principal Harrison's office. I don't think Dad even noticed Bird, he was so caught up in the lie I had told. And then he was caught up in Iris Doncaster. Bird's mom.

Of. All. People.

Dad and Iris had apparently already met. At church. I can just see it. Their fingers touching as they pass the collection plate, their smiles shy when the peace is shared. In Principal Harrison's office, Dad was helpless before Iris Doncaster. It was the way her voice shot across the paperwork, ricocheted like light through a crystal, piercing everyone in the eye, starting headaches like small fires around the room, and helping me understand, at last, why Bird always wants to kill everyone.

———

The first time Bird and Dad really met was when Dad looked Iris up in the phone book, the actual ink-and-paper phone book full of God's promises for the good people of Rosary, and under *D* for *Don't do it, Dad*, and *Damn it all*, there she was, of course. Iris Doncaster of Rosary. And he invited her to dinner at our house. Invited them.

I have imagined that phone call, how when Iris answered, it was like God's promise shining through a dark cloud, how when Dad spoke, it was like a tomb creaking open. I'm sure he said something about "making peace." She said something about "making dinner." I have imagined how her voice went extra-breathy as she offered to "make us real food from scratch." Scratch.

Like fingernails on a blackboard.

Iris makes chicken suffocated by bread in our kitchen with her hair done up and her lipstick attacking her face. Dad and Bird sit at the kitchen table and Dad forces me to sit there too. He'd been stern, for him. His voice was rasping and slow, but it was even more painful to hear than usual because not only was he trying, he was trying for her. When he'd seen my lack of enthusiasm about the dinner plans he'd made without thinking of me even one little bit, he jumped to a conclusion and told me not to hold a grudge. I knew he would. He understood enough to know that I don't want Bird to come over but not enough to know this is because of what I do want Bird to do. This faulty assumption on Dad's part is what he would call a small mercy.

So, while he was running with that, insisting that I need to forgive Bird for the violence on campus, raising his hands to his head and pointing his fingers like horns, I interpreted for him. "Only the Devil keeps score," with as much sarcasm as possible before he had a chance to say it himself. "I know, Dad."

"And are you the Devil, Helen Dedleder?"

If there is a God, He is well aware how much I hate this

question. It gets old. I mean, really old. Eternally so. Still, here was Dad speaking in full sentences, so I went along.

"No."

"Then pray for zero."

Pray for zero basically means to mind my own business. Since Dad doesn't know about Fast Eddie's, he doesn't know that Bird and I are already in each other's business and it is all I can do not to get in deeper. By inviting the Doncasters over, Dad is mixing up worlds that I want to keep apart. Our kitchen is miles smaller than the tire yard, and here we are all painfully sober. Here, there is no safe distance between truth and dare.

I sit down with them. I move my chair far away from Bird, who is wearing his best wifebeater tank top and has a fresh scar just along his nose on the inside of his left eye, no bruise yet. Whenever Dad isn't looking at him, Bird looks at me, so I look anywhere else, watch Iris working over at the counter, watch the kitchen grow heavy with smoke and silence, none of us saying a word. Bird doesn't look at me at the tire yard, much. He's busy with Mo.

And without Mo to distract him, his eyes are everywhere I want him to be.

Finally, Iris asks how school was, *zing!*, her voice through the room, and I know the Devil has his little scorecard out then because I zing right back, "How *was* school today, Bird?" I look him right in those eyes, hold myself back from looking past the basic brown to the golden specks, the shiny sparkles that make promises about him.

He hadn't been at school today, I had looked for him, as if it were possible to miss him. When I didn't see Cy either, I thought he could be sick and had reason to hope we'd cancel this stupid dinner after all. Now I am hoping he'll have to admit he didn't go, hoping to get him in trouble like a good Christian does. But where I thought Bird might freeze up, struggle with a lie, his eyes don't squint or narrow, nothing. Instead, they crinkle. He smiles. Just like the Devil, Bird came to play, but before he can spit out his lie, Dad interrupts.

"Bird?" Dad asks, confused by the nickname. I take a long drink of water from one of the good glasses Dad must have taken down from the top shelf and cleaned and dried himself, and I go back to not looking at anyone.

"Yeah," says Bird. He has this slow way of saying "yeah" that turns every room into a bedroom, a bedroom in which things are going just the way he likes it.

Dad doesn't seem to notice the bedroom vibe, though. He just waits for Bird to go on.

"That's me," Bird says.

Iris clatters the frying pan on the stove. "Gas stoves!"

"Bird?" Dad repeats it as the kitchen goes crisscross with frying-pan noises and I empty my water glass, intent on the climbing vines etched around it that remind me of Mom. Her favorite glasses. Shined up for Iris. I think about the scorecard I am not supposed to be keeping and with my stubby mental golf pencil I make three marks.

A tie.

Score one for Bird, one for me. And the Devil makes three.

"Do you prefer the gas range, Elijah?" Dad's name is a lullaby on Iris's lips, though the cradle breaks when she goes on with her nerve, with her utter bitch nerve, to say, "I suppose Evelyn used it more than you do."

The kitchen grows so quiet then it seems like even the meat stops sizzling. Like we are an exhibit at a museum, frozen in time, *Awkward Rosary Dinners of the Early Twenty-First Century.* Iris stares straight ahead, into the hood over the stove, the yellow metal of it, and I can't tell if she is wishing she could pull those words back in or if she's done it on purpose, brought up Mom to turn attention from her son.

Dad finally speaks, but he doesn't talk about the stove and I love him then for not answering Iris, for the way this tiny act of discourtesy quiets her from hopefully ever speaking Mom's name again. "And why is it that your nickname is Bird, Spencer?"

Spencer. What Bird's mama named him and what no one calls him. She named him after his dad. The dad who left them. And she has to watch now, watch her son wave away this choice, this father, this leaving, and explain the choice he'd made for himself.

I should have to write one thousand times on every chalkboard at Rosary High, *I will not fuck Bird Doncaster.* I should have to write my own first name and my own last name on all of my notebooks, imagining a future with only myself. I should have to do all the things that girls with crushes do but do them backward in order to undo this, this thing that makes me want to take my clothes off and take Bird's clothes off and then start working on seeing what's under each other's skin.

Bird hates his real name, but he loves to hear this name, the name he gave himself. He will even reintroduce himself to Cy if no one new is around to mess with. Bird and Cy are always re-getting-to-know-each-other this way, by egging each other on, beating each other up. Rain says they should just fuck and get it over with.

Like fucking someone ever clears things up, I say.

Like you would know, says Rain.

But anyway.

In the kitchen of my house with the gas range that my dead mom did or did not prefer and the smoke and quiet forming layers like an archaeological dig, Bird flexes his knuckles. He interlaces his fingers, and with his fingers still entwined, he stretches his arms straight out. At this moment, for those who can't take their eyes off of them, the muscles in his arms and shoulders ripple like heat on asphalt.

Then he flicks his hands apart like a switchblade coming open, joins his two middle fingers tip to tip. Right in Dad's face. No church or steeple, no congregants here, and in place of a sermon, just Bird, almost whispering, "Because fuck you, that's why."

I should have to carve my own name into all the cafeteria tables using only a plastic fork, until the fork breaks and my fingers bleed. *Helen Dedleder Forever.*

Iris drops a pan or a lid, something loud, onto the stove. "Spencer!" There is no miracle in her voice this time, she says his name as if she really has never heard or seen him do this before.

But of course she has.

And when neither one of them, Dad or Bird, turns to look at her, take their eyes off of each other, she laughs. It is like her laugh makes the record skip, one of those long-playing LPs, all dusty in the corner of our living room, and the Doncaster Family Singers are back in their groove.

"That is not appropriate dinner talk," Iris says.

And then Bird starts to laugh, really laugh, and Dad, who seems paralyzed except for the way his eyes hold Bird's as if he can't tell if he should punch him or pray for him, says, "Your mother is right." And then he says this next thing, a word I have never heard him say, and I feel somewhere there must be a fallen angel licking his pencil tip, writing a little mark on a scorecard. "Son," my dad says. "We won't have that kind of talk."

I actually make a noise here. It feels like a scream but no one hears.

"The fan! There it is!" Iris sings out. The fan doesn't do shit, the smoke lingers around us heavy as the word that just came out of Dad's mouth. But the kitchen fills with whirring and this is somehow better.

"Yes, indeed, dinnertime. Almost dinnertime! Who's hungry?"

Iris notes Dad's unwillingness to withhold forgiveness, trusts in it, because she starts bringing her spawn over for dinner every single week, sometimes twice. After the sixth or seventh dinner, after as many weeks of imagining ways to poison the shepherd's pie, I start to think about how long it has been since our house had any life in it. Since I'd last seen Rudolph, how long it had been since my furry baby cat had curled onto my bed at night, had spilled my homework onto the floor, had purred along to my prayers as he fell asleep. And I start to think about how, whether the Devil's keeping score or not, I'm the one always losing.

LOST

RUDOLPH THE CAT
GRAY, SKINNY, WHITE PAWS, SHORT HAIR BUT A FLUFFY TAIL.
LIKE THE TAIL CAME FROM ANOTHER CAT.
NINE YEARS OLD.
LAST SEEN ON AUGUST 25TH BUT NOW I SEE HIM EVERYWHERE.
ANSWERS TO: BABY, RUDY, RUDE, RUDE BOY, COME HERE.
LIKES: RUBS ON HIS BELLY, TO BE TOLD THAT HE IS VERY GOOD
AND BEAUTIFUL, GIRLS WHO WILL LOVE HIM FOREVER.

REWARD OFFERED.

SIGNS

I offer Fast Eddie a one-second look at my tits if he'll let me make twenty-five copies on his greasy copy machine, but it's the start of the workday, so my copies are free. He waves me on and goes back to his phone call.

Our phone number, and Aunt Bev's too, is written in the tiny little squares on the bottom of the flyer I copy. I make a cut between each square so they'll be easy to tear off, take home, and hold, as the numbers are dialed with news. I hang up my lost-cat signs all over the ten blocks of Rosary I imagine Rudolph would have been likely to roam. But no one calls.

The telephone poles around Rosary are white with flyers. It didn't used to be like that, Dad says, before the county tore. Back then, Rosary had regular internet, the real kind, like a real living way to connect, and people lost and found things, and each other, that way. Now computers are pretty useless here, but the telephone poles are crammed with flyers, everybody buying or selling. Or begging. These poles are the real Yellow Pages of Rosary, full of desperate phone numbers from Single White Males, mostly, and they are seeking hard. There really aren't anything but white males in Rosary, so I don't know why they bother with the description, like it's a selling point or something. I don't even know why they call them telephone poles anymore, since every real phone is wireless and only a legal adult with two forms of identification can purchase one here. Aunt Bev says it's a holdout from when people used to be proud of progress instead of terrified of it. Now it just sounds weird and you can hardly read through all the flyers before your neck gets sore from looking up. But I still post mine anyway, right between the offers and the promises, and I hope.

MUSICAL CHAIRS

The seating arrangement at our house used to look like this in the mornings:

—three empty chairs and then one mostly filled by Dad when he would sit down to have a cup of coffee and a piece of toast before going to work. He'd fold his hands over his toast, never touching the coffee until "the gratitude's been added." The blessing. Dad's best part of waking up.

And like this in the evenings:

—a dark kitchen because Dad is working overtime, as usual, all the overtime he can get, or he is at his Thursday night council meeting, or men's prayer group, and I'm at Fast Eddie's, which Dad unknowingly refers to as Aunt Beverly's, because

he never acknowledges that her shoppe is a business and certainly not a psychic one, because he never acknowledges that I
might be somewhere else drinking myself into a readiness to
come home. Dad calls this "doing my homework," which is
kind of poetic if you think about it.

Or:

—the light is on over grilled cheese and tomato soup or boxed
macaroni and cheese and salad from a bag because we're both
home. Still, Dad won't touch his, or the iced tea, until his
hands are folded over it, until he whispers those words I can
barely make out except for my name in them and what he is
always asking his God to do when he says it. "Bless Helen." And
I don't fold my hands, rest my forehead on them like Dad,
but I wait. I look out the window, at the bushes that we seem
to keep watering just so the spiders have a place to string their
webs, up at the clock with the abalone shell numbers and its
hands covered in dust, at the mess of orange cheese fakery and
noodles on my plate. As Dad prays, I make an inventory of
things right in front of my face, things to believe in that require no faith at all.

The mornings are the same since that day in Principal Harrison's
office, except Dad's prayer is longer, which seems impossible.
Now there are more names in it to perk my ears up, the Doncasters, Iris's name and Bird's real name. Bird, who perks up other
parts of me.

The evening prayer is very different from before, though. Now it
looks like this:

—there are no empty chairs. One is mostly filled by Dad, one is tipping back on two legs, leaning against the wall, filled by Bird. Next to Bird and inched as far away from him as I can move, there's me. The fourth chair is empty then full, empty then full, as Iris is cooking and sitting, stirring something on the stove, sitting, getting more iced tea, sitting, getting one more thing no one asked for, sitting. For goodness' sake, woman, would you sit?

When the food is ready we hold hands.

And when Bird's hand touches mine for those seconds over the table, his middle finger circles around and around in my palm.

THE MARK WHERE THE NAIL HAS BEEN

Bird is a piece of ass. Everyone knows it. Including and especially Bird. Until Winthrop arrived, he was the tallest kid at Rosary even though, like me, he is only a junior this year. And he wasn't even held back. A fact that is a source of constant surprise. Bird's hair is golden and thick and he pushes it straight back so it adds to his height, but still, stray curls manage to hang into his eyes, locks of hair that are easy to imagine swaying back and forth over you. He doesn't look like Iris at all. Like his dad, I guess, and so I forgive Iris a little bit for being unable to resist making just one hot mistake.

Bird sees right into you. He has that gift, like Aunt Bev's, except he can only see this one part, one thing. Bird can only see that piece of you that wants him. He zeroes right in on it and then he smirks, shakes his head like *tsk tsk tsk*, but it's my name he says, the only time he says it in full, on nights after these mandatory suppers, when Dad and Iris have taken their tea out onto the porch.

Bird and I clear the table. I'm working too fast and he's working too slow. I am not looking at him, I am not going to look at him. But when I hand him another plate to dry, he doesn't take it. He stands there, the wet plate dripping onto the linoleum between us, he waits for me to look at his face. When I do, he shakes his head slowly, that lock of hair falling between us, and he whispers with a *tsk tsk tsk*. "Helen, Helen, Helen."

I watched him do this during Vacation Bible Camp, to girl after girl after girl on those afternoons after lunch when Pastor Ted would check his watch and stand up, saying, "Okay, I'll be back in twenty minutes," when he'd point heavenward and add, "I'm leaving my boss in charge."

The afternoon after that first inner-space lecture, Bird stood up as soon as the door closed on all of Pastor Ted's earnest goodwill. Bird stood up and took over. He didn't exactly point, but he looked right at one of the girls seated around the long table where our lunches were spread out. He stared at this Thumper named Jessica who blushed constantly and could hardly look any of us in the eye, much less Bird. Jessica wore her long hair in a French braid, her lunch was obviously packed by her mom and came with fruit chopped in a plastic container, a napkin rolled up. And Bird was staring at her. It was like watching one of those nature shows when you feel sorry for that deer straggling behind the herd even though nothing has happened to it yet.

I don't think Bird even knew her name, but when Jessica finally looked up at him, because she had to, because the room was still and silent and everyone was looking at her now, he nodded toward the closet door and said, "Do you want to go to Outer Space with me?"

And she said yes.

Well, not exactly. She didn't say anything. But she stood up so fast that she knocked her official Vacation Bible Camp binder onto the floor and she didn't even pick it up. Bird went to the closet and held open the door for her then, as if the old rusting vacuum and the forgotten scarf and empty hangers inside of it were the finest accommodations. And, just like he was a guest at a fancy hotel, he knew they would not be disturbed when he shut the door.

At first no one moved. We sat as hypnotized as Jessica had been. Listening. I don't know for what. Then we were all watching the clock over the refrigerator, the second hand moving busily along, the way I imagined Bird's hands were doing down the buttons of Jessica's blouse, up under Jessica's bra. Up. Down.

Then only Cy watched the clock. The rest of us passed around Jessica's plastic cup of strawberries. Said nothing. When there was only a minute or so until Pastor Ted's return, Cy knocked on the closet door and Bird and Jessica popped out, sweaty and ruffled. And hot.

The next day, the sticker with Jessica's name was gone from her Vacation Bible Camp binder and stuck instead to the cover of Bird's actual Bible. The white square with her nervous handwriting fit perfectly over the "Holy" embossed there.

Her sticker was followed by stickers from the camp binders of Celeste, Zoey, and Allison, until the entire cover was full. Then Marie's sticker appeared along the Bible's spine, and on its back, April's, and no less than two Kats'. The Kats were distinguished by a cavalier underline on one, a drawing of a whiskered cat face on the other. Jessica was distinguished by having been first, and by managing to make it through to the end of camp despite being so brokenhearted that Jesus wept again. Bird was distinguished by having the camp's most desecrated Bible by virtue of his having gone to Outer Space with every girl at camp. Every Thumper, anyway. And what distinguished me was that Bird and I never went to Outer Space. Even though it was all I thought about. Or because it was all I thought about. Like he knew. Like it would be too easy that way and he wanted to make it harder for me.

So to speak.

When Iris and Bird have gone home after another dinner from hell, I can't help it. Teeth brushed, lights out, and while Dad's kneeling at his bedside, likely thanking the good Lord for bringing the Doncasters into our lives, I'm saying a prayer all my own. My hand flies inside my pajama bottoms as I remember the feel of Bird's knee pressing into mine under the table, the way his muscles flex when he cuts into Iris's chicken-fried steak, his smell that carries over whatever spices she dumped into the pan. His smell that is like old tires and fire. How he says my name over and over again like he knows this, what I'm doing right now, in my bedroom, in the dark. I go to church, find my steeple, open the door, and come to my own personal Jesus.

STAPLES

The next week, when Bird and Iris are over for dinner, the dinner when she says she wants me to start calling her Iris instead of Mrs. Doncaster, Bird says, "Hell, I didn't even know you had a cat. And now it's gone?"

"Now, Spencer," Iris says. Her voice takes on a clucking as she peels potatoes at the sink, the potatoes she said she needed no help with. I asked. I ask every time if she wants help with something, but mainly it is to hear her say no. Because I don't want to help. Except with cyanide.

The sound is the same kind of clucking like Bird does when we're washing dishes, like she knows someone is being naughty and she likes it. *Tsk tsk tsk.*

Just then, Dad shuffles in the front door. He's late today. And because Iris goes to greet him, neither of them hears Bird when he leans in close to me, his hand on my knee under the table before I can push my chair back. "Isn't your aunt in the business of helping people find some pussy?" He says "pussy" casually, like he's been reading porn with me and Winthrop, saying all the words aloud until nothing, not a single one, can make us stumble or blush. And I don't. Usually. But Bird says it like he's just had some and is ready for some more, and when he says "pussy," in that whisper, with his hand hot at my knee, I feel my face flush and it is still warm when my dad comes into the kitchen.

Dad has one of my lost-cat flyers in his hand, apparently brought over by the woman I should no longer call Mrs. Doncaster. When I see the look on Dad's face, scrunched with worry, I know we are going to have a talk. And after dinner, when we're alone, we do. Iris's potatoes au gratin settles like stone in the quarry of my stomach. All the things I want to say to my dad, to explain to him, and all I want to say back to Bird, to do to him, are swallowed there, waiting to fill my dreams tonight.

GRACE

Maybe I want him to worry. For Dad to think about me for a few minutes, notice me, our house and our life, and how what we are missing cannot be replaced. When Aunt Bev worked that magic trick in our kitchen with Mom's letters and fire, she gave back to Dad what he'd actually never lost, put it right in him forever. Where it always was. Mom's love. And I was still out here, outside of him, but I had never felt forgotten until the Doncasters started becoming a fixture in our house. So, yeah, maybe I was being a little bit of a drama queen with the lost-cat flyers. But it was a cry for help from a telephone pole, it isn't like I need an intervention.

And it worked. Too well. If I had tried to hurt myself, Dad would know what to do. There would be doctors, a mess to clean up. This is a little trickier, and it shows on Dad's face. The door has barely closed behind Iris and Bird after dinner and dishes and plans for next time when Dad catches me in the hallway trying to slink away.

"Helen." He has the flyer. I had hoped to hide it but couldn't get out from under Bird's stare to grab it and I knew Bird would bring it up again if I gave him the chance, knew he would love a reason to say "pussy" again, right in front of my dad, and then laugh it away while I tried to figure out how to act, how to pretend to be shocked and not turned on at the same time. *Tsk tsk tsk.*

"Helen." Dad smooths the paper out, unfolds a corner. "Are you feeling okay?"

I look at the flyer in his hand, how he holds it, gently, like he doesn't want to get his fingerprints on it. Like it is some kind of X-ray and maybe by examining all the shadows that fall between its whiteness and blackness we can figure out just how sick I am.

He holds it out to me and waits. Like the letters on it are leaves at the bottom of a cup and he doesn't want to jumble them up before I have a chance to see what they foretell.

And I say nothing. Because I'm not a doctor. And I'm not telling anyone's fortune. I am just a kid and one who is trying not to speak before knowing how much trouble she is actually in.

Dad starts pulling out a staple still stuck in a corner from where Iris ripped the flyer down. It is bright purple, from the special rainbow set Dad bought for me with the brand-new heavy-duty stapler and the all-color set of Sharpies. So I could make lost-cat flyers when Rudolph first disappeared.

Six years ago.

Right after Mom died.

I said I was being a little bit of a drama queen.

The markers, staples, and stapler. This was the only gift, the only thing, the only action Dad took in my direction, from the day we rushed to the hospital to say goodbye to Mom until that morning, almost a year later, when Aunt Bev made him swallow all of Mom's words, swallow them down, so he could finally find something inside of himself to say to his own still-living daughter.

And here he is now, pulling one of those staples out like our lives depend on its preservation. Not looking me in the eye. Not saying anything more. And then it is like he is the one who knows he has done wrong and is wondering just how wrong this time. How much trouble has he caused? Is his daughter losing her mind, finally, like he had done once?

We stand there. Two big kids trying to figure out who is in charge, looking for the directions for a game too advanced for us. Playing pretend, just like we did while he was lost because Mom was lost and then the cat got lost. Like we did when Dad went out and bought me some tools for finding whatever there is that can be found. Because he at least seemed to understand this much, then: when your faith leaves you, when there is nothing but silence and an empty bed, sometimes you have to make your own signs.

LAZARUS

I felt Rudolph's weight and warmth and reached for him, for his skinny, furry self on the side of my bed, but he wasn't there. Instead, it was Dad, his big bunch of keys cold on his belt loop. His face was puffy like usual back then, the months after Mom died, like he hadn't so much been asleep as buried, the sheets and pillowcases creasing into the creases already etched into him.

Mom's dead, I thought.

I thought this because this is what you think after someone dies. Every morning when you wake up you lunge for this thought because thinking this as fast as you can saves you from the splintering pain of not remembering, of thinking they are still alive even for a single second. If Mom is already dead, I thought, why is he looking at me like that? I could feel the bad news in the air and it was so heavy hanging there, I was surprised not to hear

Aunt Bev's cowboy boots on the stairs already, come to help us with this tragedy, with this new grief, whatever it was.

"Dad?"

"It's time to get up for school, first day of sixth grade." He stood up, then started talking fast, like a shy person making a toast. "Helen, I have bad news."

He held out his hand, it jingled as he did. He was holding Rudolph's collar, a circle of frayed and faded leather with a rusted bell and a tag that said his name and our phone number and, on the back, *Please call, she misses me.*

It might as well have been the first day of kindergarten, the way I burst into tears.

Dad tried. He tried to interrupt me, to stop my racing thoughts. "No, Helen." He knelt down beside my bed, put his hands on my knees. "He's . . . I don't know. I found his collar in the driveway."

"I'm going to look for him." I grabbed the collar as if it were a clue.

"You need to get to school," he said, and then he took a deep breath and his voice was stronger. "I'll call in sick today, I'll find him."

And I believed him right then, every word. I needed to, not because of the cat, but because Dad was there, helping. Dad was giving a fuck. So I buckled Rudolph's collar around my wrist and wore it to the first day of school. And then I wore it all year.

After school that day, there was no Rudolph. But there was Dad. And the stapler, the staples, the package of Sharpies he had bought. These were the atonement for the only lie I bet he ever told. The weirdest thing is, when the last bit of comfort we had between us was gone, Rudolph's gray fuzzy self totally disappeared except for that collar, Dad did not once mention prayer. He handed me permanent markers and industrial-strength staples instead. Faked some hope. And told me to write it all down.

Dad traded his perfect, sinless record for this single falsehood. For me. And I knew better, but that didn't stop me from writing my signs that night and it didn't stop me from posting them up or walking until dark every evening for weeks calling Rudolph's name. Dad had to suffer through hearing this, his daughter's voice crying in the wilderness of Rosary, and knowing it would go unanswered, because he had already cried himself hoarse.

SHARPIE

In the morning, the morning of now, I empty all the leftovers, wrapped and sealed and labeled in Iris's frilly cursive. I shove them into the garbage and I walk the long way to school so I can take down all of the lost-cat signs I hung on every telephone pole for half a mile. Baby Rudolph isn't coming home. I wouldn't either if I were him.

MARRY FUCK KILL

This isn't necessarily a drinking game, but drink anyway. It helps.

It goes like this. You are given three people to choose from. They might be famous people or people you know in real life, they can be alive or dead, and, in some very specific instances, both. You categorize them according to who, of the three, you'd be most inclined to marry, to fuck, and to kill.

For example, Sissy offers me the following three choices, "Bird. Eddie. Cy."

First, I say, "Cy." The marrying part of the game is forever and does not include sex, so you want to choose someone you can put up with but don't want to fuck. Cy is already like background music. Without Bird to prod him into action, you barely notice him. I imagine him to be the perfect husband of my three choices here.

Then, "Eddie." You only have to—or get to, depending on your desire—fuck the person in the second category one single time. If any of the people you are choosing from is listening as you play Marry Fuck Kill, a good strategy is to lie your face off, especially if the person you actually want to fuck is on the list. Knowing it. Waiting for it. Waiting for you to say his name.

Save that one for last. Kill. Kill. Kill.

MOUTH

If I were going to put Iris out of my misery, I'd start by melting all of her lipsticks. All the Mary Kays and the Avons, I'd roll their little dick-shaped selves up and up, out of their plastic shafts, until they toppled over like every erection must do when brought close to Iris's face, when it hears her trying-too-hard voice, feels her breath burning with metal from too much iced tea washing against her silver fillings.

I'd ruin all of her lipsticks, but that is only the beginning.

When she goes to open up her makeup case, instead of finding tubes of shellac to color her hole, she'll find the Sunset Pink and RubyFruit Red and Pleasure Purple penis I'd made by melting all of her lipsticks together and then shaped and smoothed, glistening and erect and waiting to be spread across her lips. On the tip, right in the center, I'd have stuck a sequin using the Bedazzler she keeps hot in her holster, ready to sparkle up anything in reach. Just that one sequin there, a shiny little arts-and-crafts piss hole for her pleasure. And when she beholds this creation, her Avon Commemorative Porcelain Heart, the one that beats Tepid Rose and GoldDigger Peach and BitchFace Wine behind her Maidenform bra, will freeze, pucker up, and stay that way as she runs for the door.

DISCIPLE

The parable of the dog shit begins with Principal Harrison losing her old fat basset hound, Marlon. Harrison posts this loss to enough Rosary telephone poles that even I am impressed. And I can see from that picture of Marlon, from his cloudy, worried eyes, his graying fur, what Harrison can't, or refuses to, see. Dogs, like cats, like moms, try to do their last bits of suffering away from the pack, to save us from that. I almost feel sorry for Principal Harrison.

The rest of the Dickheads, and the entire population of Rosary High, learn that Marlon has gone missing when Harrison actually makes an announcement about him on the loudspeakers after the Pledge of Allegiance. Her voice breaks in the middle of it, after she says Marlon's age, twelve years old. Advertising this moment of weakness is, let's face it, a very dumb move.

Principal Harrison lives just a block away from Rosary High.

Her yard, like mine and Winthrop's and everybody's, has the same four bushes that never flower, the same gravel circles beneath them. And it is there in that gravel that Bird sends Cy for three nights straight, to take, as near as we can figure, a truly basset-hound-sized shit.

Cy does it, of course, drops trou and breaks dumbass Harrison's heart. On the fourth night he is going to do it again but there she is, our principal, sitting on her porch with a flashlight and a box of dog treats. She has seen the signs Cy has been leaving her, obviously thinks they are evidence of Marlon coming home every night, that he is just confused and unable to find the door, old dog that he is. So Principal Harrison sits there with her dog treats and believes, like all the rest of us, what she needs to believe.

POST NO THRILLS

Principal Harrison never takes down her flyers, but they eventually disappear, just like Marlon did. Every few months, the Thumpers get the spirit so hard it is like they have blue balls for the rapture. Some try to speed salvation along by nailing scripture to the door of the Rosary Psychic Encounter Shoppe. Some do the Lord's work legally by getting the street sweepers in.

The streets are swept in Rosary once a week, just like everywhere else, but the sweepers also come through late at night every season or so. On these nights, they move from one telephone pole to the next ripping down the flyers posted there, every single one, no matter what kind. Church flyers about the never-ending white-elephant sales, single white men and their never-ending hunt for companionship, pictures of lost dogs and cats and people, they all come down. Rosary's desires are washed away. In the mornings after, all that's left are the naked staples running the length of every pole like the bark of a petrified forest.

THE ALLIANCE

The Dickheads don't care that Rain is trans. Or, in what might seem like a shocking turn of events, they actually do. Like, in a good way. The Rosary Bible Thumpers also care. And not in a good way. Thumpers cringe at the idea of hanging new signs on the bathroom door, the same way their ancestors did at the prospect of using a community water fountain.

Did I mention that Rosary is pretty white?

The Thumpers would heal Rain. Which is a sentence that reads like a word jumble for all the sense it makes, reads like fridge magnets someone was trying to put in a comprehensive order and then left hanging there while they made a sandwich instead.

The Thumpers would heal Rain.

Would Rain heal the Thumpers.

Rain would heal the Thumpers.
There. I fixed it.

It might be easier for the Dickheads to accept Rain because we know a little bit about feeling like we are on the wrong planet, but mainly, Dickheads owe the fact that we aren't complete morons to Sky Radio. Its hosts offer practical advice, like reminders about peeing both before and after sex, and, when exploring multiple orifices, the importance of going in reverse-alphabetical order. Vagina to anus. Never anus to vagina. And finally, that while ass play can be healthy, smoking cigarettes kills.

Sky Radio's advice when encountering people for the first time, especially ones going through changes, or who want to be going through changes, in a world that insists everyone remain just as miserable as God made them, is this: mind your own fucking business.

BOOKS OF JOB

Unless I'm relentlessly judging them, I do stay out of people's business. For example, whatever Cy's business is. The second time his tent pops up in the empty lot, its dark shadow against the evening sky, I walk over without taking off my shoes.

"Cy, it's Hell," I say, and he doesn't say anything. And when he unzips the tent, he doesn't offer me a beer. There is no beer. But that isn't why I am here. I mean, I don't know why I am here, but it isn't for beer.

This time, instead of beer, there is a stack of magazines shoved under the sleeping bag. Cy is kind of leaning one leg against them, like maybe I won't notice them there, casual, like maybe we are used to seeing each other read. He sits hugging his fancy flashlight to his chest and the light comes up around his face in that spooky, sad, underneath way that flashlights do.

Cy says, "I can't." Just that. And he lets the flashlight go. It rolls onto its side, so the light shines right on the magazines. I recognize the slick and torn pages from the dank bookshelf in the tire yard's bathroom. The porn that time forgot.

Cy's too nice to be a Dickhead, he doesn't have enough religion to be a Thumper, and whatever else he is, he's still trying to figure out. No wonder he keeps building his tent in no-man's-land. He doesn't talk much, but we hear him loud and clear. He isn't about the straight porn in the tire yard's disgusting bathroom and he isn't about making out with anyone, so much that no one even dares him to. The whole point of Truth or Dare is that you get to do the thing you wanted to do, and you don't have to take responsibility for it. You get to tell that ugly truth, you get to take that stupid risk, you get to kiss that filthy mouth.

But no one is kissing Cy.

The one time a day Cy can be counted on to speak is just as we're leaving. We're pulling on our backpacks, pulling out sticks of gum to cover our breath, and saying we'll be back the next day. Like we have somewhere else to go. This is as future tense as the Dickheads get and there are few variations:

Tomorrow.

Yeah, tomorrow.

Tomorrow, fuckers.

I listen when Cy says he'll see us tomorrow. Because if he ever doesn't, I'm going to get in his business and stay there.

Have you ever noticed how, in small towns like mine, there are these kids who commit suicide, and no one ever saw it coming, and it is always because of drugs? And how no one in these cities that are suddenly awash in drugs is ever homosexual? I never noticed it either. But the guys on Sky Radio did, and I think they are on to something. I'm no anthropologist or statistician or whatever, but if I cooked up one of those Venn diagrams to illustrate this point, with the circles overlapping to prove commonality, where the Rosary circle and the suicide circle meet, there'd be this valley. And in that valley, there'd be some Thumper with a bullhorn shouting about drugs, and the noise that he is making there is louder than understanding and almost louder than grief.

Meanwhile, the circle with homosexuality inside of it is nowhere near Rosary. Gay kids are off in a bubble of their own, far away from that noise that ignores their lives and masks their deaths. Not in My Graveyard, says the bullhorn. Not in a grave at all, I say. So, when I see Cy, when I really see him, I imagine him in that circle, floating like a balloon let go. Safe. And when it's time to go home, I listen for his tomorrow.

THE GAME OF WHO NEEDS WHO THE WORST

I never thought that Bird and Winthrop had actually done much more than nod at each other over beers at Fast Eddie's until this afternoon under the blanket-slash-porn fort in Winthrop's room. We just finished reading through *Working Bend-Overtime* and are talking about whether anyone might still be hanging out at the tire yard, if we should try to do something more productive with the rest of the day than read more porn. Like drink. This is when Winthrop makes the following incredibly surprising announcement: "Spencer said he'd be there late tonight."

"What?" I can sometimes fail at expressing confusion in a way that leads to clarity.

"Spencer's mom has plans. The tire yard's open late."

"Bird's *mom*?"

"The woman who is right now making out with your dad. Yep."

One, this is not true. And two, it makes me sick. I ignore it. "Bird told you his plans?"

Here, Winthrop stands up, throws the bedspread off with a dramatic shrug like it is a disguise he no longer needs in order to keep his superhero identity secret. He strikes a bodybuilder pose. "Helen"—he turns from side to side for me, showcasing his physique—"Spencer Doncaster and I are . . ." Here he squats, grunting like he is breathless from all the flexing, then he drops the bodybuilder guise and in its place becomes a bad stereotype of a French person still learning English.

"How do you say . . ." He twirls an imaginary mustache, squints. "We are, how do you Americas say . . . le bros?"

TAROT BEFORE BROS

Aunt Bev's laid out on her couch. It's a flowered thing that is faded in a perfect square from where the sun shines through the window of the shoppe. She has the small, worn green pillow over her eyes, is resting from the last client, a woman in an old car with a smiley-faced ball topping the antenna. She was one of those people. The main sort. She had come to hear only good things because she felt she had nothing good to look forward to and, as it turns out, had a pretty good insight into her future already. She could have saved herself the cash.

I knew her future was bleak because Aunt Bev charged her five times the regular rate. It would have been cheaper if she'd brought her to the back room for an after-hours reading. Aunt Bev calls this the sugarcoating fee, her hardest work. She doesn't like to dress up doom. "It already has on a suit and bow tie," she says, "but people want a carnation in the buttonhole."

We had been talking about Bird and Iris and the never-ending dinners. That is, I had been complaining about Bird and Iris, and Aunt Bev had been mostly listening. And then she asks me about Rudolph. Why I am missing him so terribly, so suddenly. She has seen the flyers.

I don't have a good answer.

Which seems like a good answer. At first. "Because I want some answers," I say, before realizing that I sound like one of those people.

"She wants some answers," Aunt Bev mutters. Her voice is weary all over again. It's the voice she uses when she is trying to save herself from putting a top hat and tails on doom.

I hold my breath.

"You met your match in the principal's office that day."

Her lips are all that moves below the green pillow, one hand steady on the water she drinks between clients to keep herself clear. "No matter how it feels now, you are lucky. You've saved yourself a lot of time because you're young and strong and you will figure this out. Later on, you're tired. You don't fight so hard. Keep your eyes open around that boy."

I think about Bird's shoulders, the muscles pulsing under his shirt. "I'm watching him. I promise that," I say. A hot guilt. Does Aunt Bev see me at night, rubbing one out while I imagine him over me? I've met my match, all right. And he has already won.

"Some people have the One. That's how it was for my sister. And I thought it was that way for your father too. But now, with that Iris, now I'm not so sure."

She takes a deep breath and the room fills with what feels like static electricity. Her glass of water sparkles in the sunlight and I rub my hands over my forearms where the hair has started to rise. My eyes water. I swear the room is tilting.

Aunt Bev sits up and holds the eye pillow to her chest. Her

eyes are watering too. "Helen," she says to me, "with my sister's blessing, I am sharing what is none of your business. Your father is alive. And unlike you, he knows what is good for him."

She lies back down again. Replaces the eye pillow. And then she laughs quietly and falls asleep with a smile on her face.

VIII: STRENGTH

Great-Grandma Helen spread the tarot for Aunt Bev when she was just a little girl, and it was clear right away that she and that pack had a thing for each other. On nights when she was with her grandchildren, their grandma Helen would first sing my mom to sleep in her crib, then she would move to Aunt Bev's bedside with a book. Only, hidden inside *Heidi* or *Rebecca of Sunnybrook Farm* or whatever they were supposed to be reading, would be a single card from Great-Grandma Helen's tarot, the pack she had received in her own childhood. The same pack she learned to hide away as the years went by and Rosary started attracting people with a more singular idea of belief. Still, she would slip a different card out every night for the little girl she knew was destined to take her place in the Hill family legacy, and Aunt Bev would study that card as she fell asleep, tucking its meaning into her dreams.

Aunt Bev has that pack now, it is the one that sits on her velvet-covered table. It is the one that will come to me when she dies, like the rest of my gift will supposedly come when she dies, the same as it did for her when Great-Grandma Helen passed. Because nothing in this life is free.

POM-POM

Mom was a cheerleader in high school but she wasn't an asshole. She was an actual dancer, and she danced all the way through to her graduation and then gave lessons to little girls at Rosary Dance School. Until I came along. Then she stopped moving, of course, became stuck, with me and then in a hospital bed where they stuck tubes in her arm and then a tube in her throat and then she got stuck in a grave.

She told me she didn't mind, didn't miss it. "A dancer's life is a short one," she said. But I could see her toes tapping to any rhythm, to the ticking of the stove lighting up, the clicking of a zipper going around and around in the dryer, the beeping of the machines connected to her body before the pain got too bad to keep a beat. Mom's rhythm disappeared slowly, like the rest of her, the way her breasts did, one after the other, like the way the Cheshire cat disappears on Alice, until all that was left was Mom's smile hanging over us, her voice cheering us on to have good and full lives. Rah. Rah. Rah.

LOVE THE SINNER

Fast Eddie's Tire Salvage is five driveways down from Aunt Bev's shoppe. The driveways in between belong to Rosary Cleaners, the Donut Hole, and the last two to the same empty lot that is always threatening to be something no one wants to look at and especially does not want to work at, like a big-box store.

At the shoppe and at Fast Eddie's, it's about being vulnerable. Or having people think you are. Eddie trades all the beer we can drink for all the tits he can see. Aunt Bev trades all the future she can see for whatever part of themselves folks will bare to her—money, body, soul. And yet Aunt Bev is the one who is the bad guy, the criminal. The shoppe gets hate mail, gets Bible verses nailed to its door courtesy of Thumpers so devout they make Dad look like an aging Dickhead. Hypocrites who can't see that everyone wants a revelation.

Sometimes there is graffiti too, quick and ugly on the glass and bricks of the shoppe, ASK JESUS, the spray paint suggests, or ABOMINATION, complete with a sinful number of exclamation marks. But none of these paint and judgment wielders ever look twice at Fast Eddie's, where the real sins are being committed. The letters and graffiti are also never geared toward the actually illegal work that Aunt Bev does, only the kind she is licensed to do.

When Aunt Bev is giving an "extended reading," as she calls it, she keeps her eyes open and upward, on Saint Mary Magdalene embroidered on a cloth she has tacked to her bedroom ceiling. At first I thought Aunt Bev had hung Mary Magdalene up there to soften the light in her bedroom, but as usual there was something more at work.

"I say a prayer to the Magdalene for the men's wives," Aunt Bev says, "that they will find a way to tell their husbands' futures again, to tell them they have a future, and it is there, where it all began, within arms and between legs they have grown old alongside. I ask that the men never feel the need to come back. Then I pray they will release any burden of guilt by leaving me a huge tip as they walk out the door." And she drops an envelope full of cash into the safe.

CUMMITTEE MEETING

There is a pretty notable difference between coming and cumming. Every porn book is clear on this matter.

There are special ways regular-seeming words are spelled in porn books and some regular words that never appear between their pages at all. In porn, no one has a *penis* or *vagina*, for example, none of the usual equipment. There are only *cocks* and *slits*, words people whisper or scream at each other in real life, not the ones they use at the doctor's office, unless, of course, that doctor's office is found inside of a porn book, and many are. No one ever has *intercourse*. They *fuck*, but mainly they *hammer* and *pound* and *pile-drive*.

It's more like working on a construction site, I guess.

And everyone, every single person in these books, is ready to get it on, even when they say they don't want to. You get used to it after a while, that world, its code. Like anything. Like with friendships. Each one has their own code and you have to figure out when they need you to pry, get right up in there and *tear them apart*, and when no means no.

Winthrop and I are in the middle of *Debbie's Dairy*. Things on the farm are just starting to get milked when Rain comes in and flops down on her bed, her face in the pillow. We put down the book and wait until she finally lifts her head.

She looks at us a long time before saying, "Will you two be my date for prom?"

Prom is months away. I thought the collective we did not care about prom, but if one of us cares, prom it is. We say yes, of course. But we don't go back to the porn. We wait. Obviously. We know the code. We are waiting for information, so we know how to proceed: if being present is enough, if asking questions will help, or if this is a real emergency and ice cream is required.

Rain talks. "Win, you have to wear a bow tie and we'll all wear flowers and dance our asses off. Sex is optional." She adds, "BYOP."

"Parachutes?" I say. "Bring Your Own Parachutes?"

"Pharmaceuticals," Winthrop says. He is confident, even hopeful, but Rain shakes her head no.

"Push-up bra?" This is also wrong, but it doesn't matter because she's starting to cheer up.

"Puppy?"

"Peanut butter?"

"Peanut butter puppy?"

"Protection!" Winthrop shouts this one. We pause because it feels like a winner. Rain just stares, so he clarifies, "Condoms. Dental dams. Rubber gloves. Hazmat suits."

Rain shakes her head again but says, "Always a good idea, though. You be in charge of that, Win."

"I've got it. Aunt Bev. Bring Your Own Psychic," I say.

"Oh yes," says Winthrop, he moans it, "bring Beverly, Helen, please bring her. I just want one dance with her. She needs to see"—and here he runs his hands up and down along his body in a caressing motion that would make Farmer Johnson in *Debbie's Dairy* grab his rooster—"all of this at work."

He is ignored.

"Is it Be Your Own Prom? Like, be the prom you wish to see in the world?"

Rain sighs. "You are both in serious denial. Bring Your Own Porn. Duh." She settles back against the wall. Nelson Mandela peeks over her shoulder from the poster Winthrop gave her when she came out. The words to his speech about not fearing being great and brilliant and the rest outlined with glitter marker.

"Now read to me, freaks," she says. "Read to me about how supposedly normative people do it."

RADIO FREE SKY

If there is only Aunt Bev's old red pickup in the shoppe's parking lot when Winthrop and Rain and I are walking home from the tire yard, we stop and peek in the window to see if she's still awake and if she is alone. The Epsworthys are the only friends I've ever brought to the shoppe, but even on the first night we knocked on the door and waited, me tense in the stomach, unable to decide if it would be trick or treat, Aunt Bev opened the door like she'd been expecting all three of us.

On late evenings, she meets us in one of her sets of flowing pajamas that make her look like she's part liquid. She wears these slippers with bright red cloth peonies sewn to the tops of them. The petals are so big I don't know how she can walk.

"You tune the radio," she says, "I'll make the tea." Winthrop follows her into the kitchen to help, trying to pretend he doesn't notice the way her pajamas do more than suggest that she is wearing nothing underneath them.

Rain and I sit on the floor by the radio and hold our breath until we hear the Sky voices. I keep my tuning arm steady until I find that sweet spot on the dial where they can be heard, if you really try, between snarling static on either side. And we really try. All the truth we can bear to hear is hidden there and the voices from Sky know we're listening.

"Rosary peach fuzz, we've got you when you cross that bridge," they say during every show at least once, like they know we each have a backpack ready for that moment we're going to run. "Your future fam is here, from every religion and every race, and in all the colors of that rainbow flag you aren't allowed to fly."

We sit there waiting for that, to be noticed, as quiet as we ever are, holding cups of kava-kava tea warm in our hands. Aunt Bev listens with us, sitting on the floor. At least, she's listening to something with us. She makes her tea a lot stronger than ours and after a while she's so quiet and so still, cross-legged and spine straight, you have to wonder what frequency, exactly, she's on.

It can be hard to be quiet when what we're hearing is so shocking or funny, even for less-than-pristine Rosary ears. Kids call in to the show because they want to know if they should get birth control even though their partner or parent or pastor believes birth control is murder (yes), if they should still use condoms during anal (yes), if they should tell their mom that their stepdad keeps walking in on them in the shower (yes). Porn stars are often guests on the show and share that they could never talk to their parents about birth control, or anything at all, that they don't use condoms during anal, even though they should, that their stepdads walked in on them in the shower and they never told anyone. And there are porn stars who come on the show, sometimes literally, who have never had any of these problems. But just love sex. Love their bodies.

It can be hard to be quiet.

The hosts judge everyone, but they do it with a tough love, emphasis on the love. Even when the kids calling in say stupid things like, "I can't stop thinking about having sex with my step-brother." Even when the porn stars say outrageous things like, "Do you want me to tell you how nipple piercings make my clit water?" The hosts say wise things, kind things.

"Do not have this baby, the prisons are already full."

"You know it's time to get some help. That's why you called."

"What happened to you? Let's figure out what happened to you."

And we sit there in the darkness of Rosary, listening as hard as we can to this forbidden noise, and we try to figure out what happened to us.

OR DARE

Whether you pick truth or a dare depends on who is in the room. If you want to be made to kiss one of those people drinking with you, or rub your tits on someone's face, or tweak or suck a nipple until it's hard, then definitely go dare. Even the Dickheads stay above the belt during drinking games, so you're safe enough unless you don't want to do something along the lines of what I've just described with any given person in the room. Then get ready for the truth.

That said, if you have never actually been kissed yet but would be embarrassed to have to admit it, well, choose your poison. Dickheads don't lie to each other. It's not that we respect the truth. We respect the game.

Mo. Sissy. They have their arms around each other, Mo's head is on Sis's shoulder, pillowed by Sissy's curls. Then there's me. Alone.

Bird and Cy are hanging upside down from the tire racks. Winthrop and Rain are late.

"Truth or dare, Hell?" Sissy is asking.

I drain my beer, take a deep breath. "Dare."

I never pick dare, and even Mo is surprised. She lifts her head and Sissy looks around the tire yard, considers her options. Her eyes land on the guys, hanging like bats in a cave, and she nods to them. "Spider-Man," she says.

The 2002 version of *Spider-Man* has been playing at the Rosary Theater since junior high, it feels like, but it's better than *The Shaggy D.A.*, which played for years before. As a result, we all know *Spider-Man* by heart. And this includes the famous hanging-upside-down kiss.

I am on my feet fast to hide how nervous I am. At the tire rack, I consider my options. I thought maybe the guys didn't hear, but when Sissy starts chanting, "Spider-Man! Spider-Man! Spider-Man!" everyone picks it up.

I hope Cy will forgive me, I hope I will forgive myself, but at the last minute, just a foot above my head, I see his belly button. At first I think it is just super-hairy, especially compared to the rest of him, but then I see that it's actually full of lint, dark, dirty lint is swirled around inside his belly button like a curly tail.

I kiss Bird.

And the truth of this dare is that it is better than it looks in the movies. Much better.

I'm so fucking tired of the truth.

TEA LEAF READING: A PRIMER
FOR THE UNWILLING

1. The Icebreaker—The first thing you will see in the bottom of the teacup, the most obvious thing, is what is already known. This is to reassure everyone, to make clear who it is you and the tea leaves are discussing. Not that the tea leaves are actually talking. Not that I have any idea who is talking. With Aunt Bev, I skip this step. She already believes. I don't need to tell her that I see a giant hand or a pack of cards or some other clue about her life in order to earn credibility.

But supposing Aunt Bev was a stranger to me, the following conversation would ensue:

Me: *I'm seeing a pair of cowboy boots, they feel fancy. Does this mean anything to you?*

Aunt Bev: *Oh yes, I adore cowboy boots! I have twenty pairs.*

Note: Aunt Bev does not have twenty pairs of cowboy boots but people wishing to have their fortune told usually fall into one of two categories: believers or cynics. Believers are so excited to find themselves seen, they overstate. A cynic, on the other hand, will grumble that everyone has at least one pair of cowboy boots, so what is the big deal?

2. The Faithtester—The next thing you see is a bit more challenging to translate. It takes teamwork. If the customer isn't willing, isn't a believer (see number one), it will go nowhere. They will blow it off. And the same goes for you. You'll blow it off. Until something happens, a day or a week or a month later, and it all makes sense. And then you'll do your best to blow it off anyway, chalking up your sight to coincidence, the poor man's miracle.

Using the example of Aunt Bev again:

Me, after a long pause to consider phrasing and build suspense: *There is an extremely busy . . . chicken. It is in a panic. If you see someone who is very afraid, or if you see . . . chickens, you should stay away. Does this mean anything to you?*

Aunt Bev: *Oh yes, it means something to me! It means I would like a refund. This is bullshit.*

Note: Aunt Bev would never say this, but step two still feels like a risk. The Faithtester tests everyone's faith, most especially yours.

3. The Dealbreaker—There is not always a Dealbreaker. If there is, you won't wish to share it. This is the vision you don't want to tell because it grabs onto the vague doom chasing up your spine, puts a collar on it, and brings it home for keeps. And even you will have trouble avoiding jumping to some kind of conclusion, thereby sounding even less sane than you already do.

For example, supposing Aunt Bev didn't ask for a refund after the chicken business but hung in there with me, I would say something like this:

Ahem. The extremely busy and panicked . . . chicken, that you should stay away from, it is laying broken eggs. There are broken eggs everywhere and they seem, well, dangerous. Are you trying to conceive?

To which Aunt Bev would respond with hysterical laughter at the thought of being pregnant at her age, leading to sobbing as she realizes Great-Grandma Helen's gift must have skipped a generation.

PIAZZA DE RESISTANCE

Outside of Aunt Bev's shoppe, I'm nobody's accountant. In my unprofessional opinion, though, Rosary must be giving some kind of tax break to nursing homes, because there are a ton of them here. I'm also not a politician, but it seems like all of the old white people in the nursing homes and their old white people votes are part of what keeps Rosary such a stubborn old-fashioned red. And I'm no political analyst or conspiracy theorist or anything, but it seems like these two things might be connected. I'm going to leave this one for the Reconciliation Council to pray on, though. When it comes to old white people, I've got my hands full.

Rosary High requires both juniors and seniors to spend part of their spring semester doing volunteer work at a Rosary nursing home. This injustice will teach us fellowship, respect, and civic-mindedness, or so says our history teacher, Mr. Sturm. Meanwhile, the lesson actually learned by performing forced labor at a nursing home is that getting old is a terrible idea.

It turns out there are worse places to end up than Rosary High. It turns out that old people, even really old people, don't suck or anything, it is just that no one cares about them anymore. So, here we are with our "elders," as Aunt Bev calls them, elders who are so forsaken that teenagers like me are blackmailed with the threat of not graduating high school just to hang out with them.

After weeks of boring preparation, we are assigned the Piazza Convalescent Home. It is called the Piazza, I guess, as a constant reminder to the old people rotting within that if they had made better retirement plans, they could be in Italy right now. So that's nice.

There is a lot to get used to at the Piazza. First is the smell, like a layer of bleach over a layer of empty bottom drawer. And underneath that, piss. The smell doesn't so much hit you as it seeps into you, until you feel maybe a little bit high on your way home, a little bit low. And then all you want is to shower and curl up in a ball.

You can get used to the smell, though.

It is harder to get used to how the bunch of us from Rosary High, me and Rain and Winthrop and a handful of Thumpers, are the only ones moving around through the Piazza's main rooms. The dining room, which is decorated with pictures of James Dean and Marilyn Monroe and old cars. The living room, decorated with a big television, and facing it, a mess of old people in wheelchairs with quilts draped over them.

The old people are pointed at the television and the television is pointed at them.

And that's it.

The folks who work at the Piazza, they're called "aides," roll the old people out to the television in the morning, unless they can roll themselves there, and most of them cannot. The aides roll them into the dining room to eat their meals, then back into the living room that should be called the opposite-of-living room, the dying room, the slow-death room. Then the aides roll them back into their bedrooms at night. Judging by the scrawl I can make out on the shower chart outside the huge wheelchair-accessible bathroom, they are also rolled into the shower once a week or so.

When they are not rolling people this way and that or feeding them or undressing them, bathing them and re-dressing them, the aides are doing laundry or folding laundry or rolling laundry here and there. The aides are tired from all this rolling and laundry. Their hands are so dry and red it hurts to look at them.

Maybe this is what we're really here to learn. What it is we don't want to be when we grow up.

There are no real visitors. At least, I never see one, and judging by the way the old folks look up at us, if they are able to pay attention enough to notice we are there in the first place, well, they would really, really like some visitors.

The ones who notice us latch on, excited, like they are waiting for us to perform. The expectation is so strong, it feels like we should break into song. And that's what Winthrop does. Sings. There is nothing else to do. No games, no music, no arts and crafts. Roll in, roll out, roll in, roll out, roll on forever, amen.

Mr. Sturm says he hopes we will "make a special friend" with one of the "residents" at the Piazza. He says that here we have "the opportunity to make connections that will last a lifetime." And it is pretty clear whose lifetime he means.

And we do make friends, it turns out. On accident. Some of us.

TUPELO HASSMAN

Mrs. Gillespie is always stuck on the end of the row of wheel-chairs because her room is farthest from the television and she can still get herself moving, so she rolls in last. I sit next to her on our first day, in one of the folding chairs Mr. Sturm has stra-tegically placed throughout the Piazza.

Winthrop has turned his chair toward the man he's decided is his special friend, leaned in, and after a while I can hear him singing quietly, a song I don't know. Rain is already holding the hand of another old man. She isn't trying to talk, just sitting there, being Rain. Meanwhile, most of the Thumpers around us are squirming, all but gagging. I am embarrassed for them. Mr. Sturm, unconcerned by their behavior, stands off in a cor-ner by a dusty rack of videos, talking with the aide in charge.

At first my old person doesn't notice I'm there, and I am only pretending to pay attention to her anyway because I'm busy judging the Thumpers. Then I hear Dad's voice in my head muttering about scorecards, so I remove the stone from my own eye or whatever and that's when I realize that underneath the quilts draped over the body of my Piazza companion, the ones pushed up all the way to her shoulders, there is a circular move-ment, around and around and around. A little flurry in her lap.

I don't stare, but I am kind of clocking how long this goes on, which is seven minutes and fifteen seconds, and then noth-ing. Stillness. And the woman whose body and hands are under the now-still quilt says, loudly, but to no one, "I did it."

She sounds so proud. She says it again, louder. "I did it!"

Here she is in a race to nowhere with a team of wheelchair zombies and she's winning, because if this isn't winning, I don't know what is. But no one notices.

So, I say, "Good for you."

She looks around then, not toward me, but around, up at the

ceiling, in the corners. Then, finally, to her left, at me and my folding chair, unusual additions to the room. She looks me up and down and then she repeats, "I did it!" And smiles with a set of full and strong, real and hungry teeth that surprise the heck out of me.

"Good for you," I say. To her teeth. To her bright joy. To the simple, human experience of getting off.

And then she pulls a trembling, painful-looking hand out from under her blankets. I watch the lump of it travel from her lap, up and up toward her shoulder, like when I used to watch Rudolph crawl out from under the blankets in the morning. And then it is out in the air, her hand. And she presents it to me.

"Well, hello, dear. I'm Beatrice Gillespie."

I could do a couple of things when faced with this quivering husk of a hand, and only one of them is reach right out and shake it, firmly and with respect, even though only a minute before, this same hand was working itself into a gnarled frenzy inside an adult diaper.

Beatrice Gillespie's skin feels silky smooth for all of its wrinkles, and her grip is stronger than the warped shape of her fingers promises it could be. Still, when I shake her hand, I can tell that a lot more work went into this single act of masturbation than it might seem possible to someone as young and nimble-fingered as me.

"Hi, Mrs. Gillespie, I'm Helen Dedleder."

"Well, Helen Dedleder"—and there is that smile again—"I did it!"

"Good for you, Mrs. Gillespie."

You can tell a lot about a person from their handshake.

BLOOD TIES

Even though the Rosary Psychic Encounter Shoppe has a reputation for the minor issue of being in league with the Devil and all his lesser demons, Aunt Bev doesn't mess around with anything really creepy. She makes an herbal tea on Sky Radio nights, a brew that kind of brings the room together, helps us listen in, but there is no backward writing or newts' eyes or anything like that to be found at the shoppe. And there was just that one time she poured deer's blood all over me while I slept, in order to put a spell on Dad. It couldn't have been more than a gallon and it wasn't even warm.

Aunt Bev's the expert on how women always get a bad rap for being witches because of bleeding on the regular and not dying, and how all of this has been freaking men out since Eden gave us the big heave-ho. She'll go on about the patriarchy for a week or ten days before she realizes I stopped listening on Tuesday. But this business of soaking me with blood was not really a witch move so much as a political one, and even then, a medical one. Aunt Bev would talk for a month of Tuesdays about how these are one and the same.

The thing was, I started my period. I was fourteen and it's not like I had any friends, much less like I was about to do the deed, but Aunt Bev had been looking into the future like it was the new copy of the *TV Guide* and she needed to know when her shows were on. She was sure that if I wasn't extra-careful, I'd be pregnant before you could say, "Bubble, bubble, toil and trouble."

Or, maybe, she was looking into the past and remembering being a teenager and making decisions that she later wished she'd had more guidance about. I don't know how she prognosticated this one, exactly. What I do know is that she acquired and then poured about a gallon of fresh deer's blood on me, so I wouldn't become pregnant until I planned on it.

This is an old witch's trick for when a girl crosses the line into womanhood. Deer are a symbol of both fragility and fertility. Once a deer's blood has been poured onto a young woman, the dead deer's spirit stays with her, acting as a guide across the threshold. Thereafter, its spirit settles in the woman's womb, curling up there like her uterus is a wooded glen and the deer is guarding its fertility. It's called Deer Moon.

Just kidding. I made all that up about the deer's spirit. I can't explain all the shit that Aunt Bev gets up to, but sometimes she asks me to try, to sell it in some occult-style way as practice for the future I don't see myself having as her psychic sidekick. Like I need more homework.

So, there's no Deer Moon. This thing with the blood has a nearly scientific basis. Rosary, for obvious unscientific reasons, doesn't allow any teen to have access to birth control and does its best to deny birth control to adult women as well. However, if a girl's period is out of control, she can get help. If she is bleeding too much, say, soaking through, as the old-school pamphlet from the nurse's office says, "more than twelve pads a day," that is out of control. Thus, she can get a legal prescription for birth control pills. Birth control pills help turn the bleeding down to non-torrential levels. Among other things.

Despite the intense and irrational fear of women's menstrual blood, hunting and all the bloodshed it brings is very popular in Rosary. Aunt Bev had no problem acquiring some fresh deer blood for me. She made a trade for it, to celebrate my coming of age, handed it to me in a cleaned-up plastic milk jug, and said to hide it in my room. The first morning of my next period, she let herself into our house before the sun rose, came into my room, and poured the jug out onto my bed, my pajamas, and me.

"You can open your eyes," she said. Then she whispered, "A good long shower is coming up," in that reassuring way she has, and I gave her a big bloody thumbs-up as she clicked my door shut. A second later, she slammed the front door like she had just come in.

"Good morning!"

I could hear Dad snort in his bedroom, could hear him getting up. Aunt Bev's visits are unusual, and he always makes the most of them. He considers it his duty to make little dents in Aunt Bev's damnation, and so he was out there in a hot second, talking, the coffeepot gurgling.

I climbed out of bed and, looking down at myself, I felt sorry for my dad and the heart attack he was about to have. But this was his own fault, a curse he'd brought on himself. I'd seen his council letters stressing the importance of keeping clinics out of Rosary. So I turned the door handle, went into the hall, and tried not to touch anything. In a shaky voice I said, "Dad?"

It's a real horror show, becoming a woman.

ELDER GOALS

Beatrice Gillespie and I are becoming fond of each other. Some of the other kids bounce from old person to old person, but I always put my folding chair next to Mrs. Gillespie's rolling chair when I come in to the Piazza, and I spend the afternoons only with her. I wait to speak until she's done getting off, which she seems to do precisely at 1:45 p.m. every Thursday. I can only hope it is the same every day of the week, because watching this triumph gives me renewed hope for mankind. And America. Which, I'm pretty sure, is what history class is meant to teach.

Each day, she makes the same smiling report. "I did it!" And then she'll pause, like she is sure she knows me and is reaching for my name.

"Helen, Mrs. Gillespie. Good for you."

Sometimes she gets confused and adds, "Good for you," to her greeting, like that's my name. I sit down, and she looks over at me and says, "Good for You!" and then she studies my face for a while. Sometimes she takes a nap, warm in her own afterglow. Once in a while she makes some small request.

"I would like some water, dear."

The first time she asked, I found one of the aides and told them and twenty minutes later, long after she had forgotten she was thirsty, Mrs. Gillespie was given her water in a paper cup. Then I watched the aides moving around in the kitchen, figured out where everything is, and now I get water for Mrs. Gillespie myself. In a mug.

The aides seem relieved that I'm not bothering them, and I feel pretty good about myself. And that is a new way to feel.

Soon enough, the other residents start wanting water too. It's a riot. No wonder the aides avoid meeting these small needs.

Not really. It's not a riot. It isn't a problem at all. It is just people daring to want anything in a place that every second is telling them their wanting days are over. Most of the residents are so used to being ignored that they never notice any of us or anything, but when they see me walking by with that mug, their eyes follow it across the room like it's the old Mustang they used to drive. The tips of their tongues poke out as they prepare to speak, testing the air. Remembering.

Oh, how good it felt to be behind the wheel with a full tank of gas.

I get water for everyone who asks.

I feel like I should run for mayor.

Sometimes Mrs. Gillespie asks me questions I have to create answers for. This is commonly known as lying, but in a political arena, like a U.S. history class being conducted in a questionably located nursing home so old white people's votes are funneled where Rosary wants them to go, the act of lying feels quite natural, even required.

For example, she'll ask, "Did I get a postcard today, dear?"

I feel this hollowness inside my rib cage when she does. It's like the aide with the industrial vacuum, the one who is always vacuuming, every single day vacuuming, because the residents can't hear the television anyway, because this is a more attractive chore than actually talking with forgotten people, I feel like that aide has turned the vacuum's hose on me. He's suctioned it straight to my rib cage and is cleaning out all the pesky feeling bits in there.

And on this Thursday, April 11, the anniversary of my mom's death, I wish the vacuum on full blast.

I say, "Let me go check," and then I get up like I'm going to the front desk where the mail is supposedly dropped off but really I get up and go to the wheelchair-accessible bathroom. The bathroom has no lock because none of the doors here have a lock. Because if there was a lock, these old people might lock themselves inside in a fit of human desire for the dignity of a little privacy while they sit on the giant plastic safety seat that goes over the toilet so their old and tired asses don't fall in. Instead, the bathroom has a child-safety plastic ring around the outside knob so that it is hard for confused and arthritic people to open. This way they won't walk in on someone being showered, and this way it is the safest room for me to catch a breath and stop feeling sorry for myself.

HOW TO NOT FEEL SORRY FOR YOURSELF

1. Find a potentially private space, hopefully with a mirror.
2. Look in the mirror at your own dumb face. Look hard.
3. If there are tears in your eyes, rub them with tight fists like the little baby you apparently are.
4. Say the following words to yourself in the order they appear: *Do not cry.*
5. Cry.
6. Add your own name. Maybe you weren't clear on who you were talking to: *Do not cry, Helen Dedleder.*
7. Even better than adding your own name, add a nickname given to you by someone who actually has a right to feel sorry for themselves but chooses not to: *Do not cry, Good for You.*

SAD CRABS

It is an actual Saturday, the kind that only happens on a weekend, and Dad insists that we spend it "as a family," by going to the beach with Iris and "her family." For a terrifying second I am lost in the fear that there are more of them, more Birds and Irises, coming at us like the undead, tearing away the plywood we've put up to protect us like it is so many thin pages from Dad's Bible. But he just means the two of them. And he means the two of us.

The sky and the water of Rosary are like bookends to the city, holding nothing up. They are both gray and they both stink. There is really not even a beach here, only a tiny bit of sand that is barely a dune, just close enough to the refinery to still see it. People come to throw tennis balls into the water in order to strengthen their dogs' immune systems, I guess, and that's it usually but here we are today anyway. Dad and Iris stand at the edge of the water where a flock of sandpipers run in and out with the waves and they are laughing like we are on vacation in Hawaii or something. That is, Dad and Iris are laughing like they're posing for a tourist brochure for someplace you never want to go to. The birds are full of murder, chasing the crabs as they send their feelers up through the sand, making it bubble up when the water rolls away. The birds stick their beaks into those holes the bubbles leave behind, sucking up as many crabs as they can before the next wave.

Bird and I are sitting on the sheet Dad brought. Sheets, he says, are better than blankets because they don't hold the sand when it is time to pack up. I didn't know my dad had any hot tips about the beach before. I didn't know he could relax so easily, bask in the circle of life displayed before us again and again as one crab after another is swallowed up, killed just for trying to be.

"Don't you just want to smash them?" Bird asks.

"Our parents?" I don't know what he's talking about and I hate how he does this, throws me off guard. I wish I could throw him off guard for once. Yet another thing I wish I could do to Bird.

His stupidly perfect white teeth flash against the gray sky. "Yeah," he says, and looks at me for too long. As usual.

"No," he says, and he pours out the root beer Iris had given him and digs into the sand. He fills his plastic cup with tiny crabs and holds it to my ear. "Listen," he says, "these would make great cereal. Mmmm."

I shiver at the *snap crackle pop* of the crabs' desperation, at the way Bird's Adam's apple vibrates when he says, "Mmmm," and at the way his fingers brush against my ear when he moves the cup away.

An older couple, even older than our parents, have come down to the water from the parking lot. The woman is wearing a long red dress, and as she sinks into a folding chair next to her husband the dress puddles beneath her.

"What do you think her job is?" I ask Bird. A stupid question. To change the subject from all of the above.

"She's the wife," he says, his words weightless, not even heavy as a thought. Because Bird doesn't think.

"You are a caveman."

He smiles at me like this is a compliment. "Yeah," he says. At least he spares me the obvious joke about his giant club.

He points to the waves. "There's stingrays out there," he says. "What do you think you'd need to catch one?"

I shrug.

But I think of light.

I don't tell him this because I don't know why I think of it and because I'm afraid I'm right. If I was, I know what he would do. He'd hook a piercing strand of light to a fishing line somehow, sink it into the water, hypnotize a stingray, drawing its cold, curious body closer and closer, and when he had it there, slippery in his hands, he'd shake his head at it for being so willing and ready to be caught.

Tsk tsk tsk.

LIKE A GIRL

Cy's head flops back on the couch and he snaps it up straight, takes another big sip from a beer that might actually be empty, acts like he's totally with us, and then his head drops back again. He's wasted, and he does this over and over. Sissy, sitting next to him, whacks Cy on the head every time he doesn't pop right back up, and in the midst of this Cy vomits. But only into his mouth. He holds it there, his cheeks puffing out a little, and then he swallows the puke back down like it never happened, like no one noticed. I noticed but I'm not going to say anything. It's impressive.

No matter how much I drink, I can't get wasted. I feel the beer going down my throat, rough with bubbles, sour-sweet, but then it is like I don't feel any different at all. My head stays up, I don't puke in my mouth. I'm just like before.

Watching Cy get hit on the head over and over, the glossy,

easy look in his eyes as it happens, gives me an idea, though, so the next afternoon I get to the tire yard early. It is just Sissy and me, which is what I hoped.

Sissy's eating from a bag of pork rinds. She walks through an industrial park to get here—everything in Rosary is a church, a retirement home, or an industrial park—and some days she passes a food truck. The Dickheads put in "roach coach" requests with Sissy, usually for packaged meat-like products like this one, bags of meat or salty tubes of Slim Jims, which they inhale before burping in truly life-changing ways.

I sit down next to Sissy and she offers me the bag.

"No, thanks." My hands are sweaty and I wipe them on my pants. I feel ridiculous. Like I'm on a first date and trying to be cool. Which is not to say I know what it is like to be on a date.

"So, Sis."

"So." She crunches. The pork rinds have more of her attention than I do.

"You've been in fights."

More crunching. "Yeah." Sissy fights, she fights at home and at school. She has bruises, a wide shiny scar on her forearm that seems like it must be from a knife.

"Not me," I say. "I've never been hit."

There. I said it.

The crunching stops.

"Not, like, at home?" Not many families in Rosary spare the rod. So few don't spank or hit or use a belt like the good Lord intended that those who don't beat on their kids are shamed into silence. I am pretty sure that Dad doesn't talk about all of the nonviolence at our house when he's at the men's weekly prayer group.

"Not so much."

She looks at me then, really looks at me, maybe for the first time, and it is clear that she has figured something out.

"Because your mom died." Pork rinds again. "She'd hit you if she was here." It's like she's trying to reassure me, like she wants me to know that even if my dad is fucking up, my mom would've done it right. I am loved.

"Anyway. I want to get in a fight."

Sissy has another realization. "Bird never hit you?" It dawns on her that the world is failing me.

I feel like I have never really understood Sissy until this moment.

"Not . . . directly," I say.

"That's fucking weird."

The conversation is getting away from me and I want to do this before the rest of the Dickheads show up. "Listen, will you just punch me?"

WHAM.

It's like the tire yard's heavy door slamming down. Onto my head.

I was going to ask her to take me by surprise, but I was also going to ask her not to break my nose and not to knock me out and offer to trade some beers if she would do it. None of this matters now, because it's done.

She didn't even put down the bag of pork rinds.

There's a smear of salt and grease across my cheek and I can smell it on my hands when I take them away from my face where I've been holding it in surprise, without even realizing I was. I'm feeling pain. But mostly what I'm feeling is something like joy.

There aren't really stars in Rosary. The smoke from the refinery smudges their glow and its bright twenty-four-hour lights reflect off any clouds, so whether it is clear or overcast, night never feels real here. We don't get to make wishes and appreciate how small we are. We don't get that gift of perspective. But this gives me some.

There are stars now, twinkling brightly behind my eyes where I sit on the tire yard couch.

"Thanks," I say.

I feel hungry.

Sissy does not ask if I'm all right.

"Sorry about your mom," she says, adding, "And yeah, anytime." She offers me the pork rinds again. We sit together then, crunching through the rest of the bag, and every bite is delicious.

SHOTGUNNING

Dad is sitting at the kitchen table when I come in from the tire yard. He's alone but I can smell dinner, grilled cheese with pickles, which is my favorite sandwich in the universe, and I'm still hungry from getting punched and there are plates on the table, forks and glasses. Just for two. I act like I don't see him, just like I'm acting like I am coming in from Aunt Bev's and nowhere else, drop my bag at the computer desk in the living room, and turn down the hall for the bathroom and the mouthwash to cover the smell of beer, to check that my face isn't bruised, but he stops me.

He is standing in the kitchen doorway.

Grilled cheese with pickles. He hasn't made that in years.

This can't be good.

"Helen," he says, "you're home!"

Like he's been coached. Like he just got a copy of *Appropriate Things to Say When a Known Person Comes Home.*

"How was your day?

"Are you hungry?

"I made some dinner.

"I'm going to propose to Iris."

He says all of these things right on top of each other and I forget about smelling like beer and having a punched face. He's staring at me and I'm staring at him and the kitchen goes long, stretches the way a room does after you shotgun a beer. Dad had only been a few feet from me when he started talking, but now he is far away and drifting. Dad's on the other side of the world and that world is paved with linoleum and the smells of grilled cheese and pickles. On that side of the world, everything is upside down. The dead love again, or think they do, and they make favorite dinners, and they make conversation, and they make choices their daughters can't ever live with.

LOST

DAD
WHITE AND GRAY, SKINNY, SHORT HAIR THAT IS
RECEDING, A MUSTACHE THAT IS NOT.
FORTY-SIX YEARS OLD.
LAST SEEN AT THE KITCHEN TABLE.
ANSWERS TO: DAD. WHATEVER IRIS CALLS HIM.
LIKES: RUBS ON THE BELLY, TO BE TOLD THAT LIFE IS VERY
GOOD AND BEAUTIFUL, FORTY-YEAR-OLD WOMEN
WHO CANNOT SHUT UP.

REVENGE OFFERED.

NOPE

It isn't necessary to sneak in a window or through the back door at Winthrop's house. His parents aren't home. I mean, someone is usually around but they just aren't home, as in the question, "Hello, is anybody in there?" The answer to that is nope.

So I take the key from under the roof of the stone pagoda on the porch and unlock the door. There is no other house in Rosary that I know of with a pagoda, with artificial grass rolled out on the porch, but these intrusions into Rosary's sameness, like Mr. Epsworthy's voice coming from the Lost City Bread van's speaker on his eternal rounds of dire warning–slash–insurance commercial, are the only constant signs that Winthrop's parents are with us.

Tonight, I walk past Mrs. Epsworthy, who stays asleep in her spot in front of the television. I walk down the hall to Winthrop and Rain's room. And then I crawl into Winthrop's bed.

Winthrop is the biggest spoon ever created. He's a soup spoon, a ladle, and cuddling up with him usually makes me feel better right away, makes me feel all together, like I know where all this little spoon that is me, I know where I am. Spooning with Winthrop gives a body perspective. Or it usually does, but even with my arm over his big belly now, I don't feel better.

"Helen." That's Rain, asking. Asking without a question mark. She was on her phone when I came in, with all the someones she is always talking to who are not going to be her date to the prom because they live in Sky and are waiting for her there, in her future.

That's all she says. "Helen." Rain and Winthrop always call me by my full name.

And you know how sometimes you think you're doing pretty fine, like you've got it together, and then just one person says a teeny-tiny nice thing to you and that is the end of the bullshit you've been telling yourself about how you're feeling? And how sometimes just someone who loves you saying your name is that one nice thing? The only nice thing you need? Maybe the only nice thing there is?

Well, imagine if you were just barely keeping it together and then you were double-teamed like the Epsworthys did to me right then. Just as Rain says my name like that, Winthrop closes his hand over mine, links our fingers together. And I start to cry, and not just a little bit. I press my face into Winthrop's back to hide myself and the sad fact of my ugly cry face, but they know anyway. The room that was lit only by Rain's phone when I came in goes black as she puts her phone away. And they listen, even though I'm not saying anything. And they don't ask questions looking for answers I don't have. And I love them.

And I hate everything and everyone else.

So basically, a normal day.

When I finally catch my breath and explain about Dad, about the impending disaster, Rain lets out a long slow sigh, almost a whistle, and Winthrop squeezes my hand harder, like he's wringing me out.

When I'm quiet then, no more snuffling and sobbing, and there is snot all over his T-shirt, Winthrop says what is really the only appropriate thing to say at a time like this. The single, only sentence that makes any kind of sense.

"What you need is some ice cream."

Winthrop's belief that few things are more powerful than ice cream sounds stupid until you give it one chance. And there's always ice cream at the Epsworthys'. Usually Rain doesn't join us for midnight ice-cream runs but tonight she does, because tonight it's for a cure.

Rain turns down the television in the living room and tucks the remote back into the pocket by Mrs. Epsworthy's seat. Winthrop gets out three half gallons of fancy ice cream plus a giant tub of cheap Neapolitan. He sets them all on the kitchen table and removes the lids. Then he gets down to business. There is magic in every ritual.

He lights the stove and puts the kettle on, then gets out bowls and spoons, sets them carefully before us, and just when the kettle threatens to whistle, he turns it off and pours boiling-hot water into a coffee mug. Next, the industrial-grade ice-cream scooper is stuck into the mug long enough for the metal to heat, so it can cut smoothly through the ice-cream flavors. He turns to me, and I point. Mint chip. Coffee. A stripe of Neapolitan. He rinses the scooper and reheats before each flavor, delivering perfect round scoops to my bowl.

Once we're all served, Rain raises her spoon and says, in her most serious voice, "I scream. You scream."

She pauses. And we all say together, solemn as a prayer, "We all scream."

FROM THE EDGE

After I go "check the mail," on those afternoons when Mrs. Gillespie asks me if she got a postcard, I get my shit together in the privacy of the bathroom, so I can answer her question properly. Then I go back to my seat at her elbow and say, as bright as if I had just come back from vacation myself, "Mrs. Gillespie, there's no postcard today, but didn't you get one yesterday?"

There hasn't been mail at the Piazza for any of the residents on the Thursdays I've been here. I'm relying on a different kind of yesterday. The rich one that made Mrs. Gillespie who she still is, the most alive person here, including myself.

"Oh yes! I did receive a postcard just yesterday!" she answers, and then her smile isn't only for me, it sticks with her as she remembers fondly now what it is like, being remembered.

———

"Will you pull my quilt up a bit, dear?" The top blanket in Mrs. Gillespie's mobile blanket fort is a quilt, like nearly everyone's here. But where most are knitted, hers is patchwork. Tons of tiny squares of fabric of every pattern and color, with here and there a bit of yarn pulled through to secure the squares where they meet.

I don't know if she really needs this pulling up of the quilt she asks for. Securing blankets over frail, cold bodies is probably the first thing they teach you in caring-for-old-people school. But I fuss around with it, smooth it over her shoulders, and look into her bright brown eyes when I'm done. "How's that?"

"That is just fine," she says. She surprises me by saying my name: "Thank you, Helen Dedleder."

THE SACRAMENT
OF THE PRESENT MOMENT

Winthrop has a carton of eggs. Aunt Bev said that he would.

Even before we got out of the truck I could see the splatter all over her front window, the red palm of the fortune-telling hand painted there shining with goo. As if the giant the hand belongs to had jerked off and then, instead of one of his dirty giant T-shirts, he used the Rosary Psychic Encounter Shoppe to clean himself up. Aunt Bev didn't say a word about the yolk dripping down her window, across the life and love lines and the $10 promise she's never kept. She didn't sigh, didn't do anything, not even look down at the concrete, at all the eggshells broken there. I started to wonder if she'd noticed, but once we went inside, she put down the bag of groceries we'd just bought and started filling a bucket in the sink. She squeezed some soap in, poured in some salt, and as she watched the bucket fill, the bubbles rising and reflecting the light, I knew to keep on keeping quiet.

"Your mind must be clean to create clean," she always says, has said to me since I was little, whenever she'd hand me the broom. We sweep after every customer, sweep right out the door, and shake the dust we cannot see into Rosary's already-polluted wind.

As she lifted the heavy bucket out of the sink, Aunt Bev said, "Winthrop is still sitting back there. Go get him. And bring the eggs. We'll eat."

Hang out with psychic people long enough and you learn not to ask. Not them. But you ask other people. I'm not surprised when I do find Winthrop sitting back behind the shoppe on the old plastic chair under the bird feeder. I am surprised that he is holding an egg in his hand, almost like he's going to throw it at me. There's an open carton of eggs at his feet.

"Winthrop, what the fuck?"

"That's nice, Helen." He puts his hand down. "That's a lovely way to talk."

"Why didn't you call the police?" I say, pulling him up, but when he looks hurt, doesn't make a joke, I stop. "She wants the eggs."

Inside, Aunt Bev hands me the bucket and the squeegee for the front window and fresh rags. She crooks her finger at Winthrop slowly, her eyes drawn to a squint. Seeing her face, I am kind of glad to escape to window-washing duty. It's not that Aunt Bev would have wanted Winthrop to call the cops when he caught someone egging the shoppe—she wouldn't. It's that Aunt Bev doesn't appreciate heroics. She's the kind who will punish you for trying to save her, because, she says, "If I did not want to be in this mess, I would not be in this mess."

When I come back from rinsing, and wiping until the squeegee squeaks clean across every line on the giant red palm, fate and life and love all shiny and new, Winthrop, who is always so bold when we talk about Aunt Bev and so quiet when he is actually around her, is sitting at her kitchen counter with a big plate of scrambled eggs in front of him and he is laughing.

Aunt Bev sets a plate for me. "Now, tell me about going to the prom together."

"It's not like that," we say, nearly at the same time, and Winthrop adds, "Rain is our date too."

"Rain asked us to be her date," I try to clarify, but Aunt Bev stops me.

"I understand," she says. She smiles at Winthrop. "I hear that you are a good dancer." Before he can agree—and Winthrop does agree—she is up and at her old radio, turning the dial from the classics station, which is her favorite, to an oldies station. "Duke of Earl" sings through the room and Aunt Bev puts her hand out to Winthrop, who is already on his feet. This is a dream come true for him. Aunt Bev doesn't need a crystal ball to figure that out.

He twirls her across the old Oriental rug and he sings along like he listens to oldies or something, sings like he does at the Piazza, "You know I'm gonna love you . . . for I'm the Duke of Earl," and his voice, like his moves, is full of surprises.

When "Duke of Earl" ends, "Stand by Me" comes on, and Aunt Bev makes a big show of needing to sit down, like she's been dancing for hours, fanning her hand in front of her face. "I'll let you cut in this time, Helen, but next time, you'll have to fight me for him," she says, and Winthrop takes my hand, pulls me close, and we move around the room together like two teenagers in love.

HOW TO SHAKE YOUR HIPS

We make individual trips to the Rosary High nurse with complaints of headache or upset stomach or, in Winthrop's case, what he insisted was "the vapors," as he held the back of his hand to his forehead in a faint. Once in the nurse's office, we each took our opportunity to grab a stack of the pamphlets eternally available there, *Abstinence and Teens: A Hot Couple* and *1, 2, 3, No!* The paper is kind of heavy but the cartoons on them are in full color and the corsages I'm making, using every trick Mom ever taught me, are turning out beautifully.

Rain is in charge of cosmetics, "the Special Effects Department," she started calling it when she began construction on my eyebrows. A process that involved tweezers and scissors and had Rain talking to herself in a mutter.

Winthrop is in charge of choreography, obviously, and I need all the help he can give. You'd think dancing would be in my bones, in my blood, but I was born with both of the left feet Mom never had.

Since we are already going as a threesome, we decide to keep bending the prom until it breaks. Rain and I are wearing matching strapless dresses, denim with bloodred ribbons that tie around the back, silver fishnets, and black high heels that only Rain has any practice walking in. Winthrop has one of Mr. Epsworthy's suits. It's plaid and will never button over Winthrop's stomach, but with the same satin we are using for our ribbons, Rain and I make a cummerbund, and no one will be able to tell that a rubber band is holding his pants up underneath the satin. He's leaving the coat open to better display this, along with the ruffled tuxedo shirt that we also couldn't get to button all the way down.

"Maybe two rubber bands?" says Rain, when we're testing the cummerbund.

"I'll wear my fancy boxers, just in case," Winthrop says, and then he stands there and, without seeming to do anything, his entire body shimmies in that dance move he's trying to teach us and that I, for one, will never learn. But Rain and I stand up, and we do our best, like backup dancers, just glad to share a little of the spotlight that shines wherever he is.

GET A LIFELINE

"My time costs actual money, you know. I can look in a mirror if I want to see tits."

The curtain is drawn around Aunt Bev's kitchen nook, where I'm on my stool putting receipts in date order before entering them in the paper ledger she still uses and says she always will. I'm lucky she doesn't make me use an abacus to better put the ancestors at ease. I didn't even look up when I heard the chimes on the door tinkling quietly. My house is full of wedding plans, my house that will soon be full of Bird. I'm tired of the future today, but this line about tits is definitely not Aunt Bev's usual opener, and I sneak a peek to see who has caused her to start so roughly. Aunt Bev says you have to speak their language if you want their attention. Whose language is this?

Mo's.

Sooner or later everyone shows up at the shoppe.

Mo doesn't blink at Aunt Bev's attitude. "I have twenty dollars. What can I get for that?"

Most people would melt into a puddle if Aunt Bev looked into them the way she is looking into Mo right now.

Aunt Bev doesn't speak until Mo takes the money out of her pocket and hands it over.

"For twenty dollars"—Aunt Bev's voice is more relaxed than her eyes—"I read your palm."

She takes her time straightening the bill, smoothing it, before she places it under the crystal ball on the table. Sometimes she doesn't need a palm to read at all, she says, just this act can be enough, this undoing of whatever people do to their money. She can feel Mo in every crease of the bill as she unfolds it, can find her, as if the bill were a map pulled out of a glove box on the side of a country road.

"Sit down," she says. "Your right hand," she says.

There is supposed to be an "Ah yes" now or a "Hmmmm," like Aunt Bev is agreeing with the way the lines in the palm crease, like she is listening to a good friend tell the story of her day. And then she'll ask, "You would like to know if your summer will be one of love?" Or something banal but enticing. A question that is really a statement, something she already knows how to answer. That's the script, but as soon as she has Mo's hand, Aunt Bev makes a noise like she's in pain, like she's burned herself on the incense smoking at her elbow, and I have to stop myself from going to help her.

She pushes Mo's sleeve up, holds the palm flat against the velvet. There is a burn there, another, more. There is a messy star burned into Mo's forearm and it's like the heat is all around us then. The Rosary sun is a hot coal pressing down onto the roof.

Parents come in all kinds of monster.

Aunt Bev's face starts to shine, but Mo looks perfectly cool. Calm. She looks straight at Aunt Bev, doesn't notice me, doesn't see my Converse under the curtain, or if she does, she doesn't care.

They sit together inside this blaze until Aunt Bev pulls Mo's sleeve down. She folds Mo's fingers into her palm, holds her hand shut. She whispers, "Maureen, you're going to have to start making some decisions for yourself or that heat is coming back for you and it always will."

It is so hot, too hot, in here.

Aunt Bev closes her eyes. And she doesn't say anything else.

"But you didn't read my palm," Mo says. She is looking down at her hand, empty on the table, where the velvet isn't singed, where the tarot cards are not ash.

And then I cannot believe my eyeballs because I've never seen Aunt Bev do anything like this before. You do not give a refund just because the future is bleak, you have your own future to worry about. Those are her words. She has told me in no uncertain terms that I cannot feel sorry for customers. But Aunt Bev hands Mo's money back to her. And then she says, "For your protection," and she doesn't open her eyes when she waves Mo away.

CHILDREN OF THE TORN

Mo and I know each other from the time before Dickheads. We know each other from the time of moms.

Mo's parents—she still has both of them—go to the same church as Dad and Iris, the Life Fellowship of Rosary. My family used to go there too, together. Mo and I would sit next to each other in Bible Study, swing on the jungle gym in the church's tanbark yard, singing about Jesus's love for us. Maybe Mo still goes. I don't know weekend Mo, I don't know at-home Mo, but I used to, so I can guess she probably does go, puts in an appearance to keep the peace in the Swanson household. Blessed are the peacemakers, for they shall inherit not getting the shit beat out of them. Mrs. Swanson is a true Thumper and her thumping is what powers the little motors of rebellion in the Swanson children. It's her thumping that keeps the battery running on the tattoo rig hidden in Mo's brother's backpack when he comes to visit. It's what powers Mo's lips on Bird's mouth and all the other parts of him too, what is pushing Mo down so hard she thinks Bird is a step up.

Mrs. Swanson and Mom were pregnant with Mo and me at the same time, they made friends over that same hope they carried inside of them. And once their girls were born, Mo and her mom would come over to our house and Mom would read the Bible with Mrs. Swanson while Mo and I played. Mom let us play with her miniatures on those days, a white porcelain phone, watering can, and bread box painted with blue flowers. We could play with these as long as we were careful and so were our bears and dolls. The bears and dolls called on the phone making doctor appointments for each other, watered imaginary plants, and opened the bread box to offer each other pretend muffins with jam, while in the real-life kitchen both books of Daniel or Kings or whatever were being read aloud by our moms over iced tea and saltines.

Sometimes on those afternoons, Mo would just stop playing, kind of freeze. She'd be tracing a finger over the cool porcelain of the miniature phone, its perfect smooth flowers, and the look on her face was pure hunger. I would watch and wonder where she'd gone, and then she would come back and hand the phone to me.

"It's for you, Helen," she'd say, still far away. Still my best friend.

Mrs. Swanson got pregnant again and again. The Swansons are one of those quiver families. They read that psalm about children being like arrows and sign their wombs right up to be weapons factories. While Mrs. Swanson was building her army, Mom and I started going over to their house more often, so Mom could help. On those days, Mo and I had to read the Bible aloud at the kitchen table, loud enough for "the new baby to hear," the one who wasn't an arrow yet, piercing Mrs. Swanson's future enemies. And from where she would sit in the living room with her feet up, Mrs. Swanson would thank my mom every time she walked by with this load of laundry or that dirty diaper.

"Oh, thank you so much, Evelyn, God bless you, Evelyn."

And when Mom was sick, Mrs. Swanson helped us all the time. It was like we couldn't get rid of her.

Not.

When Mom became sick, Mrs. Swanson never helped us, never came over and busted her ass while Mom put her feet up after chemo. But at church, if Mo and I were ever even close to one another, there would be Mrs. Swanson, quick on her feet even while pregnant with her bottomless quiver. "Maureen Swanson," she would hiss at Mo, her voice low and wet like a log in a fire.

Mrs. Swanson homeschooled like the true Thumpers do. At least until their kids get to high school and they realize that math is hard. Mo and I were never alone together after that. We would stare after each other at Life Fellowship, locking eyes across the pews, until the Sunday when Mrs. Swanson noticed this and, clamping her fingers around Mo's head, turned her daughter to face the pulpit. The half-moons from her fingernails left deep marks in Mo's cheek that still shone after the sermon was over. It hurt me to look at Mo after that. It hurt to see.

For a long time, I thought it was because Mom was sick that Mrs. Swanson couldn't be near us, she didn't want to catch it, especially pregnant. Now I know it's because Aunt Bev came back to Rosary to help Mom. To help us. When Aunt Bev took over the shoppe, the Thumpers ran from our lives like rats in the light. Cancer isn't contagious, it turns out, but magic is.

WHEN THUMPERS ATTACK

I'm in the giant, nearly private bathroom at the Piazza, giving myself the usual pep talk before returning to report to Mrs. Gillespie that yesterday was the day a postcard came for her and it always will be, when there's a knock.

"Just a minute," I holler, but the door opens.

It's Rain. Of course she's noticed my bathroom trips. She twirls the plastic safety device on the doorknob and laughs at it. Then she shuts the door and looks me over.

I decide I'm going to tell her about Mrs. Gillespie's stupid hunt for mail and how I feel like stupid shit about it and probably blubber my face off. But there's no time to say anything because Beau and Roger, two Thumper boys, walk right in like they've been working against child-safety locks all their lives.

"Wait a minute," says the big one, Beau. "Is this a guy's bathroom or is it a girl's bathroom?" He's pinch-faced, like a squirrel, but if you don't include his brain or heart and probably one other essential organ, the rest of him is huge. Beau is a squirrel-boy-man who loves the Lord and will defend His Kingdom, as he was raised to, starting with the assault on the freedom to piss that Rain represents to him.

"Fuck off," she says.

Beau's pinched eyes gleam and he turns to Roger. Poor Roger. Roger is a true believer but with the all-around fashion sense gained from the few uncensored R&B videos we get in Rosary. He's wearing some pretty cool baggy pants and looks almost like a normal person, but then there is a long chain with a giant gold cross on it dangling from around his neck all the way to the top of his boxers. It's too much. Jesus would agree.

"Roger," Beau says, "did he just tell me to fuck off?"

He.

There's a beat before the beating begins.

Then Rain punches Beau, an uppercut to the chin, and he leans right into it. Beau is not surprised at all. He wants this. And then he's on her, literally on her, in that same second. Rain and Beau are on the floor, and he's holding her throat, pushing her head back onto the linoleum, right between the toilet, with the big plastic safety seat hulking over it, and the drain in the center of the floor. He's making that gross hocking sound, bringing phlegm and germs up into his mouth, presumably to spit on Rain's face.

I bend my knee and bring it back, so I can smash it squarely into his head.

What I should have done is reach for the door to call for help, because this isn't a Dickhead brawl and this isn't high school. There's no Security Guard Jay here to cut in before we find out what we're really made of. This is the real deal. And there went the only second I had before Roger is on me too, pulling me down.

I have my own place on the linoleum now, under dumbass Roger, who has managed to pin me down mainly because the sag in his baggy pants takes up more room than he does.

Roger doesn't seem to know what to do next and neither do I, but I'm totally pissed.

And totally scared.

I notice things about the bathroom that I have never noticed before.

There is a metal bar for a shower curtain that is pulled closed once the old people are seated on the plastic chair under the showerhead.

Even as I'm trying to get my knee in between the legs of Roger's baggy jeans to send his balls straight through to his stomach, I am wondering if the aides ever actually close the curtain. If the old people are ever allowed this moment alone.

I start to scream.

Roger's hand over my mouth smells clean like peppermint.

I gag.

Beau is kind of puffed up now. Like a balloon animal. This means that much to him. Who Rain is. Who Beau is not.

Beau's holding her arms down, still bringing up spit.

Rain could be screaming for help, but she's not. She's cursing at Beau, over and over and over.

"Fuck you.

There's a glob of spit on her cheek.

"Fuck. You.

"Fuck.

"You."

And then I see a red handle on the wall. There's a red handle with EMERGENCY written on it. There's a string hanging from the red handle so a fallen old person could reach up and call for help by pulling the string, which pulls the handle.

Because of course there is.

Roger's hand is on my mouth, his knees are pinning my chest, but he's staring at Rain like he's never seen someone say "Fuck you" before while being slimed with Thumper goo. So I try sliding Roger bit by bit, toward the string hanging from the emergency handle. This sliding causes my sweatshirt to rise over my stomach. The linoleum is cold on my back. We are getting nowhere fast.

I open my mouth as wide as I can, accepting that I'll have to allow Roger's tiny peppermint stick fingers into it at least long enough to bite down on them as hard as I possibly can.

And when I open my mouth, he lets go.

Because he looks down and notices that my tits are hanging out.

To be fair, my tits don't really hang, not out or in any other direction. But there they are. In the open. And there he is. And he certainly has never seen live tits before.

Roger leans down then, like he's going to kiss me, maybe. His face blocks my view of Beau and Rain, of the red handle, of escape.

I feel something on my stomach.

Something liquid.

Roger's cross. His giant stupid cross is against my stomach, the metal so cold it feels wet.

And I am struck by divine inspiration.

I hiss. Like a snake.

I roll my eyes back in my head and find a growl. I writhe.

"It burns. Our flesh is burning."

And like the demons Jesus released to run into the bodies of the pigs, I am free.

———

For the rest of my life, I will remember the look of pure terror on Roger's face as he jumps off me, how one hand wraps around his giant gold cross, how the other pulls on Beau's shoulder. His frantic "We have to go, we have to go, now."

Beau isn't listening to Roger. His spitting and Rain's "fuck you"s continue, so I keep hissing, edging toward the alarm.

I'm pretty sure Roger has just started in on the Lord's Prayer when the door handle to the bathroom starts to jiggle.

It's a quiet noise but we all hear it because we're high on adrenaline.

Beau makes another spit-hocking sound in the back of his throat.

Rain says, "Oh, one more thing, Beau. Fuck you."

I hiss and lunge for the emergency handle, pushing Roger out of my way. Just then, the door swings open wide as it can go, hitting Roger in the side of the head with a force that makes him fall over.

Beau bounces off Rain like a guy who's done this before.

Rain gets up.

And Mrs. Gillespie is sitting there in the hallway in her wheel-chair. She's holding one aching hand in the other, resting them on top of her quilt-covered lap, and she smiles when she sees me.

Without so much as a nod to anyone else in the room, she says, "I did it!"

THE TOOLS OF FORGETTING

And just like that, it's over. There are no more Thursdays at the Piazza. No more Mrs. Gillespie and her crippled hand like clockwork in her nightgown. There isn't a party or anything. It just ends. The students of Rosary High disappear on those old people like everyone else has.

And then Mr. Sturm expects us to write a paper about it, eight to ten pages proving that we learned something about being better citizens.

After what feels like hours in front of the computer, I take my ten pages from the printer and staple them together. I make sure that my name appears in the top left corner so there is no confusion about who has failed this assignment.

Every one of my ten pages is blank, empty as the golden years of Beatrice Gillespie's life.

What I learned at the Piazza would overflow a paper. But it couldn't even fill a postcard.

HETEROSAURUS

There is no sex education in Rosary. We are supposed to abstain. It follows, then, that we have parenting class instead. Ms. Nash teaches what passes for science, and some of it is straight bull, like the thing about the dinosaurs. Some if it is all right, almost useful, like the bit about our brains not maturing until we are twenty-five, how we take more chances before that age. If we manage to reach it. How the reason we fall so hard under the weight of peer pressure is because being "risk averse" is something you have to grow into. "It is biological," Ms. Nash says, all the while pushing intelligent design under the rug with her sensible shoes, and there is no explanation of how this embrace of risk is also a part of God's plan and not His way to make us as extinct as our dinosaur brothers.

Ms. Nash emphasizes this inability to avoid risk, risk that in-cludes getting pregnant, as she pairs us up, heteronormatively, for the start of our final project. She gives each couple a plastic baby, dressed in pink or blue, to rock and hold and care for until the bell rings for next period.

No pun intended.

Winthrop and I scramble to make sure we're partnered. And when we receive our bouncing plastic baby, we name it Porhtniw Neleh, to commemorate the backward beginning of our child's life in this backward place.

And because it's a little bit Satan-y.

SLANT RHYME

Ms. Millen in English class wants us to write a poem about the teenage experience.

She says when we're older, we'll wish we could see us. Now, "on this cusp, the edge of adulthood. The precipice."

Ms. Millen uses too many words, every synonym, for an exercise we have no interest in, especially since science class just taught us that our brains are fucked.

The only reason we have any fun is because we're trying to die before we grow up.

RISK AVERSE

if your friends jumped off a bridge
would you
oh parents
can't you remember
those friends
they are the bridge

DON'T YOU FORGET ABOUT ME

My life is like one of those movies from the 1980s they're always having weekend marathons of on TV, even Rosary TV, because the kids in them are white and their problems are sanitized for our protection. Those movies where everyone is stuck in detention together and the girl's family forgets her birthday. Where her dad, newly returned to the land of the living thanks to his horrendous but life-resuscitating fiancée, the fiancée with the son whose presence screams, "Fuck me," that one where the dad plans his wedding for the same day as the daughter's prom because that is the only weekend day the VFW hall is available and he can't wait any longer to have aged-person sex. The prom his daughter has been planning on destroying, but in the best way, with her best friends, since before he was even engaged. And she already has a dress and her eyebrows are tamed and she's learning to shimmy and her two dream dates have already planned how to decorate the Epsworthys' van better than any limo.

Have you seen that one?

It has a killer soundtrack. Mainly, it begins with me yelling, "No," right before slamming the bedroom door on my dad's face, and him saying, softly at first from the other side, "Helen."

I shout through the door, "No," and he says, louder, "Helen." Then I scream, "NO," and he loses his cool, so it turns into this:

"Hell."

"NO."

"HELL."

"NO."

"HELL!"

"NO!"

Exactly the point I am trying to make.

AND BRIMSTONE

The phone ringing in the middle of the night stops my 1980s-style, no-commercial-break marathon of feeling sorry for myself. Our phone hardly rings at all, much less in the middle of the night, and of course it is Aunt Bev and of course she is calm even though I can hear the sirens in the background, can hear a loud voice giving orders.

The shoppe was torched. The fucks of Rosary went from ASK JESUS to BURN THE WITCH at the speed of hypocrisy and the giant palm on her front window is gone forever.

But she is fine.

She had been out back, sitting in that plastic chair, her Saint Mary Magdalene tapestry wrapped around her, her phone in her hand. And she waited for the tires to squeal away before calling

911 even though she heard the glass shatter and even though she knew the brick that shattered it was followed by a glass bottle full of gasoline and that the gasoline had a bit of rag in it that had been lit on fire. She knew because she had seen it coming with great clarity, she told me. And she knew because this has all happened before, to everyone who has ever been like her.

I've seen Aunt Bev do things outside of what is considered normal, outside of what is considered possible, for my entire life. I guess that is why I have never really questioned that she spices up her psychic days with some overtime at night, that she sees little divide between climbing into someone's psyche and climbing into bed with them. Plus, it's not like she waits for customers in a negligee and high heels and hopes for the best. She picks, she chooses. Aunt Bev is the smartest person I know, so I don't worry that she has "internalized the patriarchy," like Rain says we all have.

I never have worried about Aunt Bev at all. Until now.

Because she was prepared, called right away, by the time the first fire truck arrived, the second one wasn't needed. And when I ask her how come she wasn't in bed, when I panic after the fact, imagining her sleeping through the crash of the glass, suffocating under smoke, or worse, she tells me about what she had seen. She says, in that way she has of brushing off a question, like it's a gnat, a nuisance, "I hate getting woken up by fumes."

"But why didn't you stop them." I hear my own voice as I say this. I hear that I am not asking a question. I am making an accusation.

Whoops.

Aunt Bev's face grows severe, her lips grow white as she purses them. She gives me a look that makes me feel like a child. And maybe it's the smoke still fading from the room, the scare of losing her fading with it, maybe it's the wet chemical smell from the fire hoses, but I swear Aunt Bev grows tall all of a sudden, looms over me. She shoots up through a hole in the burned roof, her body blocking out the night sky. And the room disappears. And there is only her.

Her.

Her voice is everywhere. I don't hear it so much as feel it.

"That is not what the gift is for, Helen."

I want to scream back at her, want to scream, "Fuck the gift," but I also wish I had something to hide behind and my voice comes out small. I don't forget the question mark this time.

"But why see it, then?"

I start to cry. That really pisses me off, and I manage to add, in an almost loud voice, "Why see it if you can't change it? What kind of gift is that?"

The walls are giving way around us, something necessary to keep them up was lost in the fire. Everything is crumbling.

"Change requires sacrifice."

Or I am just trembling, because Aunt Bev is shouting now.

"Never think that I have not sacrificed."

We shouldn't be allowed in here. It can't be safe. What was the fire marshal thinking?

She takes a deep breath, softens.

"I could not change what happened to your mom, Helen. But I promised to take her place in the only way possible."

The ruined shoppe steadies around us now.

"I'm here," Aunt Bev says, in her normal voice. "I'm here for you."

She is her usual size and shape again, but I still feel small. And I sob in her arms, and in this mess of smoke and loss, her arms are a gift.

ABOMINATION

It's not like Aunt Bev doesn't care about who lit up the shoppe with a Rosary cocktail. It's like she actually does, like she is interested in the state of their souls the same way they would probably claim to be interested in hers, even as they try to destroy the body and home and business that are meant to serve it. Aunt Bev would never press charges. But her insurance company does not have any spiritual qualms about wanting revenge, and neither do the Rosary police. The department may be made up of Thumpers but they leave New Testament ideas about forgiveness at home. It is an eye for an eye, and pretty much any eye will do.

Soon enough, I know, the authorities will come sniffing around the Dickheads. What I don't know is that soon enough, they will have a suspect.

Winthrop Epsworthy.

Apparently, Winthrop has a little bit of a criminal record. Apparently, Winthrop used to like to go into other people's houses. But only when they weren't home.

"And just hang out," he says. "I didn't ever take anything. I just looked around. Sometimes I'd watch TV. And one time, just one time, there was a fire."

The image of Winthrop, in his ironed button-downs, watching TV on a stranger's couch, stealing the comfort of their home while they are away without taking anything else at all, it makes a weird kind of sense. And now it makes sense that the Epsworthys have moved around so much. It's why Mr. Epsworthy has a hypnotizing speech ready for the principal's office to absolve his children, about how teenagers in particular are the lost continent. And it's why Winthrop and Rain know that speech by heart.

What doesn't make sense is why I am just hearing this now. And maybe that bit about a fire.

Winthrop is telling me this in his bedroom the night after the fire at the shoppe. We have been up since Aunt Bev's phone call to me, after mine to Winthrop and Rainbolene, when they walked down there in their pajamas and sweats to watch the firefighters pack it in. We all cleaned up together as the sun rose, Aunt Bev and Dad and me, then the Epsworthys and the Doncasters, pink boxes of donuts from the Donut Hole springing up like flowers after a rain.

Winthrop and I are in the fort we create by pulling a blanket across the two beds. There's a porn book between us, *She Drives a Semi*, but we did not get a chance to open it before Winthrop made this confession. Or whatever it is.

He's acting weird. Something like afraid.

"Helen," he says, "I don't do this anymore. I mean, I didn't do this."

I didn't think he did it. I don't. I wouldn't. I want to know how he stopped. "How did you—"

"I didn't!" He starts to get up and the blanket fort collapses around us. His voice cuts through the stripes and zigzags of his comforter, a design that has always reminded me of Charlie Brown's T-shirt.

"I swear to God."

"I was going to say, how did you stop?" I pull the blanket off of our heads. Move a pillow behind us and make him lie down then, in the valley between the two beds. The valley of truth.

We stare up at the ceiling of this room Winthrop shares with his sister, the ceiling that is covered with glow-in-the-dark stars in constellations they invented together. Kitten with Yarn is just above us. I remember my first nights sleeping over, how safe I have always felt in this spot, how lucky. How this does not change when I understand that Winthrop has a little bit of a trespassing problem.

"Before we came to Rosary, at the last place, in Alaska, I got in trouble. I got caught. And because it wasn't my first offense, I was supposed to go to juvenile hall."

I reach for his hand.

"We moved. Dad posted bail and we left." He says, "I am on the lam."

I do not laugh. I do not think this is cool or neat. The cops are looking at the Dickheads, or they will be. And we are the Dickheads. And they are going to find out these historical facts about Winthrop.

And he never told me.

"I'm sorry I didn't tell you," he says, like a mind reader. "My mom doesn't even know. Not about the last one. Dad told her we had to move for his work."

I don't know what I'm more afraid of. That Winthrop will have to go to the farm, to some juvenile detention center where they are just training guys for the major league of prison. I don't want to think about Winthrop's big soft self in a hard place. But I don't want the Epsworthys to move away either. I don't want Winthrop to get caught, but I don't want him to run.

"I'm going to miss you, Helen."

I try to hide my selfishness. Of course they should leave.

"But I want to be at Rain's graduation."

Okay, so they'll hold out for graduation. I squeeze his hand. Kitten with Yarn is all tangled up above me and I wipe my face on my sleeve.

"Where?"

"Nowhere. I mean, to juvie. Alaskan juvie. We're going to see, if I turn myself in before they find out about my record, if they will let me wait until after Rain graduates."

"Really?" I am so excited that they're not moving away, I sound happy. Which is kind of the wrong emotion to express right now. "But you didn't even do this."

"I did light up someone else's store, though. Used furniture. It was a thrift store and it had been closed for months and all these old couches just kept getting piled up outside of it, until it was like this couch graveyard and they were moldy and gross, so I poured a little lighter fluid on one and, whoosh." He sounds nostalgic. "But the fire got big fast and a little tiny bit of the store burned before the fire department could put it out. They saw me running away. Saw that a fat kid wearing a tie had been there. Dad started packing us up before the sentencing, and the next thing I know, we're in Rosary."

Rain comes in then, which is good because I don't know what to say.

"Helen, I guess you finally met my baby brother the arsonist?" She sounds all right, but she doesn't look like herself.

I sit up. "He says he's going to let them put him in the farm? In Alaska?" I say. I ask.

"Win knows what he wants," and she looks right into me in a way that would make Aunt Bev proud, "and he wants us to stay in Rosary."

"Yay, juvie!" says Winthrop. "It's the best news I've had since I found out my sister is my only date for prom." He gets up.

"You owe me more than one dance, Helen. You owe me for the prom you'll miss and for the wedding reception I'll miss." He puts on the playlist we made for our drive to prom, all the oldies and bootleg R&B that won't be played there. We were going to do our best that night with the sparkly white-boy bands and tween-girl pop, but for now, at least, Winthrop is our DJ.

He takes my hand. And we shimmy right through all the fears and all the worries. We shimmy until we are brave.

THE SECRET LIFE OF PIT BULLS

There is the supposed love story that is about to move in to my own house, I'm helping Aunt Bev restore the shoppe, worrying about Winthrop going to jail, and then, on top of everything else, Winthrop falls in love.

Fast Eddie got a dog. The fire at the shoppe has us all looking at the Thumpers like maybe they are dangerous after all, and nowhere is more flammable than the tire yard. So here is Pen. Short for Pendeja, which is Spanish for *asshole*, I guess, and somebody's idea of a joke, but no one speaks Spanish around here, so Pen it is. Pen is big enough to be terrifying, that's for sure, but she's not. And she is definitely not a watchdog. Unless you count watching Winthrop, because that is all she does.

It's that sweet something Winthrop has. A secret scent. His sweat curls up into the rolls of his flesh like sugar in a bun. Pen likes Winthrop's smell, I'm guessing, and I know she likes that way he has. She acts kind of wild, jumping and barking at us from her corner with her bowls and an old moving blanket, but Winthrop always says hello to her when he comes in. She sits when he does, sits and waits. And finally, after her first few days at the tire yard, tired of waiting for more than that hello, she makes her move.

She strains at the end of the leash but she's not yapping or frothing. She's wagging, wiggling her butt with its badly cropped tail, and she's coming right toward Winthrop. When he sees her coming at him, he moves from a corner of the couch to the armrest, from the armrest toward the dog, goes nearer and nearer until he is close enough to reach out his hand.

Fast Eddie comes out of his office when all the Dickheads start screaming.

Eddie's probably thinking lawsuit, finally, after all the laws we break in here. He's been nervous since she arrived, irritated. And he yells, "Sit." And the dog sits. Not because of Fast Eddie but because Winthrop is right in front of her at last. She sits and sniffs Winthrop's outstretched hand. And then she licks it, like he is her own pup, tastes that sweetness. Eddie pulls her back, tells her to "Stay," and for the rest of the afternoon, Winthrop keeps his eyes on her. She looks right at him, and lets out these big doggy sighs, licks her lips, and remembers the taste of kindness that fills him inside like marrow.

At Fast Eddie's the next night, Sissy and Mo have already traded for beers for Bird and them. They climb the tires, slip and fall, and when their six-pack is almost gone they start making out, with each other and Bird. I watch for a little bit, enough to be sure no one is watching me, and then I head toward the bathroom but nod at Eddie as I go by.

I don't go all the way into his office, I stand just inside the door.

"You want a beer, Helen?" he says as he comes in, not to me but to my chest. "Half a beer?"

I am very tired of this joke.

"I don't want beer."

"What am I, a charity case?"

"I want Pen."

"That stupid dog?" Then he is all business again. "But the dog has bigger tits than you."

I turn to go. I've never cared about flashing him, but I don't think I can do more. Not for that sweet dumb dog I know Eddie already regrets getting. Not even for Winthrop and the magic trick I'm trying to work here by giving him one more tie to Rosary just in case he decides to run.

"Such a bargainer." He laughs. "Let's talk. Sit down."

I keep my hand on the doorframe. "I'm listening," I say.

"A case," he says. The laughter is gone from his voice now. This is code for Eddie getting to put his hand in my pants. Eddie never fucks anyone, not that I know of, but he will trade all the beer in the world to feel you up. And down.

"No fucking way," I say. "Half a rack," and I must be a good bargainer because he nods, comes up behind me. I grab onto the doorframe, steady myself. He smells like tar. He smells empty. And then I know why they call him Fast Eddie. He lifts my shirt up with one hand and grabs at my tits with the other.

"I just need one hand," he says, and it's like he's trying to talk himself into something.

I feel like every beer I have ever chugged in Eddie's name is in me at once, spilling up my throat.

And then he's gone. Already across the room, leaning against his desk. He never even got hard.

"The dog was a mistake anyway," he says. His voice sounds almost sad.

"I'll come back for her after you close," I say, and straighten my shirt.

Rain is stretched out on the couch when I come out and she raises her eyebrows when I have no beer in my hand, but she says nothing. The dog will be waiting outside the fence just like the six-packs and half racks and cases of beer that have been left out there for Mo and Sissy before. I'll take Pen to the Epsworthys', and when I see Winthrop's eyes light up like a thousand old sofas on fire, it will be worth it.

SPECIAL DELIVERY

The night I first slept over at Winthrop and Rainbolene's, my sleeping bag on the floor between their beds, I wore gym shorts and a T-shirt, and Rain had the big idea we play post office, which she renamed Helen's Dad Delivers. We wrote letters to each other, the three of us, from made-up personalities, lovers, lawyers, bosses, delivered the letters by wadding them in balls and throwing them at each other's heads, or folding them precisely as many times as we could, and whispering, "Knock knock! Helen's Dad Delivers!" We'd whisper it and then scream it, louder and louder, until the recipient noticed the tiny correspondence just near them.

I had my feet up on Rain's bed, a notebook on my chest, my shorts riding down my legs, gaping open around my underwear. I didn't notice this until I felt Rain's toes, painted a perfect dark red, soft on my inner thigh. "Knock knock . . ." she whispered, and I moved my notebook aside, went to reach for the next letter, and saw that she hadn't sent one.

She used her toes like little perfectly manicured fingers. Once past my shorts, they gripped my underwear and pulled the elastic to one side. She was focused on what she was seeing, what she was uncovering, whatever her toes could reveal, and I felt nervous and special both at once.

"Knock knock . . ." she said again, and I opened my legs a little, so she could see, see past and into and up and through me, and when I did she looked at my face. Her toes moved my underwear back to their original position, she smiled at me, and I smiled at her. Then she winked, ripped a page from her notebook, balled it up, and bounced it off the back of Winthrop's head, where he lay with his legs up the wall, his notepad against his knees, no idea what had just happened on the floor of his room. That two girls had just made friends forever using nothing more than what God gave them, or should have.

I wrote my next letter to Rain.

Dear Rainbolene,
　　My vagina would write this letter herself, if she could hold the pen, but that would be distracting and also, she can't spell. Anyways, she just wanted to say how excited she is for you to meet your vagina one day soon.
　　Love,
　　Hell

I folded this into a pretty terrible airplane and flew it toward Rain. It went up a few feet, then plummeted. She caught it, unfolded the wings, read it, then she closed her eyes and held it to her heart before she slipped it behind the Mandela poster and said, "I'm off to dreamland, little ones."

On this night, when I take the key from the pagoda and let myself into the Epsworthys', it is harder than usual to be quiet because I have a giant, dumb dog on a leash and she is very excited to be here. Pen jumps. Is jumping. Will jump. She is like an exercise in verb conjugation, except fun.

When I arrived at the tire yard, Eddie had already gone. Like a fucking asshole, he left her tied to the fence outside, in the dark, with no water or food. Except for headlights from the freeway, the street was dark and the ground was cold and she was pretty happy to see me or anyone. She didn't bark, just whimpered, wagged her tail, and when I was close enough to untie her, when she was close enough to leap at me, she lay down at my feet.

I had brought some bread and peanut butter and I held it out. "Good girl," I said, "good girl," and she swallowed the entire piece without chewing while I petted her big square head for the first time. I rubbed between her ears and she danced a little. "Is that your freedom dance?" I asked. "Your new daddy likes to dance too. Let's take you home."

Even though my arm feels like it will fall off, it is hard not to catch her excitement. Joy is contagious. And loud. Loud enough to wake Winthrop's mom for once.

"Hello, Mrs. Epsworthy," I say, when she turns toward the front door, blinking awake. "It's just me, Helen Dedleder." She's one of those people who make you want to remind them of who you are. "I'm bringing Winthrop's dog home."

I kind of stumble through this, my prepared explanation.

"Yes," says Mrs. Epsworthy, taking in the dog. "It's late. She'll want to be in bed."

I walk Pen down the hall, and as I open Winthrop and Rain's door, I let go of the leash. "Knock knock."

For just a minute on our walk to Winthrop's, with the smell of peanut butter on my fingers and Pen's nails clicking along on the cement, I thought maybe it would be me she loved—me, her liberator. But that was a fantasy. Winthrop's bedroom door isn't even open all the way before she pushes through and leaps, no sniffing around, no investigating, just a leap, straight onto Winthrop's bed. She knows it from Rain's without hesitation and his laughter fills the room as she licks his face, as she snuffles every bit of him.

Rain rolls her eyes at me, but it is irresistible, this nonstop wiggling.

"Okay, girl, okay, enough now," Winthrop says. He wraps his arms around her and she rolls over on her back and kind of growl-moans. He rubs her belly, and her upside-down face breaks into a smile and the room is hot with the smell of freedom and wagging dog.

BOUQUET TOSS

I'm just going to say it. I did something nice for Iris.

I didn't mean to. Just like I didn't really plan to get Pen for Winthrop. I seem to be having these fits of niceness. Like allergies or something. Before I can even find a tissue, I've snotted niceness all over the place.

That I can possibly feel anything for Iris but annoyance and nausea is insane, but there it is. She had come by with Dad's brand-new uniform, fresh from the dry cleaner's, and was hurrying past me where I was pretending to play solitaire on the computer. She was hurrying to get back home so she could hand-address the wedding invitations in her love-letter cursive. And I don't know what happened.

Maybe because she could have been talking about me becoming her daughter, or, worse, giving me a speech about how she hoped I would see her as a mom, and she never did this.

Maybe because of the way she helped at the shoppe after the fire, like she actually meant to accept Aunt Bev as family. Maybe because on Mother's Day she made herself scarce, didn't even stop by after church, making it possible for me to spend that day according to tradition, in bed with the blankets over my head.

There are a thousand ways Iris could have been making me gag. And she hasn't.

"Iris, I could make those flowers for you." I didn't take my eyes from the computer screen.

I had refused before. Weeks ago. She'd come to me, knocked on my actual bedroom door with her actual hand. "Helen, I would just love it so much if you would make my bouquet with the love letters I've written your dad? I love your flowers."

Iris is the type of person who ends statements with question marks. She is the type of person who will use the word *love* in sentence after sentence until it is empty as a deflated balloon on a dance floor. I could not imagine how many times she used it in her letters to Dad, how in reading those letters, which I would have to do to make the flowers come out right, I would see it over and over again, each word like the prick of a needle in my skin because none of those letters are from my mom.

"It would be perfect to have my bouquet made out of letters when I marry my postman, don't you think?" she said at my door.

And I looked right in her hopeful, joyful, earnest, prom-ruining, life-ruining face and I said no. "I don't want to read that stuff." As I shut the door, I topped it with, "Gross."

And she never said anything about it. And never told my dad. I know because he would have been sure to give me a First Corinthians speech. The whole reason they are getting married so soon is because Dad's Bible says they have to before they can do it. That same Bible also frowns on acting like a total shit to your future stepmom.

So I said no. Before. Extremely clearly. And then, when Iris and I were alone in the small corner of hell known as Rosary Bridal, she saw my tattoo.

And hasn't ratted me out.

This one last straw of generosity from Iris apparently broke my bad attitude's back. It has been easy to hide my tattoo from Dad, he would fall over if I wasn't wearing a sweatshirt. It is not so easy to get away with wearing a sweatshirt over the bridesmaid dress you've just tried on, no matter how ugly the dress is.

And I was so busy being disgusted by the dress, the Thumper saleswomen, the entire adventure, that I forgot all about having a nearly illegal tattoo.

When I came out of the dressing room Iris actually gasped.

The saleswoman, thinking Iris was having an orgasm about the dress, gasped too. Hissed, "Gorgeous." But when Iris grabbed my arm and turned it, so she could see the ink there, the saleswoman saw the tattoo and hurried away to pray for His mercy.

Iris held my arm, read the words on it, and said, "Well."

And praying suddenly didn't seem like such a bad idea.

"Helen." Her voice was kind. There, I said it. Kind. "You should talk with your father. He might surprise you."

When I didn't answer, she stepped back, took me in as I was, bridesmaid dress, tattoo. Attitude. Then she kept hold of my arm and reached down for one of the bunches of fake silk flowers Rosary Bridal keeps in a basket in the dressing room, to give prospective brides the full picture, I guess. Iris kind of moved my arm up and laid one of the bouquets across it, curving my arm like a cradle.

"Until you're ready for that, let me see." She reached into the basket again, tried a different bouquet, a longer one.

"There!" My tattoo was completely hidden, and she was . . .

I don't actually know how to say this. Iris was genuinely happy. Like, pleased to be able to help me. "I'll order one just like this to get you through the ceremony, anyway. After that, you're on your own."

The stories where teenagers are complete monsters incapable of a single good act are not bullshit. But in the best horror stories, the monster does that shiny little deed, that one good act. So here I am. Reading Iris's letters and making a bridal bouquet, planning out the long tattoo-covering bouquet I have said I will make for myself. Trust me, though, the groaning I'm doing as I read these letters could have come right from Frankenstein's monster himself.

The letters are mostly thank-yous, because, I guess, regardless of whether the rest of him is seeing the light, there are romantic parts of Dad and they are working just fine. Here are some highlights:

Hi, Elijah, how are you? Well, I hope! "Hangin' in there," over here. I'm writing because I received some beautiful flowers and I was totally baffled. So, I read the note and you know what it said? That it was a gift from a gentleman for Mother's Day. They were the only ones I received. I take that back, Spencer picked daisies from the median for me, the darling. Thanks again, yours in Christ, Iris.

Thank you so much for the pretty heart bracelet on the scented pillow. I love hearts, you know. How did you know? Thank you, it fits perfect and I'm wearing it right now.

Dear Elijah, thunder and lightning as we speak and I'm going to leave this note under your windshield wiper since

I know nothing can keep you from your "appointed rounds."
The postman's creed! Have a wonderful day in the light
of Christ and God Bless.

I manage not to vomit, even at the Mother's Day part, and instead, I clean up and boil some water. Then I steam off the stamps, let them dry, and I set to work, just like Mom taught me. I roll the stamps tight for the stamens and pistils, crease and fold the letters into petals, making sure all the *Christ*s and *thank*s are on the outside, just like they are with Iris. Or like I thought they were. Then I wind the stems from the envelopes and all the while try to keep my mind blank, try to not add any power to their love, to make it mean nothing that I am making her bouquet, because that's the only thing that makes one bit of sense. Because no matter what happened in the dressing room, I am certainly not a nice person.

THE DEVIL YOU KNOW

That I accidentally spill some love into Iris's bouquet is unavoidable. The whole time I am making it, folding her notes and letters, I can't avoid thinking about Rosary Bridal. And I can't get a different letter out of my head. The one Dad has tucked away on his computer. The one from Dad to the Reconciliation Council. The one where he asks them to give the Rosary Psychic Encounter Shoppe their kindest consideration in extending its business license. That one.

Fellow Council Members for the Peaceful Reconciliation of Rosary and Sky,

As your brother on our esteemed council for the past decade, I would like to officially state my position on a topic of record as relates to the Rosary Psychic Encounter Shoppe's license to do business within the city limits of Rosary.

Though I am a relation of the Psychic Encounter Shoppe's proprietor, this fact is more of a boon for our purposes than it otherwise might be since by virtue of that relationship, I have been able to keep a close eye on the business performed there and as both a Christian and a father, remain ever vigilant. It is not only as a council member but as a devout Christian that I assure you now and on record that the transactions performed at this establishment are nothing more than what it is licensed for: entertainment. The Devil gains no foothold in this case. As we are working with a known element, it is my firm belief that renewing the current business license of the Rosary Psychic Encounter Shoppe, with its current proprietor, one who remains dedicated to Rosary despite violent actions aimed at her place of business, is in the best interest of the City of Rosary as a whole.

In service,
Elijah Dedleder
Council Member

There's nothing true in Dad's letter. He has no idea what goes on at the shoppe and he knows it. And it is precisely because he took the time to write out this big bunch of lies, to keep Aunt Bev here and her shoppe open, that even as his wedding day is approaching, my heart is full of love for him. All the hellfire that will come his way for lying just proves for once that we are actually family.

FOREIGN WARS

The Rosary VFW Hall is small and dark and carpeted with at least a world war's worth of beer suds and syrup from poker nights and pancake breakfasts. The veterans don't party like they used to do, at least not in Rosary, where the jobs that were so often filled by ex-military are now taken by trade-school dropouts. Still, the hall is available for weddings. On the morning of this particular wedding, Bird and I are decorating the hall, hanging up streamers and putting a cover and bow on each folding chair, like good Americans.

We work away, and soon the chairs appear to be part bride, part mummy, and there's not a speck of the gloom left undecorated, just like Iris asked. Like we could say no. As she left for her hair appointment, her voice was a commercial jingle when she said we were "the two best kids!" Of course, we rolled our eyes at her like this was a family sitcom. But when Bird goes to the storage closet now, to blow up the pink and yellow balloons with the tank that's been rusting in there since the Constitution was ratified, he comes out saying, "Because fuck you, that's why," in a helium-squeaking voice, and we laugh so hard together, it's like we are good kids. We're a version of them, anyway. Like we are almost brother and sister for the very first time.

When the hall is as cheery as it will ever, ever be, we get back into Iris's ancient blue Honda and Bird drives me home so I can get ready for the ceremony. And all that easy laughter from earlier disappears. We have run out of things to say. The car is too small for both of us, his knees are hitting the dash, and every time he shifts, his hand brushes against my leg. It's accidental, which is new, but it feels like it's on purpose. June is hot as hell in Rosary and the VFW hall was unbearable when we arrived, we had to open the windows and haul fans out from behind the bar before we could even think about decorating, and Bird's smell is all over me now, in me. He cranks the radio station he loves, classic rock. Bon Jovi is going on about giving love a bad name, and I stare out the window and try to hold my breath.

FIRST DANCE

A really loving daughter would tell the story of her father's wedding without making it all about her. I know that. And I love my dad and there is a part of me that is glad that after six years, he gets to stop being a widower and be a husband again. All day, Dad's face is glowing, full of actual life. I am happy for him. But the rest of me is focused on something else. Me.

Because I am a teenager.

And I am a teenager who is currently a cross between a flower girl and a bridesmaid in the worst dress a wedding ever saw. I am grateful that the Life Fellowship Church is small and the aisle is short. I walk in as fast as I can in my pink polyester and stand at the front, tucking my Converse in under the frilled hem so the toes don't stick out, like I promised I would. The choice was, I could let Iris Bedazzle my Converse or I could be discreet about them. This did not seem like a choice. Weddings, apparently, are not democracies.

I am clutching a long bouquet against my tattoo like it is my own precious babe. I made the flowers out of old copies of the *TV Guide* I found in a box when we were cleaning out the spare room for Bird to move in to. I told Iris my bouquet would be made from the romance novel she gave me at Easter, a Christian one with a title that would make the porn gods proud, *Fidelity at the Drive-In*. But Winthrop and I couldn't even read through it using our best voices. It was unbearably not funny. So I tossed it and used the *TV Guide*s instead.

Winthrop is sitting next to Rain and wearing his usual button-down shirt and tie, but today his hair is freshly cut. He looks too handsome to believe. Rain is wearing a dress we found together when we were hunting for the prom dresses I won't be wearing to-night. This one is a deep green that matches her nails and the silk flower in her hair. The Epsworthys are knockouts. But I have to look away, because whenever Winthrop catches my eye he mouths, "Con-grat-u-la-tions!" and I have to look away because all I can think about is how much fun they are going to be having tonight at prom and how much my night will be the perfect opposite. I told them that we shouldn't all miss the prom, that I wouldn't do that to them. It was me who insisted they should not leave early to meet me at the VFW hall, but stay for the whole night, remember-ing every detail to tell me tomorrow. I made them promise.

It seemed like such a good idea at the time.

Aunt Bev is in the first row on our side. She is wearing a long sheer silk coat with big gold feathers printed on it, and under-neath that a purple dress, and her special-occasion cowboy boots, a black that is almost blue, with a green cactus on the heel. This combination would seem especially designed to make Iris groan, but Aunt Bev is gorgeous. She sits there moving a rosary through her fingers, mouthing a prayer. I hope it's for me. Because when

Iris walks in, on Bird's arm, because he is giving her away today, I'm glad that everyone's head is turned so no one can notice the flush creeping up my face.

I don't know if I've ever seen Bird out of a sweatshirt or tank top, but here he is, in a suit he picked out himself, that fits him like he wears one every day. His hair is mostly out of his face, so that hot sparkle in his eye is clearer than ever, like the Devil himself crawled in with a Bedazzler and set to work. Bird enjoys every step down the short aisle, moves slowly and with care. Where I practically sprinted, he holds Iris back, practically struts. When Pastor Ted thanks the Lord for this day and looks to Bird, asking who gives this woman to be wed, I wonder if he notices that a famous fallen angel is giving him a wink.

Among our setup duties at the VFW was stocking the bar. With iced tea and sodas. So Bird and I made sure to stock a fifth of Jack Daniel's in a little corner in the storage closet for ourselves. We've each put $5 in the White Horse kitty, a drinking game suitable for even two players. No one around here has much of a chance to play White Horse because it is for special occasions only. Winthrop and Rain and I were going to play it hard tonight at prom, and now they'll play without me.

To win the White Horse, all you have to do is find yourself attending a prom or wedding, some special event that people invest a lot of emotion into, and then you guess who is going to be the first of the attendees to get so drunk that she loses her shit. That's your White Horse. She might do this by crying on the dance floor, or falling on the dance floor, or making inappropriate dance moves. On the dance floor. Or making out with someone other than her date. On the dance floor. It doesn't always happen that a White Horse is first revealed on the dance floor, but mostly they are, because that is where your blood gets flowing.

Also, I'm referring to the White Horse as *her* here because easy money says the person under the most pressure is going to break first, and no one is under more pressure at a wedding, for example, than bridesmaids, say, or unmarried women, or any woman. Ever.

Pro tip: The amount of pressure a potential White Horse feels is directly proportionate to how high her heels are. Look for the highest heel, the most skill-requiring shoe. She is the one who is going to lose it first, bereft not to be the bride once again or to not have captured her husband's roving eye even in this dress, or at having some other illusion of romance shattered.

It's the meanest of all drinking games because not everyone knows they are playing. The ones with money in the kitty get to laugh it up in judgment and pretend we aren't the actual losers. Usually. But this is a dry wedding, because of course it is. Bird and I don't know who, like us, will be sneaking a little something in along with their good wishes. We were going to keep our eyes open until the cake was cut, then place our bets, but apparently the race was already won.

I should have noticed that Bird's shoes, while flat-soled, have him in a high-stakes position. He's wearing dress shoes. He gave away his mom today. We have been taking turns in the storage closet in the dark with that Jack Daniel's as we wait for Dad and Iris to arrive from the church, but Bird must have had a bottle of his own somewhere else, because he is practically toast when he flicks the lights at the VFW hall and announces the happy couple's arrival with a wolf whistle that involves stuffing what seems like all his fingers into his mouth at the same moment.

It was Iris's idea for Dad to wear his uniform instead of a suit, and the guys from the USPS did the same. Even Bird's suit is that same midnight-blue the Postal Service favors, and Iris moves through these blues in her pearl-gray gown like a great white shark in a stormy sea.

Once we're done with the potluck dinner and the dancing begins, Dad and Iris start with, no lie, "Please Mr. Postman." We all stand like we're supposed to and watch them, their heads close together, Dad somehow finding his feet, both at once, moving in time to the music. He sings along too, and Iris looks, well, pretty. Like brides always figure out how to do. Bird is behind the bar, his hands on the wooden case around the stereo, and the look in his eye is one I've never seen there before. For a guy who always knows where everyone is, exactly, maybe more than they know themselves, he looks lost.

And then it's my turn to feel the pressure.

I begged Dad not to do a father-daughter dance and I almost won that battle, but he said it was that or reading a psalm during the ceremony. At least on the dance floor I don't have to pretend it isn't awkward.

When the floor opens up, the ten square feet of wooden laminate that Bird and I have sectioned off with twinkle lights and streamers becomes a place for everyone to watch Dad and I hold hands. And dance. We move around each other like we are trying to politely avoid a swarm of slow-moving bees, waiting for Stevie Wonder to finish working through all the months and seasons and holidays of the world's longest year in "I Just Called to Say I Love You." This song was not my choice. And when Winthrop was giving me dance lessons for prom, he skipped the lesson on connecting with your partner while evading bees. Awkward for the win.

I can't meet Dad's eyes. I'm trying to pretend he's not here. That neither of us are actually here.

And that's when he sees my tattoo.

There was makeup on it, foundation and powder that Rain said would last if I was careful, but that has pretty much rubbed off. Of course, Dad recognizes the handwriting on my arm. He spent most of his life memorizing its every curve, and as he takes it in, he goes perfectly still.

Then Dad lifts my hand to his heart. To his lips, where he kisses it. And then he lifts my hand higher, above our heads.

And he twirls me. Just like we never practiced. In something like joy. In everything like acceptance.

When it's over, everyone hoots and claps and I grab my purse and basically run into the bathroom. That's right, my purse. The purse is a gift from Iris, one of the many that came my way by virtue of agreeing to stand up for them during the ceremony. It's a stupid silky thing with a rhinestone clasp and long silver chain that Iris insisted would go better with my dress than my black canvas backpack with the silver Sharpie drawings of vampire cats and lightning bolts, the backpack that is my North Star if I ever want to get lost. And this would be a good time for getting lost, all the way lost.

I look up at the ceiling, but I'm really looking higher than that, to the empty sky above. Where God pretends to be. And I raise my hand, like my dad just did on the dance floor, high above my head.

And I flip God off.

Because if Dad is happy, healed, if Dad is actually . . . twirling . . . where does that leave me? I slide down the wall onto the stained carpet of the VFW hall's bathroom. And I scream.

No one can hear me. No one that matters. Aunt Bev didn't even make an appearance at the reception, and my voice won't carry to Rosary High's auditorium, where Winthrop and Rainbolene are making memories without me.

Plus, the small crowd in the VFW hall is surprisingly loud. Apparently, every member of the Rosary Postal Service knows the lyrics of "Girls Just Wanna Have Fun" by heart. The hall is filled with their singing.

For being so holy and all, God has a wicked sense of humor.

SOMETHING CHERRY

Inside of my horrid little purse is a lipstick Iris got for me, the same bubble-gum color as my dress. I even put the lipstick on before the ceremony. I can still see traces of it on my lips when I look in the mirror after I'm done screaming. And then I do this unspeakable thing. I take out the lipstick. And I reapply.

Like Rain taught me, I blot. But I don't look in the mirror again. This is not how I want to remember myself. I don't want to remember myself at all, and I know just how to forget. I go back out to the party before I lose my nerve, find Bird still behind the stereo, and I ask him if he wants to dance.

Bird holds me too close or spins me too far and I love it all except that he's wasted. Or because of it. When "We Are Family" comes on, we join the bigger circle with our parents, we jump up and down, and Bird raises my hand up like I'm a prizefighter during the chorus, "I've got all my sisters with me." Then Bird puts on "Sweet Child o' Mine," and dances with his mom while everyone coos about how sweet it is.

No matter who else is on the dance floor, all I can see is Bird. *Tsk tsk tsk.*

As everyone begins to leave, Iris and Dad start looking like they don't know what to do. This is the one part of the day we didn't plan, but without looking at each other, and almost at the same time, Bird and I say, "We're going to stay and clean up."

You would think that Dad or Iris would notice that something was going on, but they are already on some kind of honeymoon, holding hands and leaning into each other. They've been moony from the first song to the last, which was, of course, "Signed, Sealed, Delivered I'm Yours."

This happiness between them is such a real thing, it is so hard to argue with, that when Dad comes to say good night and kisses me on the cheek, I whisper in his ear, "It was a great day, Dad, congratulations." And he gives me a squeeze and they're off, leaving Bird and me alone with Iris's car keys and the mess. And each other.

And the mess of each other.

It doesn't hurt really, and the little bit it does, I like. I like how the pain makes it real, and, more than the feeling of finally, finally catching up with Rain and Mo and Sissy, with everyone at Rosary High who has already done it, is that, after that first minute, it starts to feel actually and truly good. Bird is not crazy like I thought he would be, or stupid, or even gross. He's smooth, like all that practice he gets has paid off, and just like in the kitchen when he is saying my name over and over while the water runs into the sink and a wet plate drips between us on the floor, he looks me in the eye the whole time.

Like this. We've cleared all the trash and popped all the balloons we can reach without a ladder. And we've finished all the Jack Daniel's. We're reaching up for the same streamer when we crush into each other. The streamer tumbles gently onto our heads and Bird catches me. So I don't fall. Like I was going to fall. And then he's gripping my hands and I move them behind my back, so he's got me around the waist, and I pull us back until my hips hit the folding table we've just finished clearing. The tablecloth bunches up under me like my dress does, saving my ass from splinters after the condom is on and he pushes in, slow at first, *gentle* might even be the word for it. Then faster, harder, complete with moaning, like a porno book is being written right there in the VFW hall as the table slams its legs into the filthy carpet.

When we're done, the tablecloth has stains that are not going to wash out. And for the first time since I reapplied the bubble-gum lipstick and we started dancing, Bird seems to actually remember that we are family now.

I'm going to bury the bloodstained tablecloth under popped balloons and crepe paper in the garbage can but I'm not fast enough. Bird points to the blood. "Helen?" He says my full name and there's no *tsk tsk tsk*ing in it, no shame or smirking, he says it almost like he cares.

And I almost do too. For a minute. But then I remember that Bird's mom, who is alive, is married to my dad. I remember that my mom is not alive or married to anyone. And I say what I practiced saying as I pull the tablecloth off, whisk it away.

Not that I planned this. But I didn't not plan it either.

"As if, Bird. It's just shark week."

When I smelled blood in the water earlier, I thought it was Bird's, but when he looks at me like this, like it matters to him if this was my first time and not just my first time with him, like he might be able to tell that I am lying about having my period, I wonder if maybe there's more to him, to this, than I thought. I wonder if I'm the one who's going to get hurt.

LOST

VIRGINITY
PINK, SHINY, SHORT HAIR BUT FLUFFY.
SIXTEEN YEARS OLD.
LAST SEEN AT THE ROSARY VFW HALL.
ANSWERS TO: BABY, HONEY, COME HERE.
LIKES: TO BE TOLD THAT IT IS VERY GOOD AND BEAUTIFUL,
SEVENTEEN-YEAR-OLD BOYS WHO DO NOT LOVE IT AT ALL.

SOMETIMES LOSING IS ITS OWN REWARD.

PORCHLIGHT

When Bird and I pull into the driveway of the home we now share, Winthrop is sitting on the bottom step in the dark. There is a flower in his hands, like a real flower, an orchid. Pink and white and ferocious. The first living flower I've seen all day.

Winthrop stands up as I get out of the car. He's drunker than Bird and I ever were tonight, if such a thing is possible, and he wobbles a little and kind of holds the flower out to me.

I don't know how to act.

And he doesn't know how to act. "Helen, I got you this corsage," he says, "before." This wasn't what we talked about. Definitely not part of our prom plan. Definitely not a flower folded from an abstinence flyer striped with glitter. This is real, like for a real date to the prom.

I am stuck. With Bird behind me, closing the car door. With

our house in front of me. With Winthrop in between, holding this ginormous flower that must have been flown into Sky, then trucked into Rosary, because it sure wouldn't have grown here. With my underwear still wet and my brain confused.

But Bird doesn't have any trouble figuring out how to act, it's just another night for him. So he acts like a fucking asshole. He laughs as he pushes past Winthrop to the front door. Says, "Too late, Win."

I'm about to scream, so that Winthrop won't be able to hear what Bird says next, that we did it, *It* with a capital *I*, because if Winthrop hears it, then I have to hear it. And I'm not ready for that. But Bird doesn't say that. Just, "Prom's over. You missed your chance." Then he goes in and leaves us alone.

"Winthrop . . ." I don't know what to say. Can he see how swollen my lips are from smashing my face into Bird's? From smashing all of me into Bird? I feel like I am just a smudge of lipstick, like the rest of me is fading. I'm a blur. Even to myself.

I could say, I want to say, "Winthrop, I just let Bird pop my cherry at the wedding reception like one of those girls in *Bridesmaids or Bust*." I could laugh and thank him like it doesn't mean anything, this flower, his waiting with it. Like our entire lives don't mean anything. Because it doesn't. They don't. Do they? And I start to, I blurt out, "Remember . . ." but I bite my lip on the *B* in *Bridesmaids*. I am confused. If losing my virginity doesn't matter, why does what happened at the VFW hall suddenly matter so much?

Winthrop is watching my mouth, waiting for me to finish my sentence, I think, but then. He leans in to kiss me. Like, a real, living kiss.

He looks so beautiful with the porchlight behind him, with the flower in his fist. With trust on his face. And I feel so ugly in this stupid dress with Bird's sweat on my lips, his skin under my fingernails.

I close my lips tight together and turn my face away.

And then Winthrop does know what to say. The perfect thing. "Oh."

And he drops his hand. Drops the flower. And he walks away.

CURSE

For being so full of people all of a sudden, my house is still, quiet, even though it is way past breakfast.

There's a note taped to Dad's door . . . Dad and Iris's door. It says *No Church Today, Honeymooning!*

With a heart around it.

Which is only part of the reason I feel like vomiting.

I jump in the shower, then run to Winthrop's house before anyone wakes up. When I turn onto the Epsworthys' street, I slow down. I catch my breath. I want to appear normal. Be normal. Like this is the morning after prom and we all got wasted and had a great time and now they are going to tell me all the gory details, just like we planned.

Like this is not the morning after the scene in the driveway. After the scene at the VFW hall.

I let myself in as usual but as I'm starting down the hallway,

Rainbolene comes out of the bedroom. And she closes the door behind her.

"Hey," I say. So normal.

"Hey," she says, and stands there. So not.

We both start to speak at the same time but everything I'm going to say is bullshit so I shut up and listen.

What Rainbolene is going to say is apparently bullshit too, because she can't get it out.

"Win is . . . he doesn't . . ."

She takes a breath and looks me in the eye. "He's not ready to see you, Helen."

And I say, "Okay, right, sure," all those words at once, in this goofy everything-is-okay voice as if this happens all the time and everything is okay. I mean, I'm okay.

Right.

Sure.

And she puts her hand on the doorknob and she says, "See you at school tomorrow, okay?"

And I say, "Okay."

Right.

Sure.

And I walk out the door and down the steps. And I walk past the telephone poles of Rosary and all of their lost flyers. And I know just how they feel.

LOST

BEST FRIEND
WHITE WITH BLACK HAIR. BIG. REALLY BIG.
THE HEAVYWEIGHT CHAMPION OF FRIENDS.
SEVENTEEN YEARS OLD.
LAST SEEN BY THE PORCHLIGHT.
ANSWERS TO: WIN. WINTHROP. EVERY CALL I'VE EVER MADE.
LIKES: RUBS ON THE BELLY, HILARIOUS PORN, ICE CREAM CHEERS.
ME. BUT NOT ANYMORE.

NAME YOUR PRICE.

THE BLUES

Fast Eddie bursts out of his office. He is holding the filthy plastic trash can that usually sits by his desk. The one that is usually filled with empty beer cans and cardboard boxes from the microwave dinners he eats in there. He's holding this trash can and running, first to Mo.

He says, "Beer."

She is staring up at him, blinking, but when he grabs the beer from her and drops it in the trash can, we get it. We all move toward him and drop our beers. Except Cy, who tries to drink his first until Eddie takes the can from his mouth. Some beer dribbles onto Cy's T-shirt. We are looking at those wet drops in horror, proof of our misdeeds, and right then there is a knock at the side door.

The knock isn't asking for permission. The handle turns.

And wherever we are, we all sit. Winthrop and Rain are on the couch, Mo and Bird are on the floor. I end up almost sitting on Cy on the arm of the couch, and he puts his arm around me like he's practiced this, hiding in plain sight.

It's the cops.

Eddie disappeared into his office, the trashed beers with him, and now he comes walking back into the room. Slowly. Calmly. Cool Eddie.

"Peter," he says, and nods to the officer, whose blue uniform with its badge, whose belt with its weapons and restraints, whose ability to take people away for a day and for forever, blow through the tire yard like an icy wind.

My skin prickles and I pull Cy's arm tighter around me.

"Ed," the cop says back.

There is nothing at all about Eddie that seems nervous, let alone criminal. He is a total badass. Even Bird swoons.

The room becomes thick with some history between Peter and Eddie. It becomes one of those moments that takes place between adults that makes it obvious how truly and amazingly old they are. They've got stories. Their stories have stories. It's kind of cool, if you think about it.

But there's no time for that, because the only reason Officer Peter could possibly be here is Winthrop. Because Winthrop is going to jail.

Now.

And I'm holding Cy's hand for real and there's this prayer in my head, like God and I never stopped being tight, like I have never doubted Him, much less screamed at Him and flipped him off on my Dad's wedding night.

I get straight to the point: *Not today not today not today.*

And it works. Question mark.

Because Officer Peter has come from Winthrop's house, seduced by Mrs. Epsworthy's spacey helplessness into finding her son and telling him the good news.

Good-ish.

Officer Peter doesn't ask what we're all doing here, though he does scope the room, only focusing in twice. He takes in the old map hanging on the tire yard's wall, hung before the City of Rosary insisted on itself and made that map worthless. And he takes in Rain. He blinks in shock or awe at the brilliance dazzling his eyes, but he doesn't seem to get uptight when he looks at her. More like sad, like he feels sorry for Rain. Which is obviously worse.

After he's done focusing on Rosary's past, and its future, Officer Peter makes a little speech. The authorities will let Winthrop remain a free man until Rain's graduation, after which he will go to a detention center in Alaska. Officer Peter says this delay is so Winthrop can finish up the school year, and his words feel memorized. Like, he has to give this speech about not letting Winthrop's "past tendencies" damage his "current educational prospects," but it is not hard to hear what isn't said, the same song and dance we have been hearing our whole lives. Alaska is Philistine. Alaska is Sky. No godless judge in Alaska is telling Rosary what to do with its children.

Thanks, Thumpers. Question mark.

MAKE-OUT PARTY

Because Winthrop will be gone most of the summer, he is going to miss Rain's birthday, so she asked if she could have a double celebration, a birthday and graduation mash-up. She never wants to pass a birthday without her baby brother, she says. She also says, "More presents for me," and she does make out in the present department. It's kind of like she's on a game show.

First, her parents promise that they are putting her cell phone in her own name but still paying for it. It's a Rosary anti-miracle that she has a cell phone in the first place. No one says the phone is for Rain's safety, of course, though the Epsworthys did buy it once they moved here. We don't remark on the fact that the only trans kid in Rosary is also the only one with a cell phone. What useful thing could we say about that?

———

I give Rain a candle that I made with Aunt Bev's help. It's pink and perfumed just a little bit, with dried flowers, real flowers, pressed all through it. I'd made a mess of Aunt Bev's kitchen in the process and it wasn't really very candle-shaped, but Rain hugged it to her and then she hugged me.

And then it was forgotten. Because in the next package there was that shiny ring that all girls dream of, and on it, the only thing that matters in this life.

Car keys.

The Lost City Bread van belongs to Rain now. A gift from her mom and dad and even from Winthrop. Since Officer Peter's appearance at the tire yard, Winthrop has apparently spent the days and nights before the party secretly cleaning up the van, tacking down new carpet in the back, and wrapping a leather cover around the plastic steering wheel to stop it from becoming burning hot under Rain's new sunny skies. The leather laces up and has us making bondage jokes as we gather around the old van that feels brand-new now, right down to the not-terrible editing on the van's sides that Winthrop managed with white spray paint Mr. Epsworthy must have picked up for him. LOST CITY is completely covered over but the sheaves of wheat are still there, and underneath them, two letters remain from BREAD.

The *B* and the *E*.

BE.

A brother's perfect birthday wish for his sister. And I want to climb Winthrop and wrap myself around him like a leather steering wheel cover. Or something else just as awkward.

Rain offers to take us for a drive, to Fast Eddie's, of course. She's had her license since Alaska, and so has Winthrop, useless as they are until there is someplace to go. As she goes in the house to grab it, I climb in the back of the van and sit cross-legged on the new carpet while Winthrop gets in the passenger's seat. Things felt pretty normal during the party, but now we're alone for the first time since the driveway, since the prom, the flower. Since the deflowering. Just when I start to be afraid that the silence is coming to crush us into smithereens again, Winthrop turns to me.

"What do you think?"

That's easy. Here is what I think without pause or punctuation because that's how I feel inside when I look in Winthrop's eyes right now. The opposite of grammatically correct. *You are my best friend in the world I would do anything to fix this.*

And I am sorry.

But Winthrop is asking what I think of the van. So I try hard to make my response sound like regular-grade enthusiasm and not fangirl-grade enthusiasm. I run my hands over the new carpet and I try to say, "Yeah, it's great."

Like it's totally normal that your best friend maybe isn't your best friend anymore because maybe he is in love with you and you really don't want to lose him but you can't explain how you feel because you don't really know how you feel because when did this become about feelings anyway? And at the same time, I'm trying not to act too normal, too casual, because it isn't every day your other best friend just got her first car and the first best friend busted his ass making it awesome because he is also the best brother in the world but also because he's about to go to jail for being a deviant weirdo freak. Which is part of the reason you love him. Not that you love him, love him, like capital *L* Love him. You don't mean it that way. Do you?

It's hard to find just the right tone to capture all of this emotion without really capturing it, and my cool but appreciative, "Yeah, it's great," comes out sounding strangled. "Yuhr, it's gray!"

Winthrop gives me this pained look and says, "I thought it was more of a dark green. Like a jade."

And then he turns to face the front, and we wait for Rain.

VALEDICTORIAN

Rain did all right in school. Like the rest of us, she didn't stand out and she didn't fall behind. The challenge at Rosary High is just to show up, and that has never been truer than on this day when everyone is acting like it all really matters. Because it suddenly does. Even the Dickheads are all here today, sprinkled through the football field's metal bleachers. I'm in the front row between Bird and Winthrop because irony is real and because we put aside our weirdnesses to be the first ones here. Beside us are the Epsworthys and Dad. And then Iris. Even Aunt Bev is here, sitting at the end of the aisle nearest the gate to the parking lot, fanning herself with a program. She'll disappear as soon as Rain's done.

Principal Harrison is sweating in a suit, reading off names from her stack of diplomas. As Rosary teens scoot across the stage to shake her hand, take the paper, become adults, there is some applause. A little cheering from this or that family in the audience. But overall, it's a yawn fest.

Until Rain steps up onto the stage to wait for her name to be called. The whole audience comes alive then, rustles, bristles. The Epsworthys sit up even taller and reach for each other's hands. The only word I can think of for how they look sitting there on the bleachers is: *noble*. Which makes perfect sense as Rain walks across the stage toward Principal Harrison, because she is royalty.

She takes her sweet time moving the tassel from one side of the mortarboard to the other, and when she does, the sunlight catches on its gold metal clasp. It shines a brief, bright halo around her head and I get a chill all through me. A good one. I look over at Aunt Bev and am surprised—and totally unsurprised—when she turns and gives me a wink.

And then Principal Harrison says her name, *her* name.

Rainbolene Epsworthy.

And when she does, as Harrison's voice echoes across the field, Winthrop and Bird and I don't just cheer. We roar. The Thumpers might lose their voices when they look at Rain, but we don't need their help because we've got all the Dickheads on their feet now. Together we shake Rosary High's metal bleachers like the bars of a cage, we stomp and we cheer until the whole place trembles, and we don't stop until Our Lady of Tomorrow has left the stage.

SAY ANYTHING

When there is nothing left to celebrate, I spend the afternoon at Winthrop's house even though he makes it clear that I am not wanted. Not needed. Even Pen isn't happy to see me. Her square head is down on her paws, watching Winthrop. She must know what packing means. She must have seen people leave before. Or she can tell he is not himself, anyway, he doesn't smell the same or sound the same. It isn't like he has anything to pack either, like he is allowed to have anything in jail, but he's moving his stuff around. He's making his bed. And he isn't talking. At all. He just said that same "Oh" from under the porchlight again when he opened the door to his room and saw me standing there in the hallway. Not like he was expecting someone else, but like I am someone else. Now.

I'm trying to read through some porn on my own while he packs but it isn't funny without him and the graduation balloons that are everywhere, deflating slowly, are not helping. Everything feels used up, desperate, and as juvenile as the hall Winthrop's going to, especially me. Finally, Rain comes in and offers to read with me.

We read with a flashlight under the bedspread fort and I'm glad for it, so I can stop looking at Winthrop to see if he is looking at me, which he is not. So I can stop trying to figure out what to say, because I cannot. Rain and I take turns doing the voices in *Buxom and Bi* and *The Doctor Will Eat You Now*. We suggest that someone should maybe talk to these authors about overusing alliteration and doing a disservice to pervs everywhere with puns. And when the flashlight goes dead and we are out of batteries again I can't think of any more reasons to stay. I have to go home now. I have to say goodbye to Winthrop. Like this.

And I have an idea. A stupid one. So at least that part of my life is the same.

"Can I take one of these?" I hold *Lust in the Fast Lane*, an old one that even we've read 472 times, close to her face so she can see. I'm positive Mr. Epsworthy won't miss it, or if he does, he'll think Winthrop's the one who borrowed it and once he'd stuck the pages together from excitement he was too ashamed to put it back.

"I guess you should ask Win," she says, "he's the pornbrarian."

This is either a terrible idea or it is some coded advice about how to approach her brother. It's worth a shot, I think, but as I crawl out from under the blanket she says, "I'm staying here, where it's safe."

Winthrop is just sitting on his bed. He stopped cleaning. And he speaks before I can ask him about porn-borrowing.

"I think that you have a year to give the newlyweds a wedding gift."

Rain makes a squeak from inside the fort, but I am too surprised to laugh.

Winthrop looks like he didn't mean to say this, like he just remembered who I am, and the room goes back to quiet.

"It's for Aunt Bev," I lie.

I don't know where that lie came from. This whole afternoon is a lie. It's been a lie since the prom, since the wedding. Maybe it's been a lie before that too. I should just tell the truth. I want to take this home because I am going to miss him and I want to make him a potion, do something, anything, to keep him safe in juvie, to remind him of our friendship. A friendship I still believe in.

But when my best friend is going to a scary place alone, all I can do is make up a lie about being some kind of porn mule.

I can tell they don't understand why Aunt Bev would need porn, they are not stupid. Not only did I tell an unnecessary lie, I told one of those lies that require more lies to stop the first from collapsing. But Winthrop says yes, sure. Winthrop says, "Who cares?" which kind of stings, but he doesn't say no.

So, I try to act cool.

I bop Winthrop on the head with *Lust in the Fast Lane* and tuck it in the pocket of my sweatshirt. "See you on the other side," I say. Because I am so cool and this is a cool thing people say. Because I am trying to look like it isn't a big deal that Winthrop is leaving while things are so awful between us. Which ends up looking like it isn't a big deal to me that Winthrop is leaving. It's like I forgot that we'll see each other tonight at the tire yard where Fast Eddie's opening up late for us, a post-curfew going-away party for Winthrop.

And Winthrop, who is actually cool, who is the coolest person I know, says, without looking up, "Yeah, see you tonight."

LAST DANCE

Cans of Red Bull, which are Sky contraband, bottles of Jack Daniel's, which are so easy to come by they are pretty much government-issue, and all the cheap beer Eddie could load into his Buick. It turns out the Dickheads really know how to throw a party. Winthrop is only leaving for six weeks, but no one comes back from juvie the same as when they left, so tonight we'll burn the Winthrop we know into our memories with alcohol and idiocy and hope he sticks.

Winthrop. Rain. Bird. Cy. Mo. Sissy. Me. A pack. A shuffle. People who can't stay away from each other, who have nowhere else to go. Faces that we won't know we have loved until we see them again years later, after one of us gets married, or never does, has a kid, another kid, until decades later, maybe, when one of us is finally gone and we tiptoe into a funeral parlor thinking we will be the only stranger there, and, seeing these faces, find out we never were strangers at all.

It is after-hours and post-curfew and our parents think we are each spending the night at someone else's house. This old trick kids have used since the world was in black-and-white still works like it is brand-new. So we have all this beer to drink and all night to drink it.

And we aren't having any fun.

The Dickheads aren't themselves. There is no yelling, no punching, no daring. There isn't even very much belching. Rain is not saying a word, just hugging a fifth of vodka she brought for herself, and Winthrop is quiet too, though he smiles when the Dickheads talk to him about getting ripped at the farm. "It's like a 24/7 gym," Bird says, more than once. He says it in a way that doesn't sound like he is calling Winthrop out for his weight, but also like he can't think of another good thing to say. Because there isn't any.

The tire yard is so quiet we can hear Eddie's keyboard clicking in his office as he taps away doing what, nobody cares.

Sissy finally throws herself down on the couch and says, "Someone at least make a fart." And even though there is still beer left, we start packing up.

CHAMPION OF THE WORLD

If you are a fighter, your past is right there in your fist, no palm reading required. And as everyone is saying goodbye to Winthrop, giving him a sock on the arm or a fist bump or whatever, Bird's past unfolds straight from the life line he keeps wadded up in his fist like it's some garbage he forgot to throw away.

Bird says to Winthrop, "Hey, man, seriously, don't worry about anything out here. I'll take care of Hell." It's an actual nice thing that could not have sounded less nice because it is coming from him. Because it is about me.

And Winthrop says, in the loudest voice he's used all night, "Thanks, Spencer."

Bird was already headed for the door, as eager to get out of a moment of kindness as most people are to get into one, but when Winthrop says this, he stops.

He isn't leaving now. No one is leaving now. The heavy silence falls again with a thud, trapping us all under its weight, and Bird turns around. Comes closer.

Everybody steps back.

Except Winthrop.

"What?"

"I said, thanks." And here, Winthrop takes a breath. And as he lets it out, he loosens his tie. "Spencer."

Wham.

Pow.

Shazam.

The tire yard is a comic book of sounds as Bird punches Winthrop in the face. Not once. Three times. And Winthrop doesn't flinch.

Not once.

And then Bird stops punching. Which is one of your more surprising moves when you are giving someone an ass-kicking.

"What, now?"

And Winthrop says, through the blood pouring from his nose, he says, "Thanks. Spencer."

And we all sit down. Wherever we've been standing, our bags in our hands. We sit.

And Bird hits him again. Once in the face, twice in the stomach.

And Winthrop doesn't move or fall or vomit. And he doesn't hit back.

Which is when things get really weird. So weird that even Eddie comes out from his office. Because Bird, instead of laying into Winthrop now, finishing him off, he starts hitting slower. He stops between hits. Pauses. Like he and Winthrop are having a conversation. A whole relationship is happening between and inside the punches, between the fingers tight in Bird's fist, between the blood that drips onto Winthrop's stomach from his face.

"What's my name?" says Bird.

"Spencer."

"What?"

Winthrop clears his throat now, spits blood onto the cement. Says two names, more slowly than before, more clearly, so there can be no mistake. "Spencer. Doncaster."

Fast Eddie shakes his head. He goes back into his office, comes back out, passes out beer. Free of charge.

You'd think we would do something. Or, you'd think we wouldn't, because we are Dickheads and live for this, because we don't actually care about anyone, even each other, but that's not it. We don't do anything because we do care. We are following the Golden Rule.

As the beers open all around, the sound of them cracking open is mixed with the sound of Bird asking, "What?" over and over again. The sounds of punching, panting. And then something else. A moaning, a whimpering. But the moaning isn't coming from Winthrop.

Bird has started to cry. There are tears rolling in his sweat and then, instead of asking, "What?" he pounds into Winthrop and starts asking, "Why?"

With each punch.

Why?

Why?

Why?

Aside from his stomach rippling under the hits, Winthrop doesn't move. It's like he was born for this. Like he could stand there for days, forever, or at least until the sun rises and it is time to leave for juvie with a police escort.

And finally, Bird just stops. He stops hitting.

He says, "Why?" not really to anyone. Kind of to himself.

And that's when Winthrop says, like he planned it, like he broke into Bird's house and sat in his secrets when he wasn't home, played with them, and then put them back just like he found them. Like he knows.

"Because fuck you, that's why."

Mo goes up to Bird and kind of grabs him then, before he can punch Winthrop some more or fall over or whatever it is you do when someone takes you apart and then hands you the pieces. Spencer Doncaster, no matter what he is trying to pretend with that nickname he chose for himself, is never going to be able to fly away from here the way his daddy did.

Even so, Mo looks at me like it is my fault as she walks Bird out. And so does Rain as she wipes Winthrop's face with paper towels and they go through the door.

And as I hear the Lost City Bread van pull out of the parking lot, so do I. I look at myself that way too.

THE GOLDEN RULE

Beat other people the way you would like to be beaten.

LOVE IS A DOG FROM HELL

I have the curtain open so I can see when Winthrop turns the corner.

He has Pen with him. I thought if he brought her, I would hear her first, but she is quiet. They make a perfect pair, big and slow and terrifying, especially now. Even in the streetlight, I can see where Winthrop's face is crumpled and red from the beating.

"I talked her into being quiet," Winthrop whispers. And when she sees me through the window, she doesn't moan or make the polite throaty barks she has started making to let me know she is pleased to see me and would like some scratching around the ears. This dog can really follow orders.

And we're all quiet. I don't know what to say. I answered the phone on the first ring, and not because I was afraid of it waking Dad or Iris but because I had so hoped he would call that I basically had my hand right on it. When Winthrop heard my voice, he only said, "Bedroom window," and when I heard his voice, I was too relieved to ask why.

I know the questions to all the answers I want but I don't know if I can say those questions out loud. Does he hate me? Is he scared? He has to be scared. He doesn't have to hate me.

He knows the answers to all the questions I have. Could I write to him? I've already asked, he's already said no. But I say it anyway, "I want to write to you, Winthrop."

He shakes his head. Looks away.

"I'm obviously no good at reading between the lines, Helen."

Ouch.

You know that feeling when you stub your toe against the leg of the bed and you want to scream and fall down and hold yourself but it's the middle of the night and the house is quiet and it was your own stupid fucking fault in the first place so you just hold your breath and kind of limp along?

I feel like that.

Maybe Winthrop can tell that I want to collapse on the floor now and rock myself back and forth until the pain goes away, because he adds, "I told Rain no letters either. I just want someone to help her take care of Pen while I'm gone and"—he looks down—"your aunt said you should do it."

"Aunt Bev?" Like I have another aunt, but that's not what I mean. He's talking to Aunt Bev and not me? Getting her advice? I suppose she's going to write to him. "You guys talked?"

"You'll watch Pen?" but it isn't a question and he turns to go and this is worse than toe-stubbing, that this is how he wants to say goodbye.

Pen leaps for the window then, her front paws pushing into the screen's edge, pushing through it to rest on the sill. I tear the screen up so I can rub her head. "I'm coming to see you, Pen, every day, every single day."

When she jumps down I leave my hand out in the night air. "Winthrop."

And I stretch my hand out farther as he walks away.

TIRED

Without Winthrop at the tire yard, it isn't the same. Like reading porn alone, it isn't fun. And when I get home all I want is to get the smell of Fast Eddie's out of my hair. I thank all the gods of Rosary, from Dad's to Aunt Bev's, for the small miracle that no one is in yet. Dad is at his men's prayer group, Iris is shopping, and there's no Bird.

I run a bath. I find Iris's lavender oil and I use two drops, refill it with two drops of water so she can't tell. Just as I'm getting in, I hear Bird come home, and of course he's not alone. Mo is with him. I can recognize Mo's voice, from the way it is with him, just him, only used to respond, to mirror, to say back to him whatever he might want to hear. I can hear the hair twirling around her finger. I can hear her performing this version of girl she does so well for him. I lower my ears into the water and stare at the faucet in the silence I find there, perform my version of not giving a fuck.

But then the water ripples. There's a pounding. Bird is knocking on the bathroom door.

"Piss outside," I yell, without lifting my head, but the pounding continues, and I rise up so I can hear.

"Hell, for chrissakes, Mo has to whiz," Bird is yelling, but he isn't mad, he's laughing. Probably because Mo is about to pee her daisy dukes.

When I get up and unlock the door I open it wide so Bird can watch me climb back in the tub. I hear him say to Mo, "You know what to do," and then she giggles again.

She isn't looking me in the eye even more than usual.

"Sorry," she says, breathy, as she pulls her shorts down.

"Just hurry up," I say. But she doesn't hurry up, or she can't go. The bathroom is silent.

She sits there. I sit there. Bird turns on his stereo. Maybe the noise will help her pee.

Finally, a dribble, and just as it starts, she moans softly. "Fucking burns."

I sink my ears below the waterline again, focus on our reflections in the faucet. Tiny Mo reaching for the toilet paper, tiny Mo pulling up her tiny shorts. Tiny Helen drowning herself to not think about Bird inside of Mo and how he's tearing her apart, making her swell up so peeing burns.

I never realized how jealous I was of Mo, of her being with Bird without thinking twice about it, of her being with Bird without thinking at all. There used to be this empty feeling when I thought of her, the way she would stare into space when we were kids, her finger tracing the blue flowers on Mom's miniatures. The empty space she left when her mom took her away. But now there's this, this feeling of her here, in my bathroom, back here in my house. The birds her brother tattooed, three tiny letter *v*'s, like a child would draw, flying away now from the fire burning in her crotch. Everything about her screaming the story of how the small army of God her mom was trying to raise went AWOL.

As she closes the bathroom door she actually waves at me, a little tiny wave, and I sink my head all the way under the water and hold my breath. Then I move my hand down, around. In circles. Faster and faster. I make some waves of my own. There isn't enough water to make it so I can't hear Bird's headboard hitting against the wall, even over the music, so I keep time with it. Then I pull the plug up with my toe right as my fingers stop their mad circles and let the lavender water fall away from me. I grow heavier as the water circles down the drain and my heartbeat slows. I grow colder against the tub as the water kisses me goodbye.

HOUND

Iris had been out buying feta cheese for the monstrosity she made us for dinner tonight and when we sit down, Bird says, "It smells good in here."

"Thank you, Spencer." Iris is more than usual like a pageant winner when she gets compliments on her cooking, or thinks she does.

He looks at his plate, moves the sausage around with his fork. "Not this. This smells good too, but I'm smelling, I don't know, flowers?" And he looks at me. I used two drops of Iris's lavender oil, there is no way he could smell it, but it was on the counter when I opened the door for Mo. Or maybe he can actually smell it on me. Like a dog.

Iris is not paying attention to us. As usual. "That's my new scent." She actually uses the word *scent*. "Summer Bonanza."

"That must be what it is, Ma," Bird says, and winks at me.

"Summer Bonanza. And this smells good too, I worked up a real appetite this afternoon."

Iris hears what she wants to hear. "Thank you, honey."

Bird moves his knee against my thigh under the table and Iris fades into the background like a runner-up showing she is a good sport.

WAITING

Bird. Me. No Winthrop. No Rain. Mo comes in and Bird buries her on the couch. I don't feel like a beer anymore. I go to Aunt Bev's and have iced tea. I swear off Fast Eddie's.

WAITING

The next day at Fast Eddie's, Rain is trying to swing, arm over arm, across the top rack. Cy and Sissy are betting on whether she'll make it or not. Bird and Mo have their tongues deep in each other's faces and I'm betting on whether I can stand another minute of this before I set a match to Fast Eddie's couch and join Winthrop at the State Home for the Care and Nurturing of Young Sofa Arsonists.

IDLE HANDS

If I were going to put Fast Eddie out of everyone's misery, I would do it slowly, take my time. Rub him raw with the dull edge of shame. I know Eddie's secret, and not because Aunt Bev told me, not because I saw it on the big screen behind my eyelids. I found out this secret from some plain old-fashioned detective work. Which is to say, on accident. And I spied on him.

I am running over to the tire yard, the one I have sworn off visiting, I'm trying to get there early and pound one beer before the Dickheads arrive, so the only one who gets to see my tits is Eddie. The others are rolling in later and later and Eddie has started letting them close up without him. Things are changing. It's like we all decided we were grown-ups a long time ago and now actual grown-ups are starting to agree with us. Some of them, anyway.

Today, the side door is locked, and I am just jumping down the steps to go around to the front when a car pulls into the lot. I shrink down behind the steps, frozen. I don't know why, what I'm afraid of. That it's the mail delivery and someone would report back to my dad? The USPS has eyes everywhere? But I hide, and when the car's engine turns off, no door opens, and everything is quiet for too long, I peek my head around the corner, just peek, and see Fast Eddie there in his champagne-colored Buick. Or what used to pass for champagne but is all flat now, dull as the morning after.

This isn't his usual parking spot and he isn't acting like his usual self. He is still behind the wheel, staring at a picture he's holding in his hand. The other hand has hold of something else. I can't see, but I can guess by how focused he is that he's jerking off. Or trying to. First Cy, then Mrs. Gillespie, now this. I want to make a joke here about things coming in threes, but I'm too distracted by whatever Eddie is doing in his car.

I don't know if something is wrong with his dick or with the picture in his hand, but there is something wrong with Fast Eddie's face. It's like he's constipated, he is trying so hard. It is pretty horrible to watch. Which doesn't mean I stop. And it doesn't really seem like it is worth the effort, if you ask me, but Eddie finally gets things to work, his body takes over, and when he's done he rests his head back for one moment, just this second of peace. He slides the picture up under the visor.

And then Eddie takes one finger and he dips it into the palm of his other hand that is holding whatever dusty mess he managed to squeeze out and he smooths his cum above his head, onto the roof of his car. Like Michelangelo and that painting. A masturbation piece.

As Dad is so fond of reminding me, judge not. Lest ye be totally weirded out.

When Eddie gets out of the car, finally, I shrink toward the wall, hoping he won't come around and see me and know that I know whatever it is, in fact, I now know. But he goes around toward the front.

Which frees me up to do a couple of things. I could wait a few seconds and then knock on the side door, just two feet from me, go inside, and have a beer as planned. I could walk around the corner and hop up on the bay, jump on the door with the Dickheads as they pull it down, act like nothing has happened. Basically, I could try minding my own business. Or, I could pull that picture from the visor of his car and see what all the fuss is about.

It is a formal portrait from one of those mall studios but instead of the golden imprint of the studio in the corner there's a name, *Heidi Momoca Laine*, and the dates that bracket a life, *1974–2013*. She is pretty and earnest but everybody looks earnest in these stupid portraits, earnest as the fall leaves in a golden pile behind them, or whatever backdrop they've chosen, the starry night, the calm sea. The big lie.

Heidi's skin is the color of the cinnamon-and-sugar donuts that sell out at the Donut Hole early every morning. She is wearing a purple blouse and her black hair falls silky and neat right to the pearl buttons on the collar. Her hands are set before her, folded in a completely unbelievable way, I can almost hear the photographer suggesting this pose, clicking away, and then I recognize the gold band on her ring finger. I've seen it on Eddie's own pinkie. I don't think I ever knew Eddie's last name before. I never really thought about him having one. I never really thought about him at all.

I put the picture back in its spot and I am just about to go inside when I remember the finger painting he did. I duck my head back in the car window and it is obvious that this isn't the first time Fast Eddie has labored like this, wept and jerked it to Heidi's smiling face. It would take more than once to get the letters drawn up there as clear and sharp as they are, layer after layer, shiny and stiff on the beige upholstery of his LeSabre. All caps, SORRY.

All of Eddie's emptiness and loneliness is spelled out right there. How he has that hole in him like Dad's, the kind that makes your body forget how to work, how to do the simplest things, like get it up. It is possible that I could feel some kind of kinship with Eddie myself, especially because 2013 is the same year that Mom died.

Or, I could feel joy because fuck Fast Eddie, and I could put this little secret in my arsenal and remember it whenever the Dickheads cheer in his name. I could ruin him by telling everyone what he does when he's alone and the loneliness is too much to bear, that he is soft, in his heart, in his pants. I could take that picture from under the visor and rip it up for an elixir that I would never brew to heal him. I could leave it in shreds there on the driver's seat with a note, maybe, so he would know that someone knew all about it, a note written in silver Sharpie on one of the torn strips, SORRY, NOT SORRY.

Or, I could do nothing. Because sometimes that is the only choice with any kindness in it and sometimes kindness is the only choice.

STRANGE MAGIC

I had a plan for the porn I borrowed, *Lust in the Fast Lane*. I was going to use it to coat letters I would send to Winthrop in juvie, to make sure he is safe, to surround him with the goodness of our friendship. The laughter of us reading those scenes has to have soaked into their pages, and with a bit of Aunt Bev's magic, I would bring that out. Since I can't do that, I have to hope it will be useful when he comes home, to undo whatever damage is done to him in there. I'll spray his room with it. Give Pen a bath in it. Something.

I've seen Aunt Bev work a few binds. Once for Dad, when she revived him, and once when a Walmart threatened to move into the empty lot next door, where the angel is. She washed its perimeter with a bucket of rose water and union-labor literature, binding it with the worker. She used it to brighten up the tetanus trap that is the angel's rebar halo, binding it to her. The Walmart found another home. This is powerful magic.

I wait for an early afternoon when everyone is out and then I tear the pages of *Lust in the Fast Lane* from what is left of its cover, and then I tear the pages into strips so fine my hands start to cramp. "Scissors won't do," Aunt Bev says. "You need flesh and blood and bone. A shredder can't know your mind, that's why those documents go dumb. They're destroyed by a machine. This is hand work."

When all the pages are torn, right down to the last big *O*, I simmer them in rose water, soak them through until the ink that hasn't already been smeared by sweat and cum is blurred on the strips. Then I wait until it all starts to disintegrate, ashes to ashes, pulp to pulp. I sieve it through cheesecloth into a clean jam jar, write *LFL* on the lid. I put it in the dark to strengthen until Winthrop comes home, and then there is nothing to do but wait.

ALSO, WAITING

If you were flying in a plane over Rosary, California, on most days you would have to fly low, beneath the air on fire from the refinery, just to get some visibility. This way you'd be able to make out a figure on the ground, a bony girl in black, maybe a little drunk, and you would have no trouble making out the words on the sign I'd be holding up, the letters on it outlined and colored in until all my Sharpies dried up from the effort: TAKE ME WITH YOU.

PLUMB

Dad takes Iris out to dinner for her birthday, adults only, leaving Bird and me alone to pretend we heated up the dinner Iris left us, to pretend in general. I go to my room and shut the door. It doesn't help. It turns out that ignoring someone who isn't even in the same room as you are is not easy. It's like I can feel him breathing. It's like I can feel him breathing on my skin.

I try the bath again. I fill the tub and my fingers are circling even before the water is done running, but I can't get off. I lie there for a while, keeping the beat of Bird's stereo with my palm against my stomach. I get out. I pull the jam jar from the back of the cupboard where I hid it behind a box of tampons, the jar with *Lust in the Fast Lane* inside, the potion I made for Winthrop.

"Psychic, heal thyself," I say, as I pour just the tiniest bit from the jar into the tub. I think of Cy, in his tent, trying to get off with the wrong magazines. I think of Mrs. Gillespie and her gnarled hand, of Fast Eddie and his gnarled heart, and then I pour in a little more. "For the homies," I say.

And I get back in. And try again.

It doesn't work.

So I get back out and I pour the rest of *Lust in the Fast Lane* into the tub. Every last page, and I climb in after it. Because what am I saving it for? Winthrop doesn't want my friendship. He has so little interest in our friendship that he doesn't even want me to send him letters full of magic and pretty lies. He was clear about that. And as I figure out how to work my body again, as I start to feel that familiar rush of blood, I realize that the only one not clear is me.

And I'm going to fix that right now. Or rather, have Bird fix it for me. Using his special tool.

I wrap myself up in one of Iris's embroidered guest towels and knock on Bird's door.

Bird opens the door and he just looks at me.

"Are you busy, Bird?"

"Nah." He smiles, and all of his smiles are smirks. "I was just jerking off."

We have more in common than I thought.

And now what am I going to do? I have this moment of remembering. Who I am. What this is. I tighten the towel around me, say, "Forget it," and just then, the slightest breeze flows through the stuffy air of the house, breathes down the hallway, around me, and into Bird's room.

Bird's smirk disappears. In its place is the most serious look I've seen from him since I threw away the tablecloth at the VFW hall.

"You're having trouble with the tub," he says. It isn't a question.

He closes his bedroom door and heads into the bathroom,

where he turns on the faucet and watches it flow. I watch him. The way his hair is hanging. He needs it cut. The way his ass curves with muscle. He needs it grabbed. And then he turns to me and I realize what is happening, has happened. To us.

Lust in the Fast Lane.

And there are no brakes. That was the whole point.

"What are you really having trouble with, Hell?" he says, and almost exactly like in the scene with the plumber who shows up for an emergency call in *Hungry Housewives*, I don't need to answer. He lifts me up onto the counter and sets me right.

The water splashes in the tub and I wrap my arms around Bird, wrap my legs around him, and remember Aunt Bev's warning about binding. How there is nothing like the first bind you work to make you a believer.

WHIPPED

Today is Iris's actual birthday and she swears the only thing she wants is for us to go to church with her and Dad. Even though Bird only climbed out of my bed a few hours before, we get up and take our showers and get dressed properly, like the good children we are pretending to be.

But at church, Bird is not himself. I expected him to be my partner in crime, rolling eyes with me at the sermon, anxious for it to end, but it is like some other boy is there with us, attentive, quiet. A believer. Bird sits in the dusty light coming through the windows and the stained glass colors his face, blushes his cheeks, stings his lips like the makeup ads promise every girl they'll do. And he's beatified, like the Bible promises it will do. If we were allowed saints here, if the Catholics weren't cursed, I would call this a sighting. Saint Bird is sitting in this pew just one hymnal from me, transformed, and I know why. I know where Bird really worships and I know, exactly, what's come over him.

The love of Jesus and all His angels can't compare with the glow you get from being really, really bad.

LOST

I make a lost sign for myself. All the signs are for myself. I hang this sign up on the back of my bedroom door. I hang it on the ceiling above my bed. I hang it inside my pillowcase so I can listen to it crinkling at night. I tear off all the little squares with my number written on them and chew and chew them like they are tiny pieces of gum. Then I swallow them and wonder where they went and if I should make a lost sign for them too.

FORENSIC FILES

I go to Winthrop's to visit Pen. Sometimes Rainbolene and I walk over together from the tire yard but whether she's with me or not, I walk right in, and it has become almost like Mrs. Epsworthy doesn't know that I don't live there myself. She'll be deep into whatever television show she is watching, which is all of them, and when I say, "Hi, Mrs. Epsworthy," sometimes she doesn't say anything to me. Most times she just says, "Good girl," when Pen gets down off the couch and wiggles her way toward me, rubbing against my legs, doing her best to stay down.

So it mostly goes like this:

"Hi, Mrs. Epsworthy."

"Good girl."

"I'm taking Pen for a walk now, Mrs. Epsworthy."

Then I take Pen for a walk. We stop to sniff all the important things, and when we get back I wash out her bowls, fill one with a cup of kibble, the other with cold water, and I go home or to Aunt Bev's. I don't go to Fast Eddie's anymore. Mostly. Except when I do.

I like it at Winthrop's. Not being seen here is more welcome than being seen at home, where it's either Iris or Bird or, worse, both at once. Iris's inevitable response when I force myself in my front door hardly varies: "Well, Helen, you're still alive." And Bird has developed a real fucking attitude problem, emphasis on the fucking part.

"Sunny-side up, you *are* still alive," he says, at my tits, and when I tell him to go jerk off already, it starts a whatever-a-thon. "Whatever," he says. And what else can I say to that? I'm only human.

"Whatever, Bird."

"Whatever, sis." He puts all the emphasis on *sis* he can manage.

"Whatever." And here I pause dramatically to prove that I too can be a dick. "Bro."

It goes on like that because there's no sexual tension or anything.

I suppose it doesn't help that I keep creeping down the hall and inviting him back to my bed.

Maybe it is no surprise that the responses I receive when I show up at my own house don't feel quite as good as Mrs. Epsworthy's blank "Good girl" that isn't even meant for me.

Pen sits down for the leash, pacing already with her front paws even while her butt stays planted on the linoleum. It's almost the end of the third week without Win and she's got our routine down. But today, something is different. Where Pen's neck used to rise thick and muscular from her chest, there are rolls of furry flab and another roll is folding up around her hips.

"Mrs. Epsworthy, have you been feeding Pen?"

She doesn't hear me, so I step closer, and she seems to realize this noise I'm making isn't coming from the television. "Treats? Have you been feeding Pen treats?"

"Oh, Helen!" It's like we've just met. She turns down the television. Not all the way.

"Mrs. Epsworthy, have you been feeding Pen?"

She looks confused but seems to finally understand who Pen is, or what feeding is, I don't know. "The sweet girl! I do share with the sweet girl," and Pen thumps her tail and licks her lips imagining what apparently follows anytime the words *sweet girl* are said here.

"Mrs. Epsworthy . . ." I have to do this. Whatever else he has decided about me, I don't want Winthrop to think I can't take good care of a dog. "It's just that, remember, Winthrop talked about watching Pen's weight? Pen is getting—" I start on the *f*, my teeth into my bottom lip, but that is as far as I get.

Mrs. Epsworthy bursts into tears.

"Fat! She's getting fat! I know it. I'm making her fat, I'm making her just like . . ." And here she sobs and holds her breath and the living room of the Epsworthy house is quiet except for the grim voice of the man recounting the crime being discussed on that afternoon's show.

"I ruined him. He's ruined. Look where he is." Mrs. Epsworthy has old-fashioned ideas about fat. She thinks of it as some kind of a moral failing.

It's hard to teach an old dog-lover new tricks.

Pen runs to Mrs. Epsworthy when she starts to cry, even before that, some signal of salt and sadness calling her to attention. The dog sits down by Mrs. Epsworthy's feet, rests her head on Mrs. Epsworthy's knees, her whiskers brushing the remote. Then she looks up at Mrs. Epsworthy and moans just softly, teasingly.

I shouldn't have said anything. Pen is more sensitive to people's feelings than I am. I sit on the sofa arm. There's a My Little Pony on the couch, chew marks all through it. I brush through the pony's mane with my fingers.

"Winthrop is not ruined."

"I just want him to be happy, and treats make him so happy. They didn't used to make him so . . . pudgy." She sounds betrayed. "Before he could walk he would ask for more formula, more cookies, and he was so happy, so easy to please. Rain was never like that, I could never make her smile. I mean . . . before we understood." As I watch Mrs. Epsworthy rubbing Pen's head, massaging her ears, I realize how hard she must have worked to catch up, to understand who Rainbolene is. And now she needs to learn that *fat* isn't a bad word. Next thing you know, she'll realize that TV is sucking her life away.

Pen finally stops moaning and Mrs. Epsworthy wipes at some goop caught in the corner of Pen's eye. "Because Rain always knew who she was," she says. She sniffs at the goop on her finger and rubs it into the cloth place mat protecting the arm of the chair. "And Winthrop never did. It's like he was always looking for . . . some other family." I think about Winthrop and the homes he'd broken into. Whatever Mr. Epsworthy has told his wife about Winthrop's adventures in crime, a mom knows. She knows it wasn't the houses he was breaking into. It was the families.

Mrs. Epsworthy lets out a big sigh and pulls the remote from under Pen's jaw. The sound of the television fills the room.

"I won't give her any more treats, Helen."

I want to argue with her, to say all I know about Winthrop and who he is. Instead, I say, "Okay, thanks," and grab Pen's leash, and we run around the block as fast as we can go to burn off the calories of Mrs. Epsworthy's love. We run until my chest is about to explode, but Pen has barely stretched her legs, so we run around the block again for her, Pen straining at the leash, pulling my arm as far into the future as it can reach without pulling me to my knees.

PS WAITING

I'm not going to Fast Eddie's anymore, which is bad timing, since beers are free now. It turns out Eddie will share his beer if you just ask him how his day is going. But there's nothing for me at the tire yard now but torture in the form of Bird, endlessly sucking Mo's face, as usual, but now with one eye open, on me. It's not torture so much because I want him sucking my face, I tell myself. It's torture because they're doing it in the spot where Winthrop sits. Sat. Doesn't sit. Because they are there and Winthrop is not.

CHALKBOARD

*I will not fuck Bird Doncaster. I will not fuck Bird Doncaster. I
will not fuck Bird Doncaster.*

 *I will not fuck Bird Doncaster. I will not fuck Bird Doncaster.
I will not* walk so softly down the hallway that no one could
possibly hear me except Bird with his secret psychic sex sense.
When he's waiting for me as I push open the door and his smile
lights up the room like a searchlight from a police helicopter, I
won't cover his mouth with my hand, tell him to *shhhh.* Push
him into the hall, to my room, because it's the farthest from where
my dad and his mom sleep. And I won't close the door behind
us, push him onto the bed. By the time my clothes are off, and
so are his, I won't climb on top of him, forget to be afraid we're
going to wake the house, that the mattress squeaking underneath us is giving us away, that the blood in my ears can be
heard through the walls, that the sounds of our breathing are

screams in the night. I won't bite into the pillow, to keep us quiet, bite into his neck, stuff his mouth with my tits, and forget all about my promises to not *fuck Bird Doncaster. I will not fuck Bird Doncaster. I will not fuck Bird Doncaster. I will not fuck Bird Doncaster.*

THE FIRST MIRACLE

Even though he is so deep in love with Iris he does things that would drive any sane person crazy, like whistle as he walks around the house, and exclaim over every meal as if it is the Last Supper, Dad does a thing this morning that isn't irritating at all.

He checks in with me.

Not only is this a surprising move on his part, but what he is checking in with me about is Winthrop. To see how I'm feeling about Winthrop being gone. Dad asks, "How are you doing without Winthrop this summer, Helen?"

It is such a surprise to hear this and said in this way and I feel like Dad actually already knows the answer and that answer is, "Not fucking great, Dad." I don't say this, though. I don't say anything. And he asks me again, like maybe I didn't hear him the first time.

The question comes over me too loud.

*HOW ARE YOU DOING WITHOUT WINTHROP THIS
SUMMER, HELEN?*

Like Dad is God, God Himself, visiting us during cold cereal hour. Complete with a heavenly echo. And He already knows
the answer and the answer is meek and mortal and true.

I've just poured the flakes into my bowl from one of the plastic Tupperware pourer things that Iris insists will keep our food
fresher longer, and that is what I was thinking about. The plastic
pourer thing. In this super-mean way, I was thinking about how
Iris is always trying to make things better around here, and I was
using this tendency of hers, to do good things for us, like it is a
weapon, sharpening it to a point, so I can stab her with it. Like
she's a fucking monster for not just letting things suck, for trying. And then there is Dad's voice and this question. Like Dad
cares too, in a real and useful way. It's like God just pulled the
tablecloth out from under everything to show me that, yes, He's
got something up his sleeve.

And I lie.

"Fine," I say. I pour the milk. The milk is still in the same
old plastic container as usual, but it won't be long until Iris has
it in some kind of glass carafe or something . . . and then my
stomach kind of twists. Hating Iris is making me sick. She's never,
ever done anything to me but try to make my dad happy and
keep my cereal fresh. I reach out to the plastic container of flakes
and kind of pet it. "Fine," I say.

And then I start to cry.

My lie is not very convincing because of this.

And Dad doesn't say anything, at least he doesn't say the
wrong thing. What he does next is right, biblical and otherwise.
He takes my hand. And Iris, who has been quiet this whole time,
taking out glasses and pouring juice and all the things she is
always doing between the counter and table, she takes his hand.
And then Bird comes in and doesn't even notice anything is going

on but sits and joins hands like we always do, without a word, because we usually rush through this part to get to the cereal, so we can get to the next part, where we leave the house.

Dad says, "Our Father, we thank You this morning for our food but also for the food of the soul with which You sustain us always, the gift of real and lasting friendship." And he squeezes my hand. Not harder than usual, but warmer, if that makes any sense, and the pause before we start eating is filled with this warmth too, all across the table where God's tablecloth was pulled away, warming our cold cereal, warming all our cold parts, and then Dad says, "Amen," and we all say, "Amen," and when I drop Bird's hand, I hold on to Dad's. Just for a second longer.

OH FACE

I hear Iris shut their bedroom door. This, after listening to her open and pause and then shut Bird's bedroom door on her way down the hall, like she has every single night since they moved in, like I suppose she has done every single night of her mothering years. I get out of bed. The first step in another midnight trip down the hallway to Bird's room. The first step to make him follow me back the other way, to get into my bed. God might have made an appearance this morning, but he bailed by the afternoon, and I have all night ahead of me.

I ease open my door without making a sound.

I step heel-toe heel-toe down the hallway, keeping to the right side, where the floor doesn't creak, being careful not to knock down my embarrassing school photos.

I open Bird's door. I'm hit with that smell I still can't get used to, heavy and sweaty and warm.

And I stop.

Bird isn't waiting for me. He's out cold. He isn't lighting up the dark room with his sleepy, sneaky smile, ready to go. He doesn't bounce right up so he can come climb into my bed. He doesn't move at all.

He's wearing boxers and a tank top and the blankets are pushed down around his feet. His arms are loose around his head, a knee bent up and to one side. It's like he's been thrown back by an explosion.

Like he's fallen from a plane, from that plane that's always flying over Rosary.

Like he's frozen in the middle of a fistfight, all ecstasy and abandon.

Like a child.

Like he's someone's child.

And I close the door quietly. The slowest release of the latch, because if there is anything I don't want to be caught doing, it is this. I pause before going back down the hall to let out a breath I didn't know I was holding, to breathe in all I have just seen. What I have finally let myself see. Then I take the quietest steps ever taken in this house, because I don't want to get caught now, not in the middle of this act that I can't explain or even understand. I've caught myself in the middle of loving Bird.

Like a brother. Like a friend.

WAYS TO OPEN A PRAYER

God.

This is Your frenemy Helen Dedleder. You might remember me from such powerful hits as, "Please make Mommy stop crying," and "I will do anything, just please don't take my mom away." You might remember me from all those times I reached out to You when I was a kid and You were busy dismantling my mom a piece at a time.

I was the one You ignored.

I was the one You taught that what I want doesn't matter. That what I do doesn't matter. That I don't. Yes, that Helen Dedleder. Created in Your sight. Congratulations.

I'm here to report the sin of hypocrisy. Apparently, the whole time I was on Dad's case for being dead to the world, I was missing the fact that I was too. Until Winthrop Epsworthy rolled into town. And then, just like the zombie I accused Dad of being, I woke up, and before You know it, there I was, a brain-dead maniac consuming human flesh.

Human flesh, in the form of Bird. In my bed.

Remember Your old pal Paul who had that big moment on the road to Damascus? Remember how You showed up for him and he got to hear You and see You, and then he stopped his nasty ways? Well, this is Helen reporting from my personal Walk of Shame, and You are nowhere to be found, as usual, but I am seeing the light. A light. A little light my mom left shining for me. I guess You missed a spot.

Yea, though I fall on my face on the carpet in the hallway between my bedroom and Bird's and not on some dusty New Testament road, I am still blinded by how dumb I have been to think that I don't matter. That my choices don't matter.

Yea, though I don't forgive You for Your shit choices, O God of my misunderstanding, I do forgive myself. One of us needs to start making some sensible decisions around here.

ROUGH TRADE

I go and sit in Fast Eddie's office. He is leaned back in his chair, a beer on the desk in front of him. He doesn't seem to notice me when I come in, and even after I sit down in the greasy rolling chair across the desk from him, he's still kind of staring off at the closed blinds, the streetlight slanting through them.

I feel this prickle on my skin, all through me, the kind Aunt Bev says means it is time to clock in for work. The feeling is not like a shiver. I'm not cold. It is more like I suddenly have eyes everywhere, all over my body, and these eyes have just opened themselves up and are looking hard. Right at Fast Eddie.

He starts talking.

"My high school sweetheart."

If I wasn't paying attention, I mean, really paying attention with all of my many eyeballs, I would leave the room right now. But I know when he says this, he doesn't mean me.

"She wanted to leave." Fast Eddie takes sips of his beer while he's talking. These sips interrupt his sentences, make new sentences, make lines to read between.

"Rosary. But I wanted to do what was easy." Sip of beer. "As usual. She said she didn't like the way it was going. Didn't feel safe. After the crusaders dug in."

As he talks about his wife's fears, I feel crushed. Like my lungs have shriveled up and disappeared.

"She couldn't breathe here," he says.

I want to gasp, to raise my head higher, like I'm underwater, to rise up to where all the oxygen must be.

"Her exact words, 'I can't breathe here.' At first I decided she meant the crusaders were too much for her. Her mom was from Venezuela. She had some trouble. I told her things would settle down. And I forgot to . . .'" Fast Eddie's eyes close. His jaw trembles. He reaches out a hand to his beer and the gold ring on his pinkie makes a quiet tap against the can. "Listen. I forgot to listen. I never thought." He finally looks at me now. Right at me. Like he has eyeballs everywhere too. "You know."

I take a giant breath, a gulping breath. What a small yet wonderful thing to be able to do.

I nod at him. I know. Everyone knows, whether they admit it or not. Once science was a matter of opinion, corporations like Rosario Oil could really have their way with the air and the water, with the land and everything on it. It was a free-for-all. Like Mother Nature was a cheerleader passed out at a frat party, cancer falling all around her like confetti.

Of course, I know more than most about this. And this is what Fast Eddie is saying without actually saying, in a surprising moment of sensitivity. But what he doesn't know is that I refuse to associate Rosario Oil with my mom. Because fuck them.

Because Mom made her own decisions and she wanted to stay here, wanted to live this vision of what could be with that version of my dad who made all of her sacrifices worthwhile.

If I start blaming, where would it stop? I can blame Mom for not going when she had the chance, I can blame Aunt Bev for not making her go, and I sure can blame Dad for everything. Then I'll go right to the top and blame God for making Mom fall in love with Dad and wasting the last of her health on having me. And I'll end up alone in some filthy office every night groping teenagers to prove to myself I'm still alive.

No thanks.

And I am not going to blame Rosario Oil. I will not give those people an invitation to my grief, to my heart, or wherever it is that Mom lives in me now. This is one thing they cannot buy. This is one place they will not pollute.

Fast Eddie empties his beer. He crushes the can between his hands, then he drops it into the wastebasket and stares in at it, in a daze again. It's like he's seeing something down in there, finding meaning in the ways the empty cans have fallen, the shapes they make. Misfortune-telling.

"I went to see your aunt once. Did you know that?" He doesn't wait for an answer. "To have my fortune told. Not for the other." This is a detail I had already presumed based on his poor performance in the LeSabre. But that doesn't matter anymore. Or it matters more and in a different way, how broken he is.

"Your aunt Beverly," and he is suddenly outraged here, on this night, as he must have been on that visit to the shoppe. "She said that people hold grief in their lungs. If that's true, here's what I want to know."

And he's looking at me. And I'm looking at him.

"What am I still doing here?"

He kind of beats his chest with his fist, strikes at his healthy, working lungs hard enough that I hear the dull thud. "What am I doing here, Helen?"

My psychic eyeballs are blinking back tears for this man who would wish cancer on himself so he can be with the person he loves. For this man who deserves an answer. But I've got nothing. What are any of us doing here, besides waiting?

AIRBORNE

I'm late leaving the tire yard, late walking past the shoppe. Aunt Bev's lights are all out, even the red bulb by the front door. The shoppe is gray. The sky is gray. The pavement under my shoes is gray. There's a weird warm breeze that gusts and stops and gusts and stops and I walk down the white line in the middle of the road in the gray night trying not to stumble, pretending I am a very sober plane ready for takeoff with the next gust of wind.

And then a big gray shape blows past me, across the road, toward the fence that borders the freeway.

And there's Cy, and he's running after it.

And I'm running too. Even though the tent is going to stop at the fence and there is nothing I can do, really, nothing I can offer, to help with the weather, or with Cy being stuck here, or with there being nowhere to go from here anyway, nowhere far enough from ourselves, even if the wind lifts us up for a minute and makes us pretend.

We arrive at the tent at the same time, just as it reaches the fence, and before it can snag on any of the frayed metal poking out from it. I help Cy carry it back to the center of the angel in the lot, to where I'm just now realizing would be the angel's heart.

"Thanks," Cy says, after he's pounded in the last stake with this rubber mallet thing that is just for tent-building.

I surprise myself by asking if I can come in.

His sleeping bag is already inside, and the pillow, but they weren't enough to weigh the tent down. I guess his flashlight and things are in the backpack he pulls in after us with his mallet, but he doesn't open it up.

There is no beer and there are no magazines.

There is only the wind against the tent, stopping and starting, like the angel is beating its wings all around us to carry us away.

WAITING, A DRINKING GAME

1. Swear you will not go to your local drinking establishment.
2. Go.
3. Every time you think of the person you miss, drink.
4. Take two drinks for every time you think about not thinking about him.
5. Pound a beer straight to your head if you are so much as tempted to ask anyone, especially that person you are missing's sister, if she has heard from him and when he's coming back.
6. Take a shot if you do this anyway. Pour one for her too. Repeat.

HOTHOUSE

The orchid. The orchid Winthrop brought me on the night of
the prom I didn't go to. The one that he dropped in the driveway when he walked away. What do you think I did with that?
Do you think I let it get run over by the tires on Iris's Honda,
the ones on Dad's post office jeep? Do you think I kicked it under
the porch, let it dry up and blow away? What would it mean if I
picked it up, brought it inside, and found a safe place for it, this
flower I didn't have to make with my own hands? Is there such
a thing as a safe place?

DREGS

I can fuck my stepbrother. I can jerk off like a teenager with a robotic arm. I can make love potions. What I can't do is pour myself a cup of tea and look into it.

Because that is terrifying.

But these are desperate times. So, just like Aunt Bev does, I break the tea bag a little bit. Just enough for a few leaves to spill out while I'm drinking. It's black and cheap and awful, what Iris favors, but it will still work. And that is the scary part.

I take my time drinking it and when it's almost gone I swirl what is left in three slow circles with my left hand. That's one of the things that would freak a Thumper out, the kind who would pray for the soul of a kid who writes with her left hand. But it's not like that. Using my left hand isn't sinister. I'm right-handed. In order to get myself out of the way, to let go of the wheel, I have to stop blocking the light.

I swirl the tea. And I look.

I want to see Winthrop, something, some sign that he's all right. I want it so badly that I'm saying an un-fuck-you to this gift I supposedly have, giving it one more chance to be useful. To be kind.

And what I see is a dark horse.

That can't be good. Dark horse. Dark horses? It sounds like a bad omen. Wrong.

I make another cup. I go through all the steps. I try to clear my mind. I focus on Iris's crystal salt and pepper shakers while I drink this one, to help me let go.

And what I see is a bus stop.

He's taking the bus home from Alaska? He's waiting? Is he stuck? Is he on his way home? No. Now I'm just seeing what I want to see. Wrong.

A new cup. And what I see is a loaf of bread. A fucking baguette. And then all I can think of is Winthrop's bad Frenchie imper-sonation and I miss him so much.

I don't know what any of it means. I can't. Because I'm too close, too full of want. I don't have any practice at it anyway, sepa-rating myself, myselves. All afternoon I've been shaking myself up and down like I'm a Magic 8 Ball that's refusing to give a good answer, and now my head hurts. But it worked after all.

I saw something.

I saw me, sitting here, doing the one thing I said I would never do again because what I feel for Winthrop is an awful lot like love. Whether or not loving him is in my future, this is still a truth revealed.

FUTURE TENSE

Aunt Bev likes to leave the front door open at night if there aren't any customers in the shoppe and she is still awake. This is always in hopes of some stars appearing through the smog. Then she'll read them, like tea leaves or coffee grounds. All that's left when the day's done, she says, we can either wash this away or look inside of it. Like we can with ourselves.

It isn't only about looking, it's also about listening. So I try to listen. I hear Jake brakes on the freeway that never stops rushing on the other side of the chain link. The Rosary air is almost sweet as I settle in to go through the receipts for the first time since the fire. There is a plastic sheet up over the front wall, where the new window is going in, stained glass of Saint Mary Magdalene. Instead of a jar of ointment or whatever she's been lugging around through all of her portraits since year A.D. 1, this Magdalene holds a cup of tea, the steam curling up toward the soft, knowing smile on her face. At her feet, there are flowers made from what appears to be paper, paper that appears to have been ripped right from some sacred scripture, what with its tiny, busy print. If the giant palm from the last window pissed off the Thumpers, this display is really going to get their sacrificial goat.

The stack of receipts I'm recording are mostly the same, the standard $20 palm reading, one after another. The names are those of people largely unfamiliar to me. Except one. And the night air goes still. The traffic dies.

Epsworthy. And this Epsworthy paid for more than a standard reading.

"Aunt Bev, Mr. Epsworthy came in?"

Where she had seemed tense all night so far, Aunt Bev relaxes. She's suddenly so relaxed she doesn't even answer with words, just an "Mmmhmmm."

I smooth the paper. She's so casual. She doesn't gossip about readings. I hear what I hear if I'm in the shoppe and I see names I recognize sometimes. Once even Principal Harrison's, after her dog disappeared. It's no big deal that she isn't saying more.

It should be no big deal.

But I feel something. Like a something I'm supposed to pay attention to.

And she says, "Well, an Epsworthy came in."

"What do you mean, 'an Epsworthy'?"

"You know the answer to this one," Aunt Bev says, just as I realize that I know the answer to this one.

The date on the receipt is from the last night Winthrop was home.

And I want to torch the place myself.

Burn the witch.

And then Aunt Bev looks at me. She looks at me like she loves me. And she turns down the classical music that has been playing on the radio. So I can hear when an alarm starts ringing through the Rosary night.

"Helen, it's for you." Aunt Bev points out the door, and I'm on my feet.

What pulls us to a place? Why are there people we can't help being around, people who aren't really friends and aren't family but just as sticky?

An alarm is sounding and I'm walking toward the noise like I have no other choice. All of my avoiding of Fast Eddie's hasn't mattered at all, so why should it start now. I pass the empty lot, the Donut Hole, I pass the dry cleaner's as the noise grows louder, a ringing that never stops. Until I'm in front of the bay door at Fast Eddie's, staring at the shaft of light growing slowly wider on the concrete. And through the small opening, I see sandals strapped to legs that are too bare for the cool night air, toes that have just left the floor. It is easy to imagine the birds on that left thigh I can't see yet, flying away.

I drag myself up, squeeze under the door, scream her name. The chain hasn't lifted her far, the door can't gain real traction because she is so light, because of good luck, or divine intervention, or Aunt Bev's meddling. But she's still choking, and her eyes are wide, angry. Because she's realized she's an idiot or because her plan failed. Or because she knows what I'm going to do, what I have to do, the same as she would.

I wrap one arm around her legs and hug her to me, lift her up, I pull down on the chain with the other to create slack, give her neck relief. The door slides up a little more and then her hands are in the chain, she gets it loose, and I let her go.

GIRL TIME

Mo drags herself over to the wall and sits there. I close the door and when I can't figure out how to shut off the alarm, I sit down beside her. I can still hear her loud and clear when she finally lifts her head from her knees.

"Fuck."

I agree. "Fuck."

Making this the deepest conversation we've had since we were kids. Just the two of us.

We are still sitting there, our backs to the wall, the two fucks we have to give hanging between us, when Eddie pounds up the steps and unlocks the side door. He stops rushing when he sees us, turns off the alarm, says, "What the fuck?"

Which is what we were just saying, so we don't even need to fill him in. It's great when you really know someone. You don't have to talk. They just understand.

Mo puts her head back down. Her shoulders start to shake. "Eddie," I say, "got any beer?"

Eddie even opens our beers, another thing that has never happened before on this night of things that have never happened before. And then he goes away. Back into his office. He shuts the door. Out of habit, we touch our beers together, but then we stop. We don't say, "Fuck Fast Eddie."

We just drink.

Until Mo says, "You fucked Bird."

Which means we have to drink again because we have failed the Bechdel Test.

Here we were alone, one of us just tried to kill herself, and the first thing we talk about is a dude.

"Drink," I say, in Rainbolene's honor. The Bechdel Drinking Game is her favorite. She made us all learn it, since she said we would never be hearing about it on Rosary TV. Not the drinking game itself, that's Rain's invention. But the Bechdel Test they give to movies and books to see if the female characters are really treated like people or just like atmosphere, accessories for the male characters. One of the main tests is whether, in any scenes without dudes, the chicks talk about anything besides dudes.

I say "drink" because I do not want to talk about this. Any of it. Not who's fucking who. Not atmosphere. And I especially do not want to talk about it with Mo. Or myself.

And I say "drink" because, well, that's what we do.

"He's your stepbrother." Mo adds this detail like it is important information for me to have.

"Aunt Bev fucked Winthrop," I say. "I think."

That she looks surprised makes me feel better somehow. It is surprising. "I don't know if that's super-weird or super-hot," Mo says.

And we laugh, like the Bechdel Test can't touch us because here we are, bonding for real.

But then we are back in it, to the plot being driven away without us behind the wheel, because Mo puts down her beer and says, "I'm pregnant."

THE ROSARY YELLOW PAGES

Doctor Abstinence
A Rosary favorite, and not just because his name comes first alphabetically. A visit to this practice is prescribed to all young women as soon as they think we might start giving in to temptation, as soon as they think we might become temptation. Aunt Bev says this is the doctor to be trusted least. She says, "If it walks like a duck and swims like a duck and flies like a duck, you know what it is? A quack."

Doctor God
Doctor God doesn't get up when you come in, He doesn't even turn His head, and you are too afraid to take a seat without being offered and too afraid to stand, so you kneel on the scratchy carpet and it burns little squiggles into your knees, rubs you raw as if you were down there the whole time sucking Him off the

way it takes a long time for an old, old man to be sucked off in the many porn books where old, old men get sucked off, which is all of them. And Doctor God is an old, old man. But He doesn't want your mouth, or, He does, He wants to be in your mouth, but only so He can feel himself come out of it. He wants to be in and out of your mouth like he is in and out of everyone else's. "Oh God," He wants you to say. "How great Thou art," and the like. This is His version of "Yeah, yeah, baby." And He wants you to keep that baby, keep it right in there even though He's the only one who can see it, if it is all right, if it is all going to be all right, and even though He is the only one who can see you in there, and even if, when He sees you in there, He can see that you aren't all right. You aren't all right at all.

Doctors Kitchen Table and Coat Hanger

It's like no one can bend down. So you have to get up there, haul up there, where the plates were and the forks, where the silence was, and the "Please pass the potatoes." There are potatoes being passed over you, through your knees that are up and planted on either side of where a plate has been and will be again. There's a plate between your feet, someone's food is getting cold, there's a butter knife under one foot and a fork under the other and you don't want to be impolite so you let the tines work into your heel. The flowers etched into the handle grind into the soft spots behind your toes, the spots where you aren't supposed to put too much pressure because you don't want to cause contractions. You don't want to cause contractions, do you? Right here at the kitchen table? That would not be very polite. We don't talk politics at the kitchen table and that includes all the politics around the reason you find yourself lying on this one right now, staring up at the light, watching the potatoes pass over your breasts, the bottom of the serving dish slippery with steam. Talk about how good the potatoes are or talk about sports or talk about school. "What did you learn at school today?" That would be a good question to answer, even if no one asks it, you could talk about the three *R*s now, Reading, 'Riting, and 'Rithmetic. Tell us something you learned, prepositions maybe, fragments, contractions. No, not contractions. Not here. That would not be polite dinnertime talk.

Doctor Wish in One Hand

Some don't go to the doctor at all, any doctor, not God or Kitchen Table and Coat Hanger or Doctor Punch in the Guts. Some just pretend it all away. Here is where that gets you: on the five o'clock news, because there is a baby born in a toilet stall at a school in a town no one's ever heard of. Because no one noticed. First, you are invisible to others, so it is easy to ignore yourself. You know just how you are supposed to be: tiny, unseen. It's easy to unsee yourself. Then, you know you are a pig, a big fatty eater, so it is easy to think you're getting bigger and rounder because you can't stop stuffing your fat face. Doctor Wish in One Hand, Spit in the Other, and See Which One Fills Up First, he writes you an Rx on his Etch A Sketch. It doesn't say anything, it's a maze he's drawn, a tiny square with a bigger square around it with a bigger square around it with a bigger square around it until the entire screen is one unbroken line and there you are in the center, forgotten, and trapped, and he shakes you up until one day, from somewhere in the fat elsewhere that is you, a baby falls out. But you didn't know it was in there. But you didn't know anything was in there. But you didn't know there was a there to even be in. How could you know?

Doctor You

This is the practice Mo went to when she needed to solve her problem. The DIY School. Luckily, she didn't make it to that first appointment, or I interrupted it, and got her to reschedule with Aunt Bev, who made her an appointment in Sky.

BURN THE WITCH

If I were going to put Aunt Bev out of my misery, I couldn't. Trying to catch her not paying attention is like trying to catch the future itself, and then keep hold of it while it wiggles and hisses, just like the snake that wraps around her finger, liquid metal in the candlelight. Good luck with that.

"Just lucky, I guess," Aunt Bev says when I ask her about turning off Rachmaninoff that night, the night she pointed me out the door and down the street to Fast Eddie's and I found Mo trying to push away from this life. Aunt Bev's being sarcastic when she says this, then she is serious. She asks me if anything she has ever done has confused me into thinking she doesn't know her own business.

"Don't answer me," she says. "Just think about it, Helen. Make sure you know the exact address of that doubt inside yourself, because one day you'll need to get back there and burn it all down." She walks out the shoppe door and gets into her pickup, where Mo is already waiting. They are off, so that Mo can pee in a cup to prove what she already knows and get an appointment before it's too late. Aunt Bev used a connection from her Sky days and got Mo a very believable fake ID. The newest illegal service provided at the Psychic Encounter Shoppe is free of charge: transporting pregnant minors across the bridge to Sky, where the real doctors are.

TRUTH

We've already been out. We walked around the block twice, tossed the ball up and down the walkway. We sat on the steps. Then I lay down with Pen on the plastic grass that covers the Epsworthys' porch, green as a golf course and twice as unnecessary. I'm trying to take a nap in my pajamas and sweatshirt, curled up there, with the dog that isn't mine, on the porch of the house where I don't live.

Rain comes to the door, opens it, and asks if I'll be staying until Winthrop comes home, if she should let her parents know.

She shuts the door before I can answer.

Then she comes back and yells at me through the screen.

"Helen, you are a ridiculous person if you don't think that you are in love with my brother."

She shuts the door again, and when she comes back, before

she can yell something else at me, I speak. "It turns out that I am not a ridiculous person."

And she says, sounding so like Winthrop when she does it makes my chest ache, "Oh."

And then she slams the door again.

The next time, she comes out and shuts the door behind her. She hands me a glass of water and sits beside me. Beside us. Pen's tail makes hollow thumping noises against the porch.

"It sucks here without him," she says, we could say together.

Because there it all is. The entire truth of everything. It's like Rain just came out and ripped a bandage off of me and nothing is clean underneath. Nothing is ready for the light. And I bury my head in my arm until the sleeve of my sweatshirt is soaked and snotty.

"Have you heard from him?" I finally say. My voice is hoarse and I'm asking the wrong question, not the one about whether he's okay, if he's getting beat up, whether he's still himself in there, whether he's still in there, in there. Whether I matter to him anywhere.

She looks nervous and then I am nervous. She says, "Hold on," and goes back inside. When she comes out, she's holding a small stack of letters, honest-to-God USPS mail. She holds it above my head and says, "Truth?"

And I want to puke but I say, "Truth."

"Did you tell us not to come to your dad's wedding reception because you"—she stumbles for a second—"had other plans and didn't want us in the way?"

But I didn't do that. I didn't lie to them. Did I? If I didn't lie, why do I feel so guilty? How do we ever tell the truth if we don't even know what it is?

I tell the best truth I can find. "No," I say. "I didn't want my dad to ruin prom for everyone."

As I say this, the real truth hits me in the face like an upper-cut at the tire yard.

And the real truth is a powerful motherfucker.

I didn't want to enjoy Dad's wedding. I told my best friends not to come to make sure I would have a terrible time that night, so that no one, especially Dad, would catch me having fun.

I told them not to come to hurt my dad.

The moment when you learn that the worst person you know is yourself, that is a pretty horrible moment. And every noise I make is a sob and every sob is like a backward scream, inverted, a scream at myself to do better, to be better. To start deserving what I am so lucky to still have.

Rain sits down again beside me, holds me. She says, "It's okay," over and over, and Pen is up and snuffling around my face, grunting, sniffing for the injury that must have caused all of this, until I catch my breath.

Pen settles herself beside me again, and Rain shows me the bundle of mail in her hand. She lifts the stack of letters up above our heads and then throws them up in the air, all over the porch.

As they fall all around us, she says, "This way you can say that I did not give them to you. You found them, you terrible snoop."

I reach for the closest one.

Rain's address is in Winthrop's handwriting, and there is his name, and what I guess is his identification number. There is the address of the correctional complex where he is, a PO box very far away. Underneath Rain's name and address is a stamp, slop-pily applied: *This was mailed by an inmate confined to an Alaska State Department of Corrections Facility. Contents are uncensored.*

I open it up and Rain says, "They're all kind of the same, but I told him if he didn't write me something at least twice a week that I'd start writing to him every day."

Rainbows,

 The "food" here is an actual crime being committed against my person on a daily basis.

 I hope this proof of life is sufficient as I am about to join in another rousing game of pinochle.

 Until freedom,

 Winthrop

 PS Thanks for not writing me back. I have not changed my mind.

DOG YEARS

I take Pen back out. We go to the park. I didn't notice earlier what a clear night it is. A clear night in Rosary. The sky is big and flat and nighttime-blue, shot through with silver like a nickel that's been in Dad's uniform pocket too long and spun through the wash. And I spin around, looking up at this sky until I feel dizzy and the trees become a tunnel with light at the end. When we get back to the Epsworthys', Pen drinks an entire bowl of water and curls up on Winthrop's bed. I stay with her until she falls asleep. She has a good dream. It must be good because I watch her tail go *flip flip flip, flip flip flip flip flip flip flip*, which is exactly how I would sleep knowing that Winthrop is coming home to me.

BULL'S-EYE

The next afternoon, when I hear Iris's car in the driveway earlier than usual, I get Pen to sit and stay in the closet and I slide the door shut. But she doesn't like that, so I open it just a tiny bit to let in the light and then I sit back down with my *Histories of Man* textbook, assigned summer reading. I am trying to figure out what to do, because Iris's dog allergy is something I've been warned to take seriously and haven't, because it only seems to be related to Pen, because Pen is a pit bull. So it is really a pit bull allergy. So it is really just fear. And I just couldn't worry about that today. Today I wanted to curl up with Pen in my own bed.

But it isn't Iris home early. It's Bird. And he is drunk as hell. I don't know how he managed to not wreck the car or our front door or the pictures that line the hallway when he brushes along them on his way to my room.

"Hell." He pushes the door open. I can smell him. And I can

see him. His dick is somehow stuck in his pant leg, it's pointing straight down but fully erect so the whole shape is evident. He points to it anyway. "I need you," he says.

"Where the fuck did you come from, Bird?"

"I was shooting pool and playing darts . . ." He reaches into his pants, starts to adjust himself. "I was shooting shots . . ." I am trying to figure out where he has been doing all of this when he falls back on the bed and screams. And that is when Pen, who has been watchful of him since she first sniffed Bird at the tire yard, pushes her nose against the crack of the closet door, widens it, and leaps through. She stands in front of me, plants her feet, leans forward, her teeth bared and the hair on her ruff standing out around her head triceratops-style. She growls with her entire body, and Bird screams some more.

I grab Pen's collar, pull her back, and that is when I see tiny dots of blood soaking through the leg of Bird's pants, he is holding his thigh there, where the blood is. I can't figure out what just happened, I'm looking for the missing part, the piece where Pen bit Bird. While my mind is racing, everything else is slowing down. Bird's scream sounds long and drawn out and it takes forever for my hands to reach to Pen's face, her mouth, to see if there is blood on her jaw. Will there be blood on her jaw?

Nothing. No. Pen didn't bite him, she couldn't have. And she wouldn't have. It all happened fast, but not that fast. Bird is just being an asshole, like usual, and once I understand that, time speeds back up again.

"What the fuck, Bird?"

He is rolling on the bed now and moaning and I hear the front door slamming and he says, "Darts," and I see the plastic feathery ends of his darts sticking up out of his front pants pocket, which is a very, very stupid place to put them. He rolls around. "Please," he begs, and, holding Pen by the collar as far away from him as I can with one arm, I reach over and pull the darts out.

Needless to say, Bird has lost his erection by this point. No pun intended.

And that's when Iris comes in. She sees her son moaning in pain, the tiny bit of blood, the dog whose reputation she is allergic to, and she does some math. Like, some crazy mom-martyr math. I watch Iris finish an equation she has been working on for too long, since Bird was a little boy and she first started to feel like he was out of her control, and yet how everything he did was all her fault.

DISCIPLINE

"Go, Helen, just go," Iris says, and turns all of her attention to Bird. Like I am going to just go. And miss this. She climbs onto the bed with him, my bed, and pulls him onto her lap. In her arms, Bird looks huge, but he sounds small. He is drunk begging-screaming for her to call the fire department, for an ambulance.

I don't even think his leg is bleeding anymore.

She rocks him and shushes him, and you can barely hear her saying, "No, no, no." I can't move from watching her, even though Pen is whimpering and pulling us toward the door. Dogs are smart.

Suddenly Bird remembers I'm there. He's desperate. And stupid. If there was any doubt about what had been happening between us before, it disappears when he says, "Hell, I love you."

It could mean anything, it's clear that he's drunk. But Iris knows what it means. I can tell by the way her jaw tightens up under her powdery blush, the way she holds him tighter too, and, without even glancing at me, says, "Not anymore you don't."

She doesn't take her eyes from him when she reaches underneath him, into the front pocket of her slacks, and pulls out her cell phone. Then she does this amazing thing. She slides her phone across the floor. She doesn't open it first. She doesn't use it. She makes it so she can't use it. It hits the wall underneath the dresser and that is when I finally understand what is happening, or think I do, because it is very hard to understand people who are completely losing their minds.

Iris isn't holding him tight until he calms down, she isn't rocking Bird until the paramedics arrive. The *no*s she's whispering aren't a rejection of what we've done together, him and me. These *no*s are her answer to him, his needs, his brutal wants. Him. All the *no*s she should have ever said throughout their lives, an entire mom-career of *no*s gathered up right here.

Because she thinks that Pen has attacked him and the blood is from a dog bite and not from the darts she's never noticed in my hands, which are sharp but aren't going to bleed anything dry but his pride. And Iris thinks the imaginary dog bite is because Bird has attacked me and so he deserves it and not because I have trained him to bring me his boner like an obedient mutt. And so, after all the things he has actually done and all the things she thinks he has done but he probably hasn't, not yet anyway, she is going to let him die, of embarrassment if nothing else.

Aunt Bev would say this is all because Iris only understands what her eyes tell her and she only believes what she feels, which is mainly guilt and shame, two of the most highly unreliable feelings. And here I am, the witch's apprentice, figuring out everything that's happened, inside this room and everyone in it, and I don't feel guilty at all.

HELLICORN

The biggest surprise, at first, is seeing Dad at the shoppe. This is the border that separates our family, the line between what Dad believes and what Aunt Bev practices, like we live in a tiny divided county within all the other divided counties. But here he is. And it is so surprising, it takes me a second to put the rest together. The streamers, the balloons, the cake that is frosted with white cream and red letters, that says *Happy Birthday, Helen!*

Next to Aunt Bev and Dad, there is Iris and Bird and Rain and Mo. Everyone who isn't stuck in Bible camp or juvenile hall. Bird looks kind of shy, smaller, like he is this other version of himself. And Mo looks less shy, not bigger, you can't tell she's pregnant by looking at her, but it is like all of her is here, in this room with us.

Everyone is shouting, *Surprise!* and then the door chimes tinkle behind me.

The shoppe fills with warmth like a window in the sun. Aunt Bev says pay attention to that, the feeling in your body when you're with someone, the temperatures that repeat around them.

"Surprise." Winthrop does not shout.

Even if this wasn't my birthday, it would feel like it now.

He is himself, but bigger. Not bigger around, but across, stronger. No one has been beating him up. And he is still him. I can tell when I hug him, which I do before I even think about it. And he hugs me back. He is not as much of a marshmallow anymore, but I feel like one.

There are presents. I am supposed to be gracious and excited about each one. I don't need an etiquette lesson from Iris to remind me of that, but it is hard to focus with Winthrop right there. I open the presents in a daze.

Dad has finally broken down and gotten me a cell phone, maybe because Bird got one when Iris felt so guilty for trying to murder him. The card says the phone is from Iris too. And some stuff about God.

From Aunt Bev, a bottle of rose water she pressed herself. It's in a green glass bottle with the shoppe's new logo on the front. Tied to it with a bit of twine is a business card for the Rosary Psychic Encounter Shoppe. It has my name on it. *Helen Dedleder, Partner.* Dad's smile is tighter now, as I'm reading this.

"A gift for your gift," says Aunt Bev, and everyone cheers. Like they know what the hell she is talking about.

And then, a red velvet box. From Mo. Inside there is a silver chain, so fine and delicate that everyone *oohs*. When we meet eyes across the room, Mo pulls one just like it out from under her shirt collar. There's no charm, just the chain, and no one but us knows that this means everything. Well, us and Aunt Bev.

Before things can get too sentimental, Bird hands me a gift

he obviously wrapped himself. In printer paper. It's a magnify-
ing glass. Because without a tit joke, my birthday simply would
not be complete. "Maybe you won't always need it, Hell," he says.

"But you always will," I say. Which is a lie and half the room
knows it, but he laughs, and even for one second looks a little
shy, and then everyone laughs, even Dad. Things are starting to
get pretty weird, but thankfully Rain interrupts.

"I didn't know how to wrap this," she says, and pulls a black
piñata in the shape of a unicorn from behind the counter. It is
clear that the unicorn used to be white with a pink mane and
that Rain has spray-painted it black. It is also clear that the unicorn used to be a horse and she added the horn using what appears to be a mutilated paper-towel tube. She's drawn silver lines,
stars, and hearts all over it, and the horn is mostly silver too.

We string the unicorn up behind the shoppe. I watch everyone
I care about take turns swinging at it with a broom handle until
the piñata finally breaks open for me on my second turn. There
are cheers and I pull up the blindfold to see paper flowers and
Sharpies and tiny bundles of sage tumbling onto the cement.
And it's like someone tore me open too, and there they all are,
everyone I love, whether I mean to love them or not, picking up
the pieces and calling them treasure.

WELCOME HOME

After all the cake is eaten and everyone is on their way out, Winthrop sits down by me and says, "I couldn't bring my present here, Helen. I have to bring you to it."

And it's like the adults are suddenly, I don't know, smart. Iris and Aunt Bev are chummy, washing and drying cake plates together at the counter, and Dad says, "Looks like we're all set here. Why don't you two go on." He says it just like that. Without a question mark.

I still feel blindfolded. Like I don't know where the target is, and Winthrop takes my hand and leads me toward his house. "Pen wants to be there too," he says, and we pick her up and then she leads both of us, down his street and around the corner to a bus stop. Where she sits right down. Winthrop looks nervous. And so am I. Pen even seems on edge, her fur rippling in the street-light, in the nervous night air.

On the telephone pole, behind Pen, there's a flyer. A lost sign. It is cleaner than the ones around it, like it was just put up. Its design is familiar.

On the bottom of the flyer there are little squares to tear off and take home if you feel like you can help. This is where a phone number usually appears. Only on these, there are two words, over and over again, bent and fluttering. The same two words that Winthrop says now.

"Happy Birthday."

FOUND

HELEN DEDLEDER
ALWAYS ALL IN BLACK. ALWAYS ALL IN.
SEVENTEEN YEARS OLD TODAY.
LAST SEEN EVERY TIME I CLOSE MY EYES.
ANSWERS TO: NO ONE.
LIKES: GOOD DOGS AND BAD PORN.

THE REWARD IS ALL MINE.

LITTLE BIG

I don't know how to act. If I take my eyes from the flyer, I am going to cry. If I keep reading the flyer, I am going to cry. Already the letters are blurring, the *always all in black* and *always all in* blending together to *always all always all*.

Here we both are. Finally.

Except Winthrop's not himself.

And I'm not myself.

And the strangers that we are fall into each other. Pen tries to join us. She bounces off of us on every side until she finally squirrels between our legs where we stand hugging. Her tail sticks out from between us, flipping like a flag in the world's slowest parade.

———

"I'm sorry it's so corny," Winthrop says. "Like a corn-o book?" He's trying to make me laugh, to see if I'm okay, okay with this, not like last time, the orchid on the driveway. And I choke, half on laughter, and try to speak.

"I'm the one who's sorry, Winthrop." And he shakes his head and pulls me to him. And we are holding each other. And I really think about how hard it is to hold Winthrop, how hard it must be for him to feel held, and then I really want to hold him right. I move my arms around, lower, then higher, then I pull him to the bus-stop bench and I climb up.

Now our faces are closer, and I hold on to his. I look into his eyes, no matter what-all he is going to see shining in mine, whatever last bit of truth we didn't know about each other. And I kiss him. No potion required.

AMENDS

Before we can all go ride off into our senior-year sunsets, Aunt Bev says there is one thing we have to do, and we have to do it together.

We have to help Mo terminate the pregnancy.

Not financially. That would be too easy, in its way. Not medically. That would be too stupid. We have to help her spiritually, says Aunt Bev, mentally. We have to help her recover. Like friends do.

The day that Mo is to go off to Sky for her appointment, we all meet at the shoppe and wait with her. Rain shows up in the Lost City Bread van, because Rain is an adult with her own vehicle and the best candidate for escorting Rosary's needful souls across the border, since she can hang out with friends there while she waits.

And we all hug Mo.

And when we all hug Mo, we all feel pretty weird. It turns out that we are not very good at it, this hugging. When Mo and I first try, our arms wrapped loose and high around each other's shoulders, Aunt Bev comes over. And corrects us.

"None of this butts sticking out." She pushes my hips toward Mo's, does the same with hers. "Commit to the hug."

It is a different hug when you do it with your whole body.

Mo and Rain take off and we all try not to look at Mo when she is trying not to look at Bird who is trying not to look at her and I know we're all thinking that there is a drinking game in this somewhere. Who's the Daddy, or something. And I know we all feel bad for thinking it. Because this isn't a game at all.

Then the blinds come down. The Rosary Psychic Encounter Shoppe is closed for a private event, just as the sign Aunt Bev puts on the front door explains.

Inside, Aunt Bev guides Winthrop, Bird, and me into the most surprising shapes of our teenage constellation. She might have done this with Bird alone, she said, but he is unreliable and Mo is too weak for a partner like him. Winthrop is here as Bird's reinforcement, his second.

I am here to learn.

Winthrop on the floor, on the rug, with candles all around. Bird is on one side of him, I'm on the other, and Aunt Bev is walking in a circle around us all, holding the eagle feather she usually keeps locked in the fireproof safe.

Bird on the floor, on the rug, candles all around. Winthrop and I are on either side of him. Aunt Bev is walking in a circle ringing a small bell, its tiny sound barely louder than her bare feet as she steps by us.

We start right at 1:00 p.m., the time of Mo's appointment, and though Aunt Bev got Bird to agree to be here, he still won't commit to going all the way. The *all the way* Aunt Bev is asking for is something more intense than a real hug. More intense than sex. She is asking him to lie on the floor in the supine position that a patient is forced to take, with all its vulnerability and all its possibility. The possibility that says, is saying, in some operating room in Sky right now, "I need more than this." Or "I need to wait." Or "This isn't right for me." Or maybe just "Help me."

Bird is obviously weirded out at the idea of lying down on the floor.

Did I mention that he has to get naked?

Aunt Bev is gentle with Bird, says, "You can undress behind the curtain," but Bird is frozen, quiet. For once. He has his arms wrapped around himself in a hug that speaks of his full commitment to not taking part.

Winthrop gets up then, and I've never seen Bird look so grateful.

Winthrop doesn't go behind the curtain. I guess spending time in juvenile hall got him used to being naked in front of a crowd, so it doesn't matter. Or, it doesn't matter in the first place and he knows this, just like usual.

He stopped wearing ties since he got home from the farm, but he unbuttons his dress shirt, takes off his pants and boxers, and lies down on the rug, his head on the pillow Aunt Bev has placed there. Then she kneels at his feet and pushes them up, until both of his knees are bent. She holds on to his feet. She looks at the clock. We wait.

At 1:30 p.m. precisely, Aunt Bev says, "The anesthesia is taking over Mo's body. We will gather the rest of her with us here." She had explained it to me, this thing Great-Grandma Helen used to do before, years ago, when abortions were even less legal and more dangerous, this way of holding the woman undergoing the procedure so that none of her, of her actual self, is lost in a process that has taken so much from so many.

Aunt Bev said she did this for Mom when she had her cancer surgeries too, but back then she had to do it alone. "It's good to have a partner, Helen," she'd said, like maybe if she'd had a partner then, when she was trying to help Mom, Mom wouldn't have come apart like she did. Which makes sense. And sounds insane. And familiar. I know exactly how it is to negotiate for Mom's return by blaming myself. I just didn't know I wasn't negotiating alone all these years. I felt suddenly full of love for Aunt Bev then, the love that has always been there, but now mixed with awe at all that she has done and does and is. And I said, "Yes. Partners." Because it has finally become clear to me what we already are.

"Relax your thighs!" Aunt Bev's voice is sudden and rough and loud. Winthrop's legs flop open like he is a giant white frog, his dick and balls relaxed in the warm room, in the heat from the candles. The silvery flesh of his stretch marks shines like satin ribbon on his skin.

"Relax your thighs," she says again, like a threat. She rubs Winthrop's thighs then, massages them. "Relax." And somehow, even though her hands are right there by his junk now, it gets less weird.

After Winthrop is as relaxed as he is going to get, Aunt Bev gets up and takes the eagle feather. She bows toward Winthrop and says, "We hold you."

I hold Winthrop's hand then, like Aunt Bev said to do. I was worried I would forget this part, but now that we're here, it's easy. This is what makes sense. I think of Mo, hold her in my mind like she deserves to be held right now, and then Bird takes Winthrop's other hand, and I don't look at Bird's face when I hear him trying not to cry.

When Bird gets up, a little while later, it isn't surprising either. It makes sense when he starts taking off his clothes. When he blows his nose on his tank top. When he says to Winthrop, "Thank you." It all makes sense.

They switch places. Winthrop gets dressed and Bird makes frog legs without being told and Aunt Bev puts the eagle feather back in its case and then kneels in front of Bird and rubs his thighs too before she gets up and starts ringing the world's tiniest bell, so tiny you can't believe it is being heard somewhere in another city, in some medical office in what feels like another country. But you know it is.

This is the kind of thing you do with someone and never talk about again. Like running in terror from a house you think is haunted after hearing a noise inside that you probably made. Like beating on someone until they bleed, or making them want to do that to you, and then letting them, because you need to feel something. Like fucking on your parents' wedding day even though you have just legally become family. Winthrop and I hold Bird's hands while Aunt Bev rings the bell and we all think about Mo as hard as we can, spread open and gone from herself, a Rosary girl daring to believe she has a choice.

THE KEYS TO THE LOST CITY

Aunt Bev makes tea and we sit around the shoppe. Our shoppe. Hers and mine.

We sit and wait. Most of the candles have burned out but we open the curtains, raise the blinds, and leave the lights off. No cards are being read today, no future promised. No one's even talking, but the quiet isn't weird either.

And then there they are.

We watch them through the window. Rain gets out and opens Mo's door. Mo doesn't move until Rain says something to her, something that frees her to kind of tumble out of the van and into Rain's arms, into the shoppe, where we all hug again, but like experts this time, fully committed.

And Mo's fine.

I wish I could know that. All I know for sure is that I can't know. I don't know if there's anything that Mo left in Sky that is going to haunt her someday, make her run from herself. All I know for sure is that I'll be there if it does.

SKY TRAIN

Rainbolene's stuff is packed into the van, her Nelson Mandela poster rolled safely in a tube. I think I'm going to come say good-bye and then hang with Winthrop, make sure he is okay, that we are both okay, begin sorting out how we are supposed to roll on without our third wheel. If that is what Rain ever was.

I'm trying to act like this is not a big deal, like things are not really changing. It isn't like the entire family is leaving, Winthrop saw to that, asked if they could stay another year. Rainbolene is going to Sky, and Sky isn't so far, and we'll be eighteen soon enough. But when Rain hugs her parents, Mrs. Epsworthy even gets up from the couch. And when Rain puts her forehead right up against Pen's and says, "Take care of my little bro, Snuffle-butt," I have to go out to the porch.

Winthrop follows me out. He looks like I feel.

And there's Rain, her bag strapped across her chest like she already lives in a real city, like she owns it. She says, "Okay, Win, the little one is the key to the second gas tank. It kind of sticks." And she hands him the keys to the Lost City Bread van, which is no longer the Lost City Bread van, which I can't stop calling the Lost City Bread van, and she says, "Let's get going so you can be back before curfew."

It's like a cloud of dumb has descended on the porch and Winthrop and I are breathing it in.

"Go?" he says.

"Go, to Sky. Aren't you taking me home?" Rain has already found an apartment, roommates, fellow warriors on the road to whatever transitions they know are best for them.

She talks more slowly to her new dumb brother. "And then . . . you will drive yourself back here . . . in your new van. Use it to visit me. And to do other good things." She presses the keys into his hand. "I've got this amazing thing they have in democracies, it's called . . . wait for it . . . actually useful public transportation. I'll be riding the train, big little brother, like nature intended."

I hold on to Pen's leash as they get in the van. As the best sister in the world gives the best brother in the world all the freedom she has to give him. As they drive away, Pen and I wave, hand and tail, *flip flip flip.*

HOT WHEELS

"You can see right into the apartments from the bridge," Winthrop says when he gets back from Sky.

He is still in the driver's seat and I'm sitting on the passenger side of the Lost City Bread van. Win's van. Pen practically leaped through the window when he pulled into the driveway, so I followed her, and now she is on her back in the space between us, Winthrop's hand moving slowly across her belly. His eyes are focused out the windshield, though, like he is still on the freeway, with Sky's endless high-rises giving him that welcoming hug on both sides.

"You can see televisions on, people walking around. You can see mess. It's like"—and he looks at me here, like he thinks I've known this all along—"they're living."

I want to hear about Rain's apartment, her room, her friends,

I have questions, but this is more important now. I have questions about this too.

"When I used to sit in people's houses. Break into them. That's what I wanted. To see how they really lived. How the time passed. I'd look in the garbage cans even, trying to see what I missed since the last time, what had gone on, and it was almost always the same. Mail. Food. Like those paintings of waxed fruit. Like everyone is staging themselves for a portrait and forgetting to be alive." He comes back into the van now, looks at me. "Except periods. When my neighbor Ms. Carstarphen had her period, I felt better. If it wasn't for the blood"—he shrugs—"I couldn't be sure that I wasn't the only one here. Really here. In the world. I wanted proof of life, I guess."

He takes my hand and Pen rolls over onto her belly and closes her eyes.

"You make me feel like that, Helen. Like life is happening. That's what I figured out at the farm."

I squeeze his hand, rub my thumb over his knuckles. "I've never been compared to a stranger's dirty tampon before."

It's funny, but I don't laugh.

"I'm a romantic, Helen, I thought you knew that." He manages not to laugh either, and then is truly serious when he says, almost in a whisper, "Don't forget the fire part, I like to set fires too," and because he leans across to kiss me when he says it, this line does the opposite of make me want to puke. Winthrop kisses like he talks and dances and walks and sings, like he can do it in any style, be anyone he wants to be. He fucks like that too. He makes love like that too.

"Let's christen the van," I say, when we break away, but he is already climbing over Pen and into the back, pulling my hand.

"One of us will have rug burns." He pulls off his shirt and lays it down approximately where someone's knees might go.

"Both of us will have rug burns," I say, and unzip my sweatshirt, spread it out approximately where someone's ass and back and head will go, and we fill this space, overflow it, with bodies, knees, asses, elbows, hands, fingers, tongues, and trust. Our breath coming faster and faster, fast enough to collect on the front windows, where it condenses around the marks that Rainbolene left for us there like she knew we'd be doing just this, her message drawn in the mist, a heart with our initials inside and the words GET FREE.

SPOILER ALERT

Winthrop stops for donuts every morning. Then he stops for me and the rest of the Dickheads. Once at school, he parks the van in the farthest corner of Rosary High's lot, so we aren't caught being thoughtful and friendly toward each other. We have a reputation to protect.

As we move through our classes, Winthrop and I brush against each other in the hallway. He runs his mouth along my neck as he reaches into the lockers we share on different ends of campus, and Security Guard Jay always seems to be looking the other way when he does.

On the eve of Winthrop's eighteenth birthday, I pull a sweatshirt over my pajamas and walk over to his house just before midnight. I take the key from the pagoda and go inside to his room. I crack open the curtains so I can look down on Winthrop and Pen curled up together. Pen is the little spoon and I push her out of the way. Her tags jingle as she climbs up onto Rain's empty bed, circles and circles, and settles down.

Pen's spot is warm and Winthrop's arms wrap around me in it. I pull up his T-shirt and in the light of the streetlight coming through the window I can see the stretch marks that connect Winthrop's old self with his new self, all the selves he'll be, shining silver and pink. I trace them with my tongue, speak them like a spell, this new incantation to memorize, whispered like a prayer. And I make sure he has a very happy birthday, indeed.

It's on Winthrop's birthday morning, as we're getting out of the van in Rosary High's parking lot, after the rest of the Dickheads have already gone inside, that Roger appears. Roger from the Piazza bathroom. Roger from the land of idiots. That Roger. His pants are still sagging but he doesn't have his big gold cross around his neck, and from the look on his face he might have swallowed it whole.

Roger kind of holds up his hands when he gets close, like we are going to jump him. Which does cross my mind. And his hands are shaking.

"Look," he says.

We are looking.

"I heard that you might be able to arrange"—and here he stammers, like he's going to ask for a blow job or something—"a ride. To the . . . across the . . . It's for a friend."

Winthrop looks at me. There's a decision before us and he's waiting for me to do something. It takes me a second to figure out what, that he's waiting for me to give my consent. Like the gentleman he is.

I nod at Winthrop.

He nods back.

And everything about what this means fills the air between us over poor dumb Roger's head.

RISE

I'm pulling on my backpack, the one with the silver stars and lightning bolts, and yeah, you caught me, some hearts too.

"Helen Dedleder, tick tock." Winthrop's voice is coming from the speaker mounted to the Lost City Bread van's roof, it fills our driveway and barges through the front door. When I come out, he's handing Bird a donut through the window and Bird waves it at me as he walks on to school, if that's actually where he's going. Winthrop is already halfway through an apple fritter and when I get in and lean over to kiss him good morning, I taste hot sugar and coffee.

Delicious.

On the van's dash there is a stack of flyers and a staple gun. The design is familiar. As I reach for one, Winthrop says, "I hope you like it."

I'm expecting another love note, like the one from my birthday, but that's not what this is. Or that's exactly what this is. On the squares at the bottom, there is no cute message and there's no phone number either. Instead, in place of the usual contact information, there is a code that any Rosary High kid will recognize, a letter and a number, each pair the locker of a different Dickhead.

Because we're in this together.

DELIVERANCE

NEED A LIFT?
TRY US FIRST.
LOST CITY TRANSPORT
COUNTYWIDE AND BRIDGE RUNS.

PRICE NEGOTIABLE. JUDGMENT-FREE.

GOOD TROUBLE

All the love stories and their happy endings are romantic bullshit, especially the hetero ones where the boy and the girl drive their weird van off into the sunset.

There is a big smile on my face, but this is not a romance.

And don't let the pollution from the refinery fool you either. That is not the sunset.

Our work is just beginning.

The sun is coming up. Even in Rosary. My house is only the first stop. Next is Mo and Cy and Sissy, next is every one of us born on the battlefield of someone else's war, ready now to fight for the only thing that matters. Each other.

And I know we will.

I can see the future.

ACKNOWLEDGMENTS

Much gratitude to the Sherwood Anderson Foundation for its generous support and to Susan Salser for her sustaining kindness.

Family: Daniel, Don and Tam, Jim and Windy, Steve and Carmen, Grandpa Earle and Poppi Rob, Liz and Shea, Mamasan Elizabeth and Cap'n Mark, I wish us all nearer.

Forever teachers: Vicki Forman, Jim Krusoe, and Alan Ziegler.

Healers: Julia Carpenter and Michelle Lemieux at Berkeley Acupuncture Project, Andrea Du Flon, Hilary Henson, Chad Houfek at Charleston Community Acupuncture, Francine Madrid at Mariposa, and Angela Watrous at Restorative Empathy.

True believers: Franny and Jorie, Josh and Tracy, Kris and Elizabeth, Nikki from Alaska, Elina Agnoli, Shirley and Tilden Atwell, Donna B., Burgin Bailey, Chris Baty, Augustine Blaisdell and Eric Frison, Pat Bowen and Lindsay Grant, Sarah Ciston, Daniel A. Colfax, Nicole Dietrich, Jacqueline Doyle, Daniel Duvall, Ann Endress, Jules Gilbertson, Steve Gutierrez, Michael Hacker, Regina Kammer and Jason Munkres, the Mitchell Women, Mandy Mosiman, Celine Nadeau, Leslie Outhier, Anna Padgett,

Candace Procaccini, Cyndera Quackenbush, Judith Remmes, Graham and Jess Rolak, Cathy Salser, Daniel Sanders, Laura Lampton Scott, Mark Searles, Cheryl Silver, Nancy Smith, Tavia Stewart, John Streit, Zulema Renee Summerfield, Jessica A. Walsh, Sarah Warshaw, Amanda Weisel, Laura West, Josie Williams, and Marci Mamacita Grandmacita Zeimet.

Lisa, a.k.a. Horse Face, and Paula Parnello-Copley: Dickheads forever.

Jenna Johnson, for defying the world to end. And all the good shepherds at FSG, especially Chloe Texier-Rose and Lydia Zoells. Abby Kagan's design is everything this book and I wanted. Na Kim for wielding the magical Sharpie of wish fulfillment. Dave Cole deserves all the hot-air balloon rides.

Bill S. Clegg, the only living boy in New York, here's to today. And the Clegg Agency at large, especially Simon Toop, who puts up with more Tupe/Toop puns than is proper.

Ford Aloysius and Josiah Wright, my dearest inspirations to do and be and imagine better.

And to Bradford, my eternal teen romance, for keeping me found.

A Note About the Author

Tupelo Hassman's debut novel, *Girlchild*, won the American Library Association's Alex Award. Her work has appeared in *The Boston Globe*, *Harper's Bazaar*, *Imaginary Oklahoma*, *The Independent*, *Portland Review*, and *ZYZZYVA*, among other publications. She is the recipient of the Nevada Writers Hall of Fame Silver Pen award and the Sherwood Anderson Foundation Fiction Award, and is the first American to have won London's Literary Death Match. She earned her MFA at Columbia University.